Bolan had taken on the job for old times' sake

He was driven by feelings long suppressed if not forgotten, paying an installment on a debt of loyalty he knew would never fully be discharged. In truth, he didn't want to cut that tie, however tenuous it was.

Sometimes even a scarred and bloodied warrior needed something to remind him of another time. Another life. It might be lost beyond recall, but memories were precious, all the same.

He palmed the GPS device and got his bearings, let the compact gadget point him toward his goal. A stranger waited for him there, not knowing it. Bolan had come to save that stranger from himself, at any cost.

Old ghosts kept pace with Bolan as he struck off through the jungle on a trail invisible to human eyes.

Don Pendleton's Mack Bolan®

STATE OF EVIL

A GOLD EAGLE BOOK FROM
WORLDWIDE®

TORONTO • NEW YORK • LONDON
AMSTERDAM • PARIS • SYDNEY • HAMBURG
STOCKHOLM • ATHENS • TOKYO • MILAN
MADRID • WARSAW • BUDAPEST • AUCKLAND

First edition November 2006

ISBN-13: 978-0-373-61514-8
ISBN-10:   0-373-61514-0

Special thanks and acknowledgment to
Mike Newton for his contribution to this work.

STATE OF EVIL

Printed in U.S.A.

There is no arguing with the pretenders to a
divine knowledge and to a divine mission.
They are possessed of the sin of pride, they have
yielded to the perennial temptation.
—Walter Lipmann,
The Public Philosophy

There'll be no argument with my opponents on
this mission. The plan is simple, in and out.
God help anyone who stands in my way.
—Mack Bolan

PROLOGUE

Obike, Republic of Congo

The congressman was sweating, which was no surprise, given the oppressive temperature and humidity. But climate couldn't explain the tingling chill he felt at the back of his neck.

A sense of being watched.

He turned abruptly in his chair, raising a hand as if to swat a troublesome mosquito, and he caught one of Gaborone's bodyguards turning away, suddenly anxious to avert his eyes.

It wasn't paranoia, then.

The goons *were* watching him.

Lee Rathbun wished he'd never made this trip, but it was too late now for backing out. He was the youngest congressman in California, midway through his second two-year term in Washington and looking for a chance to prove himself. The Congo trip had fit his need, humanitarian and daring all at once, solving a problem, maybe bringing justice to a charlatan while overcoming certain hardships in the process.

Naturally he'd brought a camera crew along to put the show on tape. Why not?

The problem was that he'd been misinformed, somewhere along the line. Ahmadou Gaborone had that Jim Jones/David Koresh air about him, smiling serenely while chaos churned behind his eyes. He spoke sometimes in riddles, other times in parables that could mean anything or nothing. Typically, his voice was soft, almost hypnotic, but when raised to make a point during one of his marathon sermons, it shook the very primal forest that surrounded Obike, the retreat.

Lee Rathbun's mission was twofold. First, he had promised to inspect Obike and report his findings to constituents whose loved ones had deserted sunny California for the jungle compound where Gaborone was constructing his tentative Eden on Earth. Second, he was supposed to interview the absent kin of those who had besieged his hometown office, seeking help. He would seek out the converts, take a private reading on their health and state of mind, and share his findings with their families.

Simple.

Aside from nailing down some grateful votes, the junket would earn him a page, maybe two, of fresh ink in the *Congressional Record,* when he filed his report with Congress.

Now he was almost done and it was nearly time to leave, but Rathbun couldn't shake that creepy feeling that suggested hostile eyes tracking his every move.

One of the guards was moving toward him now, a sullen six-footer whose plaid short-sleeved shirt was unbuttoned, revealing an ebony six-pack that shone as if oiled. His AK-47, Gaborone had explained, was one the group used to protect them against Gaborone's enemies, those who would harm him for spreading God's message.

"Say goodbye now," the guard told Rathbun. "Time to go."

Rathbun smiled as if trying to win the man's vote. Behind him, he heard one of the cameramen mutter, "It's about damned time."

"Smiles, people, smiles," Rathbun said to his team. "Remember where we are, and that our host has been extremely generous."

It was true, to a point. Gaborone had granted them a tour of Obike that revealed austere but functional facilities, the living quarters well tended and almost compulsively tidy. Rathbun's interviews had also gone without a hitch, at least superficially. Those he sought were all accounted for and pleased to answer questions on their life within the sect.

As for the answers, rehearsed to the point that they all came out nearly verbatim, Rathbun didn't choose to raise that issue in Obike. Not under the guns of Gaborone's security force.

Relieved to put the place behind him after three long

days and nights, Rathbun rose from his canvas chair and led his people toward the waiting bus.

NICO MBARGA WAITED with the vehicle. His scouts had left an hour earlier, to guard the airstrip and prepare the send-off Master Gaborone had ordered for the visitors. Mbarga wore the smile he deemed appropriate for partings.

The politician approached him, flicking glances at the old converted school bus that would take his people to the airstrip. Parked close behind the bus, a Jeep sat idling with four of Mbarga's men waiting stoically for his order to roll. They watched Mbarga, not the visitors, because they knew who was their master, once removed.

"Will Mr. Gaborone be joining us?" the politician asked.

"Alas, no," Mbarga replied. "He has other pressing business, but he wishes you a safe and pleasant journey home. He hopes your visit to Obike was rewarding and your fears are laid to rest."

The politician frowned. "What fears?"

Mbarga shrugged. "Perhaps that kinfolk of your countrymen have been mistreated here or held against their will."

The politician blinked. "I saw nothing to indicate that might be true," he said.

"Good, good. You're happy to be going home, then. Please take seats aboard the bus, and we shall go to meet your flight."

Mbarga watched the visitors file past him, all except the politician bearing haversacks and camera equipment. When the last of them had gone aboard, Mbarga followed, nodding to the driver. He sat behind the driver's seat, sliding his pistol belt around so that the holster with its heavy pistol wouldn't dig into his hip or thigh.

Mbarga glanced around the bus as it began to move. The visitors—a woman and three men besides the politician—all wore queasy looks, as if their breakfast of plantains and porridge sat uneasily within their stomachs. Mbarga wondered whether any of them had the gift of precognition.

No, he finally decided, smiling to himself.

If that were true, they wouldn't be aboard the bus.

Whatever they were thinking, it was now irrelevant.

"So, where's the plane?" asked Ellen Friedman, Rathbun's personal assistant, as she stepped down from the bus.

"Good question." Rathbun turned to the commander of the escorts and inquired, "Shouldn't the plane be here by now?"

"Sometimes it's late," the bodyguard replied.

"Sometimes?"

"Most times," the bodyguard amended with a careless shrug.

"We have a flight to catch in Brazzaville," Rathbun informed him, fudging in an effort to communicate a sense of urgency.

"No problem, sir."

Turning to scan the airstrip, Rathbun noted that a Jeep had reached the scene ahead of them, bearing four gunmen to the site. With those in the following Jeep and their escort, that left his small party outnumbered.

"Are you expecting trouble here, today?" he asked.

"Always expecting trouble, sir," the bodyguard replied. "Prophets have many enemies."

"I see." Rathbun glanced pointedly at his wristwatch, then saw the gunmen stepping from their vehicles. They didn't wear their rifles shoulder-slung this time, but carried them as if prepared to fire.

"This stinks," said Andy Trask, the cameraman. "I don't like this at all."

"Relax, will you?" the congressman replied, but he was having trouble suiting words to action. There was something in the way the gunmen watched him now....

"Put down your bags," their escort said, no longer sounding affable. When Rathbun turned to face him, he discovered that the man had drawn his pistol from its holster.

"What?"

"Put down all bags," the bodyguard repeated. "Leave them where you stand and line up there." His final word was punctuated with a gesture from the pistol, indicating open grass beyond the blunt nose of the bus.

"Now wait a minute," Rathbun said. "What's going on?"

"I only follow orders," said the bodyguard.

"And what, exactly, might those orders be?"

"I must protect the master and Obike at all cost."

"You still aren't making sense." Rathbun was striving for a tone of indignation, trying not to whimper. Even here, it was important to save face.

"All threats must be eliminated."

"Threats? What threats? We've spent the past three days among your people, with consent from Mr. Gaborone. Now we're leaving, as agreed. There's no threat here."

"I follow orders," the bodyguard said again.

Rathbun felt the vicious worm of panic twisting in his gut, gnawing his vitals. It would break him if he faced the others, registered the sudden terror on their faces.

"I don't understand what's happening," he said.

"Step into line. We have orders and a schedule."

"Just think it through," Rathbun pleaded. "If Mr. Gaborone is worried about bad publicity, what does he think *this* will accomplish? You'll have troops, police, God knows who else, if we don't get to Brazzaville on time."

The escort shrugged. "We're ready for the day of judgment. It will come in its own time."

It was a sob that broke the last thin shell of Rathbun's personal composure. Ellen Friedman weeping like a child. Rathbun hardly knew what he was doing when he shouted, *"Run!"* and drove his right fist hard into their escort's startled face.

He missed the bastard's nose but felt the lips mash flat beneath his knuckles, twenty years or more since he had swung a punch that way, at some forgotten enemy from John Wayne Junior High. It staggered his opponent, gave him time to turn and flee.

Too late.

A voice behind him shouted something Rathbun couldn't understand. He heard the first gunshots when he was still some thirty paces from the trees. Rathbun was the last American to die.

"MY CHILDREN! Harken unto me!"

Ahmadou Gaborone occupied his favorite chair, a throne of woven cane planted atop a dais in the central plaza of Obike. Nearly all of his disciples were assembled on the open ground in front of him, summoned by the clanging of a triangle to hear their lord and master's words. His bodyguards were shooing stragglers in from here and there, to join the tense, expectant throng.

"My children," Gaborone repeated, "we have reached a perilous, decisive moment in our history. For three days, enemies have dwelt among us. They conspired with enemies outside to fill the air with lies about Obike and myself. Unchecked, they would have turned the governments of Brazzaville and Washington against us."

Murmurs from the audience. Quick glances here and there from nervous eyes, as if his people thought the enemies might suddenly appear beside them.

"I have acted as a leader must, to spare his people," Gaborone continued. "On my order to the guardsmen of Obike, the intruders have been neutralized. They are no more."

That sent a ripple of surprise through the assembled crowd. Some of his followers were clearly frightened now. The master raised his hands, then stood when the familiar gesture failed to silence them.

"My children! Hear me!" he commanded. "Have no fear of those outside. You know that Judgment Day must come upon us in its own good time. Nothing we do can hasten or delay the hour of atonement. We shall someday face the test against our enemies. Whether tomorrow or ten years from now, I cannot say until the word is given from on high."

"Master, preserve us!" someone cried out from the audience.

"I shall," the prophet replied. "Fear no outside force or government. No man can harm us unless God permits it, and He never leaves His faithful children to be slain unless they first fail in their duties owed to Him."

"What shall we do, Master?" another voice called from his right.

"Stand fast with me," he answered. "Do God's bidding as it is revealed to you, through me. With faith in Him, we cannot fail. His grace and power shield us from our worldly enemies and all their schemes. While we are faithful, those who threaten us are vulnerable to God's holy cleansing fire."

"Amen!" a handful of his children shouted, others taking up the chant until it seemed to echo from a single giant throat.

"Amen!" he thundered back at them. *"Amen!"*

Nico Mbarga stood beside the dais, waiting for

Gaborone to step down and retreat from his throne. The chanting of "Amen!" continued even after he had left the audience, continued until he was well inside his quarters with Mbarga, just the two of them alone.

"Tell me again, Nico," he said, "why you are certain that the bodies won't be found."

"We burned them, Master, and their ashes have been scattered in the jungle."

"What of their effects? The camera? The other things?"

"Buried," Nico assured him. "Buried deep."

"There will be questions."

Nico shrugged. "We saw them board the plane and fly away."

"What of the pilot?"

"He has sisters in Obike. He will land in Brazzaville on schedule. How can he explain the disappearance of his passengers, once they departed from his care?"

"It's not much of a story, Nico." Gaborone sometimes enjoyed being the devil's advocate.

"It is enough, Master," the bodyguard replied. "We pay the Brazzaville police enough to close their eyes."

"But what of Washington? Their President wields power, even here. Their dollars buy compliance."

"You believe they'll crack the pilot?" Mbarga asked.

"Given time and the incentive, certainly."

"I'll see to it myself," Mbarga said.

"Soon, Nico. Soon."

"I'll leave tonight, Master."

"How many sisters of the pilot share our faith?"

"Three, master."

"Take one of them with you to the city."

"Sir?"

"If he should simply die, more questions will be raised. A scandal in the family, however, raises issues the police can swiftly put to rest."

"A scandal in the family." Mbarga seemed to understand it now.

"Sadly, not everyone shares our view of morality."

"No, sir. The woman—"

"Tell her she's been chosen for a mission in the city. Flatter her, if necessary. Has she any special skills."

Mbarga shrugged. "I don't know, Master."

"Think of something. Use your powers of persuasion, Nico. I'm convinced that you can do it."

Meaning that he didn't want the woman dragged aboard a Jeep, kicking and screaming. He didn't want her spreading stories to her sisters or to anybody else during the short time left before her one-way trip to Brazzaville.

"It shall be done, Master."

"I never doubted you. And, Nico?"

"Master?"

"Make me proud."

CHAPTER ONE

Airborne: 14° 2' East, 4° 8' South

The aircraft was a Cessna Conquest II, boasting a forty-nine-foot wingspan and twin turboprops with a maximum cruising speed of 290 miles per hour. It had been modified for jumping by removal of the port-side door, which let wind howl throughout the cabin as it cruised around eleven thousand feet.

The air was thin up there, but the aircraft was still below the level where Mack Bolan would've needed bottled oxygen to keep from blacking out. His pilot, Jack Grimaldi, didn't seem to feel the atmospheric change, although he'd worn a leather jacket to deflect the chill.

Twenty minutes out of Brazzaville and they were halfway to the target. Bolan had already checked his gear, but gave it all another look from force of habit, nothing left to chance. He tugged at all the harness straps, tested the quick-release hooks, making sure that he could find the rip cords for the main chute on his back and the smaller emergency pack protruding from his chest. Bolan had packed both parachutes himself, folding the canopies and lines just so, and he was confident that they would function on command.

The rest of Bolan's gear included military camouflage fatigues, the tiger-stripe pattern, manufactured in Taiwan and stripped of any labels that could trace them to specific points of origin. His boots were British military surplus, while his helmet bore the painted-over label of a manufacturer whose products were available worldwide.

His weapons had apparently been chosen from a paramilitary grab bag. They included a Steyr AUG assault rifle manufactured in Austria, adopted for use by armies and police forces around the world. The AUG was well known for its rugged construction and top-notch accuracy, its compact bullpup design, factory-standard optical sight and clear plastic magazines that let a shooter size up his load at a glance. Bolan's sidearm was a Beretta Model 92, its muzzle threaded to accept the sound suppressor he carried in a camo fanny pack. His cutting tool was a Swiss-made survival knife with an eight-inch, razor-sharp blade, its spine serrated to double as a saw at need.

The rest of Bolan's kit came down to rations and canteens, a cell phone with satellite feed, a compact GPS navigating system and a good old-fashioned compass in case the global positioning satellite gear took a hit at some point. His entrenching tool, flashlight and first-aid kit seemed antiquated by comparison, like items plucked from a museum.

When he was satisfied that nothing had been over-looked or left to chance, Bolan moved forward to the cockpit. Grimaldi glanced back when he was halfway there and raised his voice above the rush of wind to ask, "You sure about this, Sarge?"

"I'm sure," Bolan replied. He crouched beside the empty second seat, too bulky with his parachutes and pack to make the fit.

"Because if anything goes wrong down there," Grimaldi said, "you're in a world of hurt. That's Africa down there. If you trust the folks at CNN, a lot of it still isn't all that civilized."

"Worse than New Jersey?" Bolan asked. "The South Side of Chicago?"

"Very funny." From his tone, Grimaldi clearly didn't think so. "All I'm saying is, your sat phone may connect you to the outside world, if it decides to work down there, but even so, it's still the outside world. You've got no backup, no support from anyone official, no supply line."

"I've got you," Bolan reminded him.

"And I'll be waiting," the pilot assured him. "But my point is, even if you call and catch me sitting in the cockpit with my finger on the starter, it'll be an hour minimum before I'm in position for a pickup. Plus, with the restriction on armed aircraft, I can't give you anything resembling decent air support."

"Just be there for the lift. That's all I ask," Bolan replied.

Grimaldi shifted gears. "And what about this kid you're picking up?"

"He's twenty-two."

"That's still a kid to me," Grimaldi said. "Suppose he doesn't want to play the game?"

"I'll make him an offer he can't refuse," Bolan said.

Grimaldi frowned. "I mean to say, he's here by choice. Correct?"

"In theory, anyway," Bolan said.

"So he's made his bed. He may not want to leave it."

"I'll convince him."

Bolan didn't need to check the hypodermic syringes in their high-impact plastic case, secure in a pouch on his web belt, but he raised a hand to cup them anyway. The kid, as Jack called him, would be coming out whether he liked it or not.

Whatever happened after that was up to someone else.

Grimaldi gave it one last try. "Listen," he said, "I know where this is coming from, but don't you think—"

"We're here," Bolan said, cutting off the last-minute debate. "I'm doing it. That's all."

"Okay. You've got my cell and pager set on speed-dial, right?"

"Right after Pizza Hut and *Girls Gone Wild*," said Bolan.

"Jeez," Grimaldi said, "I'm dropping a comedian. Who knew?"

"I needed something for my spare time," Bolan said.

"Uh-huh." Grimaldi checked his instruments, glanced at his watch, and said, "We're almost there. You'd better assume the position."

"Right." Rising, Bolan briefly placed a hand on his old friend's shoulder. "Stay frosty," he said.

"It's always frosty at this altitude. I'll see you soon."

Turning from the cockpit, Bolan made his way back to the open door, halfway along the Cessna's fuselage.

"WE'VE GOT a quarter mile," Grimaldi shouted back to Bolan in the Cessna's open doorway, waiting for the quick thumbs-up.

Whatever was about to happen, it was out of Jack Grimaldi's hands. He could abort the mission, turn the plane around and violate his old friend's trust beyond repair, but that option had never seriously crossed his mind.

He was the flyboy; Bolan was the soldier.

He delivered Bolan, and the Executioner delivered where it counted, on the ground.

Grimaldi understood the impetus behind their mission, recognized the urgent strength of loyalty that rose beyond mere friendship to a more exalted level. Still, their small handful of allies was behind them now, and half a world away. The broad Atlantic Ocean separated Bolan and Grimaldi from the support team at Stony Man Farm. Whatever happened on the ground below, Bolan would have to cope with it alone.

And recognizing that, Grimaldi thought, what else was new?

From what Grimaldi knew, Bolan had been a kind of one-man army all his fighting life, from combat sniper service with the Green Berets, through his solo war against the Mafia at home, and in most of the Stony Man missions he'd handled since joining the government team. From boot camp to the present day, Bolan had been unique: a great team player who could nonetheless proceed alone if there was no team left to field.

Most often, in the blood-and-thunder world he occupied, Mack Bolan was the team. Grimaldi simply had the privilege, from time to time, of making sure that Bolan didn't miss the kickoff.

"Ready!" he shouted in the rush of chilling wind. The drop zone was below them, waiting.

"Ready!" Bolan answered without hesitation.

And when Grimaldi glanced toward the Cessna's vacant hatch again, he was alone.

THE WIND HIT Bolan like a tidal wave and swept him back along the Cessna's fuselage, even as he began to fall through space. He plummeted headfirst toward Earth, arms tight against his sides, a hurtling projectile of flesh and bone.

Although he was accelerating by the second, answering the call of gravity, he also felt a lulling sense of peace, deceptive, as if he had been a feather drifting on an errant summer breeze. The jungle canopy below didn't appear to rush at Bolan, hastening to crush him. Rather, from his vantage point, it seemed to be forever out of reach, a vista seen through plate glass on the far side of a massive room.

Bolan had done enough high altitude, low opening jumps in his time to recognize the illusion for what it was, and to dismiss it from his mind. HALO drops were designed for maximum maneuverability and stealth. The jumper guided himself with pure body language for the first eight thousand feet or so, waiting to pull the rip cord when it counted, minimizing exposure to watchers on the ground.

The jungle helped him there, of course. For spotters to observe his parachute, they'd have to be at treetop level—no mean feat, considering the fact that trees in the Congo jungle below Bolan averaged one hundred feet or more in height. The lofty African mahogany might double that, but climbing giant trees wasn't child's play. Unlike most temperate trees grown in the open, giants of the crowded rain forest typically boasted branches only near the top, leaving two-thirds of their trunks entirely bare except for creeping vines and moss or fungus growths.

If Bolan's parachute became entangled in that lofty canopy, he ran a risk of being killed or crippled in his bid to reach the ground. The first step in his new campaign could also be his last.

Around two thousand feet he pulled the main rip cord. There was a heartbeat's hesitation, known to every jumper who survives a drop, before the main pack opened and the chute blossomed above him. Bolan's headlong plummet was arrested as the shroud lines snapped taut, air filling the cells of the sleek pilot chute overhead.

Bolan clutched the risers, using them and the parachute's slider to guide his descent toward the treetops. This was his most vulnerable time, dipping lower by the moment at a speed most riflemen could easily accommodate. He didn't think there would be spotters in the treetops, but a hunter in a clearing on the ground might catch a glimpse of Bolan and his parachute, might even have the time to risk a shot before he ran to spread the word.

One clearing in particular preoccupied the jumper's thoughts.

The drop zone had been chosen based on aerial and satellite reconnaissance, map coordinates for Bolan's final destination matched against bird's-eye photographs of the jungle canopy he'd be required to penetrate on D-day. A natural clearing in the forest had been spotted from on high, charted and measured, analyzed for likely risks as far as a computer half a world away could take the problem toward solution. Based on that intelligence, he had been told precisely where and when to leave Grimaldi's Cessna for his leap of faith.

The dark patch of the clearing lay below him now, and slightly to his left, meaning a hundred yards or so, from Bolan's altitude. It was a black hole from his viewpoint, while sunlight reflected on the treetops all around that vaguely oval gap amid the foliage. From two thousand feet, it looked like the cup on a putting green. Up close, he guessed, it would resemble an abandoned well or mine shaft yawning to receive him.

If he didn't miss his mark and hang up in the trees.

Bolan was skilled at navigating parachutes. He'd learned the art as a young Green Beret and practiced it sporadically throughout his wars, keeping his skills and reflexes in shape. Still, there were always unexpected twists and turns in any combat mission. Wind might carry him off course, a bird could strike him in the head and render him unconscious, or the guidelines on his chute might snap, leaving him rudderless.

If none of that transpired, he had a chance to hit his mark—and only then would he find out what happened next.

The guide lines didn't break. No windy gale or suicidal bird disrupted Bolan's plan. He steered the parachute without a hitch, correcting his descent by slow degrees until the dark mouth of the jungle clearing was directly underneath his feet. Up close it was a black maw, roughly oval, thirty-seven feet, nine inches wide at treetop level.

The dimensions were precise, but Bolan had no clue what might be waiting for him at the bottom of the shaft.

Assuming that he ever got that far.

He marked a bull's-eye in his mind, steered for it, watching his target instead of the belled chute above him. Bolan pointed his toes, peering between his boots as if they formed a gunsight's V.

So far, so good.

The treetops rose to meet him much more swiftly now, it seemed, during the final yards of his descent. Gripping the risers firmly, Bolan fought to keep the parachute on course, resisting updrafts from the sun-warmed canopy.

The clearing yawned beneath him. With a hiss of rip-stop nylon, Bolan hit his mark. The forest swallowed him alive.

It was a curious sensation, being swallowed by a jungle. First, the sunlight flickered, faded, screened by treetops looming overhead as Bolan cleared the forest canopy. An instant later he felt a drastic change in the humidity and temperature. Though shaded now, Bolan had also lost the morning breeze. It felt like plummeting into a sauna, fully clothed.

Dead air didn't provide the same support for Bolan's parachute, either. The pace of his descent accelerated, but he had no room for any kind of meaningful maneuver. What had once gone up was coming down, and he could only brace himself for impact as the ground rose to accept its human sacrifice.

A glance in passing told him that the clearing had to have been created by a lightning strike that shattered one great tree, in much the same way demolition experts drop a skyscraper without inflicting any major damage on its neighbors. Eight feet below him, closing fast, Bolan saw the detritus of the forest giant's fall. A ragged stump sprouted from mulch and teeming fungus growths, surrounded by remains of charred and rotted wood.

Before he had a chance to think about what might be living, breeding, feeding in the giant compost heap below him, Bolan struck the spongy surface. He had time to veer a yard or two off course, avoid impalement on the sharp-pronged mahogany stump, but that effort cost him balance on the landing and he rolled in filth, smothered in the chute as it descended like a shroud.

Bolan opened the quick-release clasps on his harness and shed it, pulled his knife and slit the parachute, emerging from it like some mutant forest life-form rising from its amniotic sac. At once, he sheathed the blade, unslung his AUG and waited where he stood for any challenge from the jungle murk.

A silent minute passed, then two, and he was satisfied. Keeping his rifle close at hand, Bolan hauled in the flaccid remnants of his chute, and opened his entrenching tool. The mulch beneath his boots was soft and had a mildew stench about it. When he broke the surface crust, it teemed with vermin—ants, worms, beetles Bolan didn't recognize—but he dug deeper, leaving those he had disturbed to scramble for another path to darkness, out of sight.

He dug until he had a pit of ample size to hold the bundled parachute, his spare, the harness and the helmet he had worn. Filling the hole was faster, but he took the extra time to evenly disperse the surplus mulch he'd excavated from the reeking mound. The next rain, probably sometime that afternoon, would mask whatever signs of digging Bolan left behind. Searchers would have to excavate the spot themselves, to find his gear, and there was no good reason they should even try it if they'd hadn't seen him drop in from on high.

Digging ditches in ninety-degree heat and ninety-eight-percent humidity drained a strong man's vigor in a hurry. Bolan was a veteran jungle fighter, long accustomed to the hardships of tropical climates, but every day spent away from the jungle, swaddled in the chill of fans and air conditioners, reduced a subject's tolerance for enervating heat. His thirty hours in Brazzaville had helped provide a measure of reacclimation, but there was a world of difference between the city—any city—and the bush.

Bolan folded his shovel, stowed it and allowed himself a sip of water from one of his canteens. Ironically, dehydration was a major risk in the midst of a sodden rain forest, where any water he found would be teeming with germs, unfit to drink unless he boiled it first.

And Bolan couldn't risk a fire.

Not yet.

He might be burning something later, but for now he had to pass unnoticed through the forest en route to his target. Any chance encounters on the way increased the danger to himself and to his mission.

He had taken on the job for old times' sake, driven by feelings long suppressed if not forgotten, paying an installment on a debt of loyalty he knew would never fully be discharged.

In truth, he didn't want to cut that tie, however tenuous it was. Sometimes even a scarred and bloodied warrior needed something to remind him of another time. Another life. It might be lost beyond recall, but memories were precious, all the same.

CHAPTER TWO

Cheyenne, Wyoming

Five days before he stepped out of the Cessna into Congo skies, Bolan had followed cowboy footsteps through the streets of what was once a wild and woolly frontier town. He dawdled past gift shops, a bookstore with a lot of history and Western fiction in the windows, glancing at his watch again to verify the time.

Almost.

He didn't know that much about Wyoming—big-sky country, open range, the Rockies—but it didn't matter. Dressing like a tourist didn't make him one. Bolan had business here, and it was causing him a teaspoon's measure of anxiety.

He was surprised to see a pair of middle-aged civilians pass, both wearing pistols holstered on their hips. No badges visible, and Bolan took a moment to remind himself that this was still the wild frontier, in certain ways.

His own sidearm, the sleek Beretta 93-R with selective fire and twenty Parabellum rounds packing its magazine, was tucked discreetly out of sight beneath a nylon windbreaker. He much preferred the fast-draw armpit rig and had no need to advertise that he was armed.

As long as he could reach the pistol when it mattered.

Bolan had two minutes left to wait, but it was getting on his nerves. That was peculiar in itself, considering that patience was a sniper's trademark and a trait that kept him breathing, but he wrote it off to special circumstances in the present case. The message from his brother had surprised him and had kept him revved since he received it.

He wasn't nervous in the classic sense, afraid of what would happen in the next few minutes, worried that he might not find a way to handle it. Bolan had outgrown such emotions as a teenager, had any remnants of them purged by fire as a young man. That didn't mean he was immune to feelings, though.

Not even close.

He'd driven past the Chinese restaurant first thing, an hour early for the meeting, checking out the street. That part was instinct, watching for a trap. It made no difference that his brother would've died before collaborating with an enemy. Betrayal wasn't even on his mind.

The drive-by was a habit, ingrained for good reason. Johnny would've taken care when calling, but that didn't guarantee their conversation had been secure. What really was, these days? Each day, the NSA's code breakers intercepted countless e-mails, phone calls, radio transmissions, television programs. Other ears and eyes were also constantly alert. There was a chance, however miniscule, that Johnny had been singled out, his message plucked from the air or off the wires and passed along to someone who would pay to keep the rendezvous.

For one shot at the Executioner.

The drive-by had been wasted, nothing on the street that indicated any kind of trap in place. That didn't mean the restaurant was clean, simply that Bolan couldn't spot a snare if one was waiting for him. Call it eighty-five percent relaxed as Bolan turned from the shop window he'd been studying, using the glass to mirror the pedestrians passing behind him, watching both sides of the street. His windbreaker hung open, granting easy access to the pistol if he was mistaken and a trap awaited him within the next block and a half.

The call from Johnny had been short and sweet.

"Val needs to see you, bro," he'd said. "Can you find time?"

And it was wild, how a three-letter word could reach across the miles and years, clutching his heart in a death grip.

No, that was wrong. Make it a *life* grip, and it would be closer to the truth.

Val needs to see you, bro. Can you find time?

Hell, yes.

The day seemed warmer as he neared the corner where a left turn was required to reach the restaurant. Bolan could feel a sheen of perspiration on his forehead and beneath his arms. It wasn't *that* hot, and the physical reaction made him frown.

It's been a long time, he admitted. Then, as if to reassure himself, There's nothing to it. Get a grip.

The nerves were partly Johnny's fault. He could've spelled it out directly, or at least suggested why Val needed him. It had been years since they'd seen each other last, and she had been hospitalized, recuperating from one of those traumas that dogged Bolan's handful of loved ones and friends. It was his final memory of Val, and he had no idea how well she had recovered from her injuries. What scars remained, inside or out.

At least she wasn't one of Bolan's ghosts.

Not yet.

Val needs you.

Why? Presumably she'd tell him to his face.

He cleared the corner, gave the street a final sweep and walked on to the Bamboo Garden, halfway down the block. The door made little chiming sounds as he pushed through it, brought a smiling hostess out to intercept him.

"One for lunch?" she asked.

"I'm meeting someone," he replied. And as he spoke, he had them spotted. "Over there."

The hostess bobbed her head. "Please follow me."

As they moved toward the corner booth, he noted Johnny's left leg sticking into the aisle, his foot and ankle fattened by a plaster cast. A pair of crutches leaned against the wall beside him.

Val was seated on the inside, next to Johnny on his right. Her raven hair was cut to shoulder length, framing a face with the exotic beauty of her Spanish heritage. Her smile seemed tentative, but what could he expect?

He sat, back to the door, and didn't even mind. Johnny could watch the street. The hostess handed him a menu and retreated. Bolan knew he was supposed to read it, order food. He simply wasn't there yet.

"Long time," Val said. "You're looking good."

He wasn't sure if that was true, but Bolan meant it when he said, "You, too."

He turned to his brother. "What's the story on that leg?"

Johnny looked suitably embarrassed. "It's a classic," he replied. "Stepped off a ladder, got tangled up and cracked a couple bones."

"No marathons this season, then."

"Guess not."

That much told Bolan part of why Val had reached out for him. Johnny was benched for the duration, and whatever problem had arisen, Bolan guessed it couldn't wait for him to heal.

"Bad luck," he said.

"What brings you down from Sheridan?" he asked Val.

Her home was on the far side of the state, near the Montana border, some 330 miles north of Cheyenne. Bolan surmised that Val had picked the meeting place so that she wouldn't have him on her doorstep.

Just in case.

Trouble had found her in Wyoming once already, and she wouldn't want a replay. Not if she could help it.

"I thought we could eat first, catch up on old times," Val said. "Then maybe take a drive and talk about the other when we're done."

Where waitresses and busboys couldn't eavesdrop.

"Sounds all right to me," said Bolan.

"Good." Another smile, relieved.

Old times, he thought.

They seemed like bloody yesterday.

VALENTINA QUERENTE had been calling her cat the night Bolan had first seen her, in Pittsfield, Massachusetts. On the run and bleeding out from bullet wounds inflicted by a crew of Mafia manhunters, he'd staggered into Val's life, literally on his last legs, bringing unexpected danger to her doorstep. She had taken Bolan in and nursed him back to health, no questions asked, and in the process her initial sympathy had turned to something deeper, something stronger than she'd ever felt before. Bolan had been startled to discover that he'd felt the same.

The warrior and his lady had spent nearly a month in the eye of the storm, while cops and contract killers turned the city upside down in search of Bolan. Finally, they had decided that he had to be dead, or maybe wise enough to flee the territory for a hopeless life in hiding, parts unknown. His would-be killers left a million-dollar open contract on his head, uncollected, and went back to business as usual.

For some, it was their last mistake.

Bolan had returned from his near-death experience with a vengeance, striking his enemies with shock and awe long before some military PR man had patented the phrase. He left the syndicate's Massachusetts Family in smoking ruins, but he couldn't hang around and taste the fruits of victory.

There would be no peace for the Executioner, as he pursued his long and lonely one-man war against the Mafia from coast to coast. No rest from battle and no safety for the ones he loved. Before he left Pittsfield, with no hope of returning, Bolan's heart and soul were joined to Val's in every way that counted short of walking down the aisle to say, "I do." And by that time he'd known that home and family, the picket fence and nine-to-five, had slipped beyond his grasp forever.

There'd be no treaty with the Syndicate, and he could never really win the war he'd started when he executed those responsible for shattering his family. It was a blood feud to the bitter end, and Val hadn't signed on for that. She would've risked it, but he had refused in no uncertain terms.

It had been Val's idea for her to shelter Bolan's brother Johnny, at a time when every hit man in the country wanted Bolan's head. A living relative was leverage, and anyone who harbored him was thus at risk, but on that point she wouldn't be dissuaded. Bolan might roar off into the flaming sunset and abandon her, but Val knew that he wouldn't take his brother on that long last ride. She volunteered to make that sacrifice—

risk everything she had, future included—to preserve the Bolan line, and thus maintain at least a slender thread of contact with the warrior who had changed her life.

It was a good plan, soundly executed, but the best of human schemes sometimes went wrong. In time, a Boston mobster had divined Val's secret, kidnapped her and Johnny in a bid to make his prey surrender, trade his life for theirs. Bolan had recognized a no-win situation from the get-go, known his enemy would never let two witnesses escape his clutches. There'd been no room for negotiation as the soldier launched his Boston blitz and damned near tore the town apart. Mobsters and cops alike still talked about the day the Executioner had come to town, but most of those who served the Boston Mafia today had heard the stories secondhand. There weren't many survivors from the actual event to keep the facts straight as they circulated on the streets.

Before the smoke cleared on that hellfire day, Johnny and Val were safely back in Bolan's hands. He'd passed them on to Hal Brognola, then chief of the FBI's organized crime task force. He in turn had assigned FBI agent Jack Gray to handle security for Val and the boy who posed as her son.

And something happened.

Bolan's first reaction, on hearing from Johnny that Val and Jack were engaged to be married, was a warm rush of relief. Despite the love for her that he would carry to his grave, he felt no jealousy. Bolan had offered Val nothing but loneliness, love on the run and damned little of that. He knew that she deserved the finer things in life, and when she married, when her groom adopted Johnny Bolan and his name was changed to Johnny Gray, Bolan had felt a guilty burden lifted from his shoulders.

Val could live and love without a shadow darkening each moment of her life. Johnny could grow up strong and stable, without hearing schoolyard gibes about his brother on the FBI's Most Wanted list. And if the end came—*when* it came—for Bolan, they could mourn him quietly, without fanfare.

They could move on with their lives.

That should've been the final chapter, but an echo of the Mob wars had returned to haunt them all, long after Bolan had moved on to other enemies and battle-grounds, with a new face and new identity. A mobster scarred by his encounter with the Executioner, maddened by his pursuit of vengeance, had traced the Grays to their new home in Wyoming, making yet another bid to reach Bolan through those he loved. The hunter missed Johnny, a grown man on his own by then, but he had wounded Jack and kidnapped Valentina, dragging her into a private hell as he reprised the Boston plan of forcing Bolan to reveal himself.

It worked, but not exactly as the lone-wolf stalker planned. He got his face-to-face with Bolan, but he'd found the Executioner too much to handle. Perhaps the old maxim "Be careful what you wish for" echoed through the gunman's mind before he died.

Or maybe not.

In any case, Val had survived, but at a price. She carried new scars on her psyche, from her brutal treatment at the killer's hands, and Bolan wasn't sure if they would ever truly heal. He knew some women bore the strain better than others, and while Valentina ranked among the strongest people he had ever known, nobody was invincible. Some wounds healed on the surface, but could rot the soul.

Bolan had checked with Johnny over time, received his brother's reassurance that Val had recovered from her ordeal. She was "okay," "fine," "getting along" with Jack's rehab and other tasks she'd chosen for herself.

But now she needed him again.

And Bolan wondered why.

"How's Jack?" he asked as lunch arrived.

"Retired," Val said. "I guess you knew that, though. He's doing corporate security and helping me with some of my projects."

"Which are?"

"I teach a class at community college now and then. Do some counseling on the side. I've also established a mentoring program off campus."

"That must keep you busy," Bolan said.

"I'm thinking of letting it go."

He began to ask if that was part of the reason she'd summoned him here, but it didn't make sense and he kept to his agreement to eat first and ask questions later. The food was a cut above average but nothing to write

home about. Bolan ate his meal, drank some coffee and
went through the motions when the waitress brought
their fortune cookies.

His read, "You will take a journey soon."

There's a surprise.

Bolan picked up the check, dismissing Val's objections, then accepting her reluctant thanks. Reluctance
seemed to be the order of the day, in fact. Val had a
vaguely worried look about her as they left the Chinese
restaurant.

"Are we still driving?" Bolan asked. "My rental's
parked around the corner."

"Mine's right here," Val answered, moving toward a
year-old minivan. "I'll drive."

Johnny kept pace on crutches, telling Bolan, "I can
drive, but Val says no. She's such a mom sometimes."

"I heard that," Val informed him. "If it was supposed
to be an insult, you need new material."

"No insult. I'm just saying—"

"That you're handi-capable. No argument. Just
humor me, all right?"

"Okay."

Johnny maneuvered into the backseat, while Bolan
sat up front with Val. He didn't mind the shotgun
seat. It let him watch one of the minivan's three
mirrors as Val pulled out from the curb. They had no
tail, as far as he could see, but he kept watching as
she drove.

Habits died hard.

Soldiers who let them slip died harder.

"Do we need to sweep the van for bugs, or can we talk now?" Bolan asked.

Val cut him with a sidelong glance. "I didn't want to get the restaurant mixed up in this," she said.

"Mixed up in what?"

"I told you that I do some mentoring, aside from classes."

"Right."

"I doubt that you've had time to keep up with the trend," she said. "It sounds like simple tutoring, but there's a lot more to it. Counseling, sometimes. Guidance toward long-term life decisions if appropriate."

"Is there some course you take for that, like special training?" Bolan asked.

"I have my counseling credential, plus the teacher's certificate," she answered, "but it's mostly personal experience and observation. Listening as much as talking, maybe more. I don't come out and tell students they should be lawyers or mechanics. If they have an interest, we address it and discuss the options. If they have problems, we talk about those, too."

"So, how's it going?" Bolan asked, sincerely interested.

"I've lost one," Val replied.

"Say what?"

"One of my students."

"Val—"

"I don't mean that he's disappeared," she hastened to explain. "For that, I would've gone to the police."

"Okay."

"I know exactly where he is. Well, not *exactly*, but within a few square miles. And what he's doing. That's the problem."

"Maybe you should start from the beginning."

"Right. Okay. But promise you won't think I'm crazy."

"That's a safe bet going in," said Bolan.

"All right, then. His name's Patrick Quinn. He turned twenty-one last weekend, but I haven't seen him for three months. It's thirteen weeks on Friday, if you need to pin it down exactly."

"Close enough," he said, and waited for the rest of it.

"He comes from money. Anyway, a lot by how they measure it in Sheridan. His parents raise cattle. They have a few million."

"Cattle?"

"Dollars," Johnny answered from the backseat. "Four point five and change."

"You hacked their bank account?" Bolan asked.

Johnny shook his head. "Bear did it for me."

Meaning, Aaron Kurtzman, boss of the computer crew at Stony Man Farm, in Virginia.

"So, the Farm's involved in this?"

"I asked a favor," Johnny told him. "Strictly unofficial."

Ah. A backdoor job. But why?

"Still listening," he told them both.

"Pat's father wanted him in law school, but he didn't like the paper chase. Premed was too much science. What he really wanted was a job that let him work for the environment. Something like forestry, the conservation side. It made for stormy holidays at home, to say the least."

"And he wound up with you," Bolan said.

"Right. First in a class I taught last year, then counseling after he set his mind on dropping out completely."

"I guess it didn't take?"

"We made some headway, working on a new curriculum, before the Process came to town," Val said.

"You don't mean that satanic outfit from the sixties, tied in with the Manson family?"

"Wrong Process," Val corrected him. "At least, I'm pretty sure. This one's a sect run by an African—Nigerian, I think he is—named Ahmadou Gaborone."

"Never heard of him," Bolan admitted.

"He's spent a lot of time flying below the radar," Johnny said. "No flamboyant outbursts like Moon or Jim Jones, no public investigations. He's been sued twice on fraud charges and won both cases."

"Fraud?"

"The usual," Val said. "Some youngster donates all of his or her worldly goods to the Process and the parents go ballistic, claiming undue influence, coercion, brainwashing, you name it. Gaborone's been smart enough, so far, to only bilk legal adults, and they've appeared for his side when the cases went to court. All smiles and sunshine, couldn't be more happy, the usual."

Bolan shrugged. "Maybe they are," he said, catching the look Val gave him. "Some folks don't function well alone. They need a preacher or some other figure of authority directing them, telling them what to think. You see it in the major churches all the time. It's what your basic televangelists rely on, when they beg for cash."

"This one is different," Val informed him. "Gaborone's not just collecting money, cars, whatever. He's collecting souls for Judgment Day."

"You lost me," Bolan said.

"Recruits—converts, whatever—don't just pony up whatever's in their bank accounts. They also leave 'the world,' as Gaborone describes it, and move on to follow him. He used to have three communes in the States, in Oregon, Wyoming and upstate New York, but all his people have been called to Africa. The Congo. He's established a community they call Obike, also known as New Jerusalem."

"You said the Process had a compound in Wyoming," Bolan interrupted. "Am I right in guessing that your protégé was part of it?"

"You are," Val granted. "Now he's gone. I'm hoping you can bring him back while there's still time."

VAL HAD PREPARED for meeting Bolan, talked herself through the emotions that were bound to surface at first sight, considering their history. She'd braced herself, thought she was ready, but the storm of feelings loosed inside her when she saw him in the flesh still took her by surprise. She'd managed eating, barely, and was glad when they were in the minivan, moving, her story starting to unfold. But now, she had begun to wonder if her master plan was such a great idea.

"When you say, 'bring him back,'" Bolan replied, "you mean…?"

"To us," she said, too quickly. "Well, of course, I mean his family."

"Suppose he doesn't want to come?"

"It's likely that he won't, at first," she said.

"So, it's a kidnapping you have in mind?"

"If that's what it takes."

"I'm not a deprogrammer, Val. I don't save people from themselves."

"But Patrick—"

"By your own admission, he's an adult. Twenty-one, in fact. I don't know what kind of donation he's given the Process, but—"

"A few thousand," she said. Her turn to interrupt. "His parents froze Pat's trust fund when they found out what was happening with Gaborone."

"So, has he been declared incompetent to run his own affairs?" Bolan asked.

"Not specifically. His parents have a pending case, but Patrick's unavailable to testify or be deposed. It's all in limbo now, with a judicial freeze on his accounts until the court is satisfied he's not acting under duress."

"A standoff, basically."

"So far," Val said, keeping an eye on traffic as she spoke. "But money's not my primary concern."

"I gathered that," Bolan replied. "So, what's the problem, really? Do you think he's been abused? Mistreated? Starved?"

"There's been no evidence of anything like that,"

Johnny remarked. "All members of the Process who've been interviewed so far seem happy where they are."

"In that case," Bolan said, "I don't see—"

"Happy messages came out of Jonestown," Val reminded him, "until the night they drank the poisoned fruit punch. Who knows what people are really thinking, what they're really feeling in a cult?"

"Not me," Bolan admitted. "Which explains why I don't normally go in for kidnapping. Unless you've got some evidence—"

"You haven't heard about the Rathbun party, then?"

Bolan considered it, then shook his head. "It doesn't ring a bell."

"Lee Rathbun is—or was—a congressman from Southern California. Orange County, if it matters. Some of his constituents had relatives who'd joined the Process and gone off to live in Africa with Gaborone. Last week, Rathbun and five others flew to Brazzaville and on to Obike. They should've been back on Monday, but word is that they've disappeared."

"That's it? Just gone?"

"It smells," Johnny said from the backseat. "First, Gaborone and his people swear up and down Rathbun's party made their charter flight on schedule. When the cops in Brazzaville start checking, they discover that the charter pilot's killed himself under suspicious circumstances. Killed his sister, too—who, by coincidence, was also in the Process."

"Why the sister?" Bolan asked.

"Police report they found a note and 'other evidence'

suggesting incest," Val said. "They think the sister tried to end it, or the brother couldn't bear his shame. Theories are flexible, but none of them lead back to Gaborone."

"Too much coincidence," Johnny declared.

"It's odd," Bolan agreed. "I'll give you that."

"Just odd?" Val didn't try to hide the irritation in her tone.

"How were the killings done?" Bolan asked.

"With a panga," Val replied. "That's a big—"

"Knife, I know. The pilot stabbed himself?"

"Not quite," Johnny said. "Seems he put his panga on the kitchen counter, then bent down and ran his throat along the cutting edge until he got the job done. Back and forth. Nearly decapitated."

"That's what I call focus and determination."

"That's what *I* call murder," Val corrected him.

"Assume you're right, which I agree is probable. Who killed the pilot? Someone from the Process? Why?"

"To silence him," Val said. "Because he knew that Rathbun's people didn't make their flight to Brazzaville on time."

"How long between their scheduled liftoff and the murder?" Bolan asked.

"Twelve hours, give or take."

"And how long is the flight from Brazzaville to Gaborone's community?"

"About two hours," Johnny said.

"Leaving ten hours for the pilot to contact police

and spill the beans about his missing passengers. Why no contact with 911 or the equivalent?"

"We're guessing the pilot was bribed, threatened, or both," Val said. "Then Gaborone or someone close to him decided it was still too risky, so they silenced him and staged it in a way that would discredit anything the pilot might've said before he died."

"Okay, it plays," Bolan agreed. "But it's a matter for police. There's nothing to suggest your friend's involvement with the murders, or that he's in any kind of danger from—"

"That's just the point," Val said. "He *is* in danger."

"Oh?"

"The Process is an apocalyptic sect. Gaborone is one of your basic hellfire, end-time preachers, with a twist."

"Specifically?"

"Lately, he's started saying that it may not be enough to wait for God to schedule Armageddon. When it's time, he says, the Lord may need a helping hand to light the fuse."

"From Africa?"

"It's what he heard in 'words of wisdom' from on high," Johnny explained.

"I never thought the Congo had much Armageddon potential," Bolan said.

"Depends on how you mix up the ingredients, I guess," said Johnny. "In the time since he's been settled at Obike, Gaborone's had several unlikely visitors. One party from the Russian *mafiya* included an ex-colonel with the KGB. Two others were Islamic militants, and there's a warlord from Sudan whose dropped in twice."

"You don't think they were praying for redemption," Bolan said.

"Not even close."

"But if we rescue Patrick Quinn, and he agrees to talk, it may all be explained."

"Maybe," Johnny agreed.

"Or maybe not," Bolan counseled. "Even if he turns and gives you everything he knows, the rank and file in cults don't often know what's going on behind the scenes with their gurus."

"It's still a chance," Val said. "And Pat deserves *his* chance to live a normal life."

"Can you define that for me?" Bolan asked her, smiling.

"You know what I mean."

"I guess."

She saw concession in his eyes, knew he was leaning toward agreement, but she couldn't take a chance on losing him. No matter how it hurt them both, she gave a quick tug on the line, to set the hook.

"So, will you help us, Mack?"

CHAPTER THREE

Five days after he looked into those eyes and said he would help, Bolan was marching through the Congo jungle, guided toward his target by the handheld GPS device. He found it relatively easygoing but still had to watch his step, as much for normal dangers of the rain forest as for a human threat.

Contrary to the view held by most people who have never seen a jungle, great rain forests generally weren't choked with thick, impenetrable undergrowth. Where giant trees existed, their canopy blotted out the sky and starved most smaller plants of the sunshine they needed to thrive. Ground level, although amply watered by incessant rain, was mostly colonized by ferns and fungus growths that thrived in shade, dwelling in permanent twilight beneath their looming neighbors.

Walking through the jungle, then, was no great challenge except for mud that clung to boots or made the hiker's feet slide out from under him. Gnarled roots sometimes conspired to trip a passerby, and ancient trees sometimes collapsed when rot and insects undercut their bases, but the jungle's greatest danger was from predators.

They came in every size and shape, as Bolan realized, from lethal insects and arachnids to leopards and huge crocodiles. He had the bugs covered, at least in theory, with his fatigues. An odorless insect repellent was bonded to the garment fabrics, guaranteed on paper to protect against flies, mosquitoes, ticks and other pests through twenty-five machine washings. As for reptiles and mammals, Bolan simply had to watch his step, check logs and stones before he sat, beware of dangling "vines" that might have fangs and keep his distance from the murky flow of any rivers where he could.

Simple.

Camping wasn't a problem, since his drop zone was a mere three miles from Bolan's target. The extraction point was farther west, about five miles, but he could make it well before sundown, if all went according to plan.

And that, as always, was the rub.

Plans had a way of turning fluid once they left the drawing board and found their way into the field. Experience had taught Bolan that almost anything could happen when time came to translate strategy to action. He'd never been struck by lighting, had never watched a meteorite hurtle into the midst of a firefight, but barring divine intervention Bolan thought he'd seen it all.

People were unpredictable in most cases, no matter how you analyzed and scoped them out before an operation started. Fear, anger, excitement—those and any other feeling he could name might motivate a human being to perform some feat of cowardice or daring that was wholly unpredictable. Vehicles failed and weapons jammed. A sudden wind caused smoke to drift and fires to rage out of control. Rain turned a battleground into a swamp and rivers overflowed their banks.

One thing Bolan had learned to count on was the unexpected, in whatever form it might assume.

The jungle climate that surrounded him decreed a range of possibilities. It wouldn't snow, he realized, unless the planet shifted on its axis—in which case it likely wouldn't matter what a Congo cult leader was planning, one way or another. He had no reason to suspect that a volcano would erupt and drown the cult compound in molten lava. Sandstorms were unlikely in the middle of a jungle.

He started to watch for traps and sentries when he was a mile east of Obike. Bolan wasn't sure if Gaborone's people foraged in the jungle, but he took no chances. If the guru truly thought the Last Days were upon him—or if that was just a scam, and he was double-dealing with some kind of slick black-market action on the side—it was a fair bet that he posted guards. More likely now, if Val and Johnny were correct in their suspicion that the cult had killed a U.S. congressman and members of his entourage.

If Rathbun and his crew weren't dead, it posed

another kind of problem for the Executioner. He'd come prepared to lift one person from the compound, not to rescue seven. Even if he managed to extract that many souls, the chopper rented by Grimaldi wouldn't seat eight passengers. He couldn't strap them to the landing struts, and who would Bolan ask to stay behind?

Forget it, Bolan thought. They're dead by now.

If not...

Then he'd jump off that bridge when he got to it, hoping there was time to scan the water below for hungry crocodiles.

Meanwhile, he had a job to do and it was almost time.

The GPS system led Bolan to Obike with no problem. He could smell the compound's cooking fires and its latrines before he saw the barracks and guard towers ranged in front of him. And there were sentries, yes indeed, well armed against potential enemies.

Bolan stood watching from the forest shadows, working out a plan to infiltrate the camp to find one man among seven hundred people known to occupy this drab, unlikely New Jerusalem.

After an hour, give or take, the Executioner knew what he had to do.

"GIVE ME THE PEOPLE'S mood, Nico. I need to know what they are thinking, what they're feeling now."

Mbarga had expected it. The master often hatched a plan, then put it into motion, only later thinking of the consequences to himself and those around him. That was genius, in a sense—fixation on a goal, a means of solving problems, without letting daily life intrude.

But that could also be a self-destructive kind of genius, doomed to early death.

"I move among them, Master," he replied. "And as you know, my presence urges them to silence. They work harder and talk less when I am near. We have no listening devices in the camp, so I—"

"Give me your sense of how they're feeling, Nico. I don't ask you for confessions of betrayal."

Nico swallowed hard. Telling the truth was dangerous with Gaborone, but if the master later caught him in a lie that had already blown up in their faces, it could be worse yet.

"Master," he said at last, "some of the folk are worried. Naturally, they trust your judgment in all things, but still some fear there may be repercussions over the Americans. In these days, when the White House orders bombing raids, invades whole nations without evidence, they fear our actions may yet bring about the Final Days."

"And they fear that?" Gaborone asked. He seemed confused.

"Some do. Yes, sir."

"After I've told them time and time again they must fear nothing? That the Final Days will simply be our passport into Paradise? Why would they fear a moment's suffering, compared to that eternal bliss?"

"They're only human, Master," Mbarga said. "They know pain and loss from personal experience, but none have shared your glimpse of Paradise."

"They share through me!" Gaborone said, now seeming on the verge of anger. Mbarga knew he had to calm the guru swiftly or his own well-being might be jeopardized.

"They share in *words*, Master, but it is not the same. You've *seen* the wonders of the other side. Despite your eloquence, unrivaled in the world today, word pictures still fall short of all that you've experienced in Heaven."

"Paradise," Gaborone said, correcting him.

"Of course, sir. I apologize."

"How can we calm the people, Nico?"

"They need time, Master. And I will watch them closely."

"In the matter of our visitors," Gaborone said, "are they content?"

The delegation had arrived that morning, ferried from the jungle landing strip by Mbarga and his men. No more Americans this time, but men with money in their pockets, anxious to impress the master and do business with him. It was Mbarga's job to keep them happy in between negotiations, and he took the job seriously.

"Both are resting now, after their midday meal," Mbarga said. "The South American requested a companion for his bed."

"He is a pig," Gaborone said, "but very wealthy."

"I sent him one of the neophytes. The Irish girl. She'll see you later, Master, to receive her penance."

"Ah. A wise choice, Nico. And the other?"

"He asked nothing, Master. I believe he favors

young men over girls. The way he looked at some of your parishioners…"

"Enough! There is a limit to my patience." Gaborone frowned mightily, then added, "If he should insist, choose wisely. Use your own best judgment, Nico."

"Always, Master."

"When I speak to them again, tonight, we may—"

The shout came from outside, somewhere across the compound. Nico heard the single word, repeated loudly.

"Fire!"

"What's that?" asked Gaborone, distractedly.

"A cry of 'fire,' Master. I'll see what—"

"Go! Hurry!" As Nico left the master's quarters, Gaborone called after him, "And don't disturb our guests!"

Outside, Mbarga smelled the smoke before he saw it, dark plumes rising from one of the storage sheds. What did they keep in that one? Food. Mbarga wondered if the grain in burlap sacks had grown too hot somehow, inside the shed, or if there'd been some kind of accident to start the fire.

Jaw clenched, Mbarga planned what he would do if it turned out that someone had been smoking, in defiance of the master's edict.

He joined the flow of people rushing toward the fire, anxious to smother it or just to be a part of the excitement. He was halfway there and shoving rudely past the others when another cry went up, this one arising from the far side of the camp.

"Fire!" someone shouted over there. "Another fire!"

IT WASN'T ANYTHING high tech, but Bolan often put his trust in fire. It ranked among humanity's best friends and oldest enemies, holding the power to inspire or panic, after all those centuries. A warm fire on the hearth might lead to passion or a good night's sleep. Flames racing through a household or a village uncontrolled were guaranteed to set off a stampede.

He'd taken time to choose his targets, noting structures here and there around the huddled village that would burn without immediately posing any threat to human life. Storehouses, toolsheds and the like were best. And he was lucky, in that Gaborone's community hadn't invested in aluminum or any kind of prefab structures that were fire resistant. They used simple wood, often unpainted, and there seemed to be no fire-retardant chemicals or insulation anywhere.

His first challenge was entering the camp, but Bolan managed it. The watchtowers were manned, but by a careless breed of sentries, more inclined to talk than to scan the tree line for approaching enemies. The guards on foot were spread too thin, and no fence had been raised to help them keep intruders from the village proper. Bolan waited, chose his moment, and crept in when those who should've tried to stop him were distracted, feeling lazy in the heat of early afternoon. A light rain shower that had fallen while he circled the perimeter wasn't refreshing; quite the opposite, in fact.

But luck was with him. As the atmosphere conspired with Bolan to seduce his enemies, so he was shown the young man he had come to find. Bolan carried no photograph of Patrick Quinn. He'd memorized it and returned it to the slim file Val and Johnny had presented to him in Wyoming. He would know Quinn if they met, though, and the straggly wisps of beard his quarry had been cultivating in the past few weeks did little to conceal his face, when Bolan saw him coming out of the latrine.

Quinn had a listless air about him, but that seemed to be the rule for tenants of Obike. He wore what seemed to be the standard uniform for male inhabitants, a pair of faded denim pants with rope pulled through the belt loops, and an off-white cotton shirt. Long sleeves despite the heat, but no one seemed to mind. None of the sleeves he'd seen so far had been rolled up. Perhaps it was another of the guru's rules.

Quinn had lost weight since he was photographed, and there was no trace of a smile in evidence. Bolan watched as the young man walked from the latrine to one of several barracks buildings on the north side of the compound, went inside and closed the door behind him. Even with the windows open, Bolan guessed it had to have been a sweatbox there, inside.

After determining where Quinn was, Bolan set his fires accordingly. Obike's honor system helped him, since he found no locks upon the doors, and the midday siesta minimized his contact with the villagers. Bolan met one along the way, about Quinn's age, unarmed but ready to alert the camp before strong fingers clamped his windpipe shut and Bolan's fist rocked him to sleep. He bound the young man's hands with trouser twine and gagged him with the severed tail of his own shirt, then stashed him in a toolshed, propped against a bank of hoes and rakes.

He had gone on from there to set three fires, slow-burners, sited to draw villagers away from Quinn's barracks and focus their attention elsewhere. The first alarm was shouted moments after Bolan found his hiding place beside the target building, crouched in a convenient shadow.

Those cries of "Fire!" had the desired result. Guards rushed to find out what was happening, while sleepy villagers emerged more slowly from their gender-segregated clapboard dormitories. Bolan watched and waited, heard men stirring just beyond the wall that sheltered him. He couldn't pick Quinn's voice out of the babble, but it made no difference.

Leaving his rifle slung, Bolan removed the hypodermic needle from its cushioned case and held it ready in his hand.

NOW WHAT? Patrick Quinn thought. He'd barely fallen back to sleep after his trek to the latrine, and now the sounds of crisis roused him from a troubled dream whose fragments blew away before his mind could catch and hold them.

Someone shouting from a distance. And what were they saying?

"Fire! *Fire!*"

Quinn bolted upright on his cot, no blankets to restrain him in the stuffy room's oppressive heat.

Around him, others were already on their feet, repeating the alarm in half a dozen languages.

"Hurry!" someone declared.

A new round of warning shouts rose from a different part of the village, bringing a frown to Quinn's face. Two fires at the same time? Quinn wondered whether it was one of Master Gaborone's incessant drills. They'd been more frequent lately, since the incident with the American film crew, and failure to perform was bound to mean some sort of punishment.

Quinn started for the door, then hesitated. That was smoke he smelled, no doubt about it. Would the master go that far to make his practice exercise seem real? He wasn't known for using props, and yet—

When the third cry of "Fire!" rent the air, rising from yet another part of the village, Quinn knew something was wrong. The master's drills were never that elaborate. He simply sent his guards around to roust the people from their beds or jobs and send then streaming toward the sectors designated as emergency retreats.

A real fire, then—or *fires*, to be more accurate. When was the last time that had happened? Never, since Quinn first set foot inside the compound.

Sudden fear surprised him, but he had a duty to perform. Each member of the congregation had a role to play, whether at work or in response to situations unforeseen. Quinn reckoned he could be of service to the master and his fellow congregants, if he could just suppress his fear and trust the prophet's message.

Feeling childish, now that all the others had gone on ahead of him, Quinn rushed the door and made his way outside. He hesitated on the dormitory's simple wooden steps—all of the buildings in Obike had been raised to keep out snakes and vermin, though Quinn thought the shady crawl spaces beneath had to be like breeding grounds—and scanned the village, seeking out the plumes of rising smoke.

Three fires, spaced well apart, and what could be their cause? Quinn shrugged off the question. That wasn't his concern. The first job was to douse the fires before they spread and did more damage to the village. Hopefully, no one was injured yet and they would not have lost any vital supplies.

Quinn chose the blur of smoke and frantic action closest to his barracks, on his left, and moved in that direction. He had barely taken two strides past the corner, homing on his destination, when a strong arm clamped around his neck and someone dragged him backward, toward the shadows at the east end of the dormitory.

Quinn resisted, would've cried for help if he could speak, but speech and breath alike were suddenly denied him. With his fingernails, he tried to claw the arm that held him fast, but fabric stopped him gouging flesh. He kicked back, barefoot, striking someone's shin without significant effect.

The needle jab behind his ear was almost insignificant, a pinch immediately followed by a chill, the numbness spreading to his face and scalp, then downward through his body. Quinn was startled when the arm released him, let him breathe again, but when he tried to turn and fight his legs would not obey the orders from his brain. They folded, let him fall into a dark void that had opened to receive him, sucking him forever downward toward the center of the Earth.

IT WAS ALMOST TOO EASY. The young man struggled briefly, shivered, then collapsed in Bolan's arms, dead-weight. Bolan half turned him, crouched to make the fireman's carry work, and took the sleeper's weight across his left shoulder.

There was no time to second-guess the dosage he'd injected, calculated in advance to drop an active male adult of five foot nine, weighing about 150 pounds. The object of his search had clearly lost some weight since those statistics were compiled, presumably because the Process Diet wasn't big on building body mass, but would it make a crucial difference?

However Patrick Quinn reacted to the drug now coursing through his system, Bolan couldn't stop to check his vitals on the spot. The first priority was to get out of Obike before someone discovered that a tall, armed man was making off with one of Master Gaborone's happy campers. If that happened, Bolan could expect fireworks, and Quinn was likely to be injured, maybe killed, as a result.

The plan wasn't to use him as a human shield, or to discard him in the bushes while the Executioner took out a troupe of sentries. His mission was supposed to be a soft probe, in and out before the heavies knew he'd been here, carrying a package that he hoped they wouldn't miss in the confusion he'd created.

For a while, at least.

His luck held firm as Bolan made a beeline for the compound's south perimeter. As planned, the fires he'd set had drawn the guards and villagers to find out what was wrong, then solve the problem as a group endeavor. Bolan gave them points for thinking on their feet and thanked his lucky stars for the brief lapse in discipline that left his way unguarded.

A HALF HOUR ELAPSED between the first harsh cry of *"Fire!"* and the last puff of smoke from sodden embers. Thirty minutes saw the fires extinguished, leaving those who fought them at a loss to understand how they'd begun. There was no correlation of the buildings that had burned—food storage, garden tools, clothing—nor any clear-cut reason why one of them, much less three, had suddenly burst into flame.

"Arson?"

Ahmadou Gaborone wasn't precisely sure why it surprised him. He'd been warning of attacks against Obike since construction started on the village, but his sermons were theatrics for the most part, smoke and mirrors meant to keep the sheep in line.

Now he had smoke, all right, but there wasn't a mirror to be seen.

"Yes, Master." Nico Mbarga's attitude was solemn as he answered. "Someone set the fires. Timed them to be discovered all at once, I think."

"But why?"

Mbarga shrugged. "I don't know, Master. When we find the one responsible, he'll tell us."

"Only one? There were three fires, Nico."

"Master, it isn't difficult. A bit of fuse, even a candle or a cigarette can make a simple timer. Certain chemicals, as well."

"Who has such knowledge in Obike?"

Mbarga had to have felt Gaborone peering into his soul. He stiffened to a semblance of attention and replied, "As for the chemicals, Master, perhaps no one. But anyone who's ever smoked or used a candle might be wise enough to place it in a twist of cloth or paper, even some dry grass. When it burns down…" Another shrug.

"A simple matter, then. But why would any member of our fold do such a thing?"

"Master, we've spoken of morale in camp since the Americans were here. It's possible that someone wishes to depart but fears to tell you openly. In that case, a diversion might allow them to slip out while we were busy with the fires."

"A traitor, then." The word tasted bitter on Gaborone's tongue.

"Perhaps only a coward, Master."

"It's the same thing, Nico. Those among my people who lack faith in me are traitors to the Process. They betray me and themselves."

"Of course, sir."

Another moment made it clear to Gaborone what had to be done. "We need a head count, Nico. Have your men assemble everyone, immediately. No excuses. None. If someone is too sick or lame to walk, have your men carry him outside. I want to *see* my people. If there is a traitor in the village, I must know his name and look into his eyes."

"Yes, Master."

"Go, then! Do it now!"

Mbarga ran to do as he was ordered, calling to his men along the way. Within five minutes, he'd retrieved the megaphone that Gaborone sometimes employed for sermons, braying orders now for every person in the village to assemble near the mess hall, falling into ranks by dormitories to be counted.

Mbarga did it well. He didn't mention traitors or betrayal, rather claiming that the master wished to reassure himself that no one had been injured by the fires. It was a good excuse and went unquestioned, since Obike's residents were long accustomed to surprise assemblies, lectures and the like.

Gaborone stood apart and watched as his people assembled, lining up in groups of ten or twelve, depending on the barracks they inhabited. He searched their faces, tried to scan their souls, seeking the foul rot of betrayal that he felt should stand out like a lesion on the flesh. It pained him that he couldn't spot a traitor in the ranks. That failure made him wonder if his gifts were fading, if the secret voices had deserted him.

Impossible!

The gift of prophecy wasn't a transient thing. When someone was selected as a messenger of God, that designation was a lifelong calling. Still, prophets were only human. They could make mistakes. And sometimes they could be deceived.

The head count took another thirty minutes. Some of Mbarga's men were bad with numbers, lost their place and had to start again, forcing Mbarga to be harsh with them. When they were done, there should be 732 assembled congregants, including guards.

And if no one was missing, what came next?

Mbarga jogged back to offer his report. Anxious, the master asked, "How many?"

"Seven hundred," Nico said, "and thirty-one."

"One missing, then. Who is it?"

"An American from dormitory number 7. Patrick Quinn."

The name inspired vague memories. Resentful parents and a battle over money. It was nothing Gaborone hadn't experienced before, mere trivia, considering his greater plans.

"Find him!" the master ordered. "Bring him here to me!"

CHAPTER FOUR

Patrick Quinn might've lost some weight since moving from Wyoming to the Congo, but a quarter mile into the Executioner's forced march, the body slumped across his shoulder seemed to be gaining more poundage with every step.

Bolan knew that the feeling was a combination of fatigue, deadweight and the oppressive jungle atmosphere, but understanding didn't make his burden any lighter. He experimented with his speed, plodding, jogging, looking for a happy medium between the two, but nothing eased the chafing or the dull ache that had started in the left side of his body.

No hunters were pursuing him, so far. Bolan was confident he would've heard them coming through the forest, but he couldn't say when the pursuit would start. His rest stop had to be a brief one, and perhaps he'd shift Quinn to his other shoulder for the next half mile or so.

When he was two miles from the village, he could use the satellite phone to contact Grimaldi, and his ride home would be airborne within minutes. There was still a long, hard march in front of him, but if he reached their rendezvous without a swarm of trackers on his tail, there would be time to rest while he waited for the chopper.

And by then, Bolan knew he would need it.

He was forced to lower Quinn by stages, to avoid a sudden drop that might inflict concussion or a list of other injuries. First Bolan crouched in front of a looming tree, then braced one knee against the spongy soil. He set down his rifle and gripped Quinn's torso with both hands, leaning forward an inch at a time until his passenger was seated on the ground, reclining with his back against the tree trunk.

Perfect.

Only when he saw Quinn's face did Bolan realize that something had gone wrong.

The young man's skin was clammy, deathly pale. His breathing was a shallow whisper, barely there. When Bolan checked his pulse, two fingers probing for an artery below the bristly jawline, he discovered an erratic, feeble beat.

Bolan had never gone to med school, but he'd passed the basic first-aid course required of every Special Forces soldier, and he recognized a classic case of shock. Quinn's vital signs were fading fast, and if the trend wasn't reversed, Bolan's inert companion would become a true deadweight.

Some people panicked in a crisis; others did what had to be done. Bolan has lost his panic gene in mortal combat, long ago and far away. Younger than Quinn, he'd learned that those who lost their head in crisis situations often lost their lives, as well. All things being equal, cooler heads and steady hands had better chances of survival.

Bolan's life wasn't at risk this time, not yet, but it was still a case of do-or-die. He guessed that Quinn's condition represented a reaction to the sedative—either some kind of unexpected allergy or possibly an overdose occasioned by his recent weight loss.

In either case, if Bolan's supposition was correct, he had the answer in his pocket.

Stony Man had planned ahead, as always. While the sedative injection had been judged appropriate and safe for adult males of Quinn's expected size and weight, the Farm's medical officer had left nothing to chance. The hypo kit furnished to Bolan also included an all-purpose antidote, a sort of steroid-adrenaline cocktail designed to suppress allergic reactions and to jump-start failing hearts.

It would be either Quinn's salvation or a waste of time. If something else was killing him, or if he suffered some adverse reaction to the antidote itself, Bolan had no more remedies on tap. He couldn't operate, couldn't keep Quinn alive with CPR and still meet Jack Grimaldi for their pickup. He would simply have to watch the young man die, then take the bad news back to Val.

Screw that.

Bolan removed his last syringe from its high-impact case, peeled back one of Quinn's denim sleeves and found a vein. He pinched Quinn's bicep, made the vein stand out more prominently and administered the dose with steady pressure on the hypo's plunger. Ten long seconds saw it done, and Bolan stowed the kit, now useless to him, as he settled back to wait.

Some fifteen seconds after the injection, Quinn began to twitch, as if experiencing a mild seizure. Warm color rose from underneath his collar, tingeing throat and cheeks. Quinn muttered something unintelligible, batting weakly at his face with his left hand.

And then his eyes snapped open.

"EXPLAIN THE PROBLEM once again, if you don't mind," Pablo Camacho said. His frown was thoughtful, almost studious.

It angered Gaborone to have his concentration interrupted, but he couldn't show impatience to Camacho or the man who stood beside him, likewise waiting for his answer. One of them would soon pay millions for the key to Armageddon, and until the contract had been executed, Gaborone couldn't afford to vent his spleen toward either one.

"The fires were set deliberately," Gaborone replied in even tones. "Having discovered that, I realized that someone might be injured, or else missing from the camp."

"The fire setter." Adnan Ibn Sharif remained impassive as he spoke.

"Perhaps. In any case, a survey of our people has

revealed one absent from his dormitory. An American. My men are searching for him now in other barracks, the latrines, mess hall."

"You have guards here," Camacho said. "Can anyone simply walk out, unseen?"

"It's a community, Mr. Camacho, not a prison camp. My people stay because they wish to. They have faith in me and in the Process. We await the end times here."

Camacho fairly sneered. "Someone grew tired of waiting, it would seem."

"We don't know yet if the young man in question set the fires. He may still be in camp, somewhere. In any case, he will be found and questioned."

"Found in any case?" Sharif was plainly skeptical. "What if he's run into the jungle? Can you find him there?"

"Some of my men are native hunters. They can track a leopard through the thickets to its lair."

"This is a man," Camacho said, "not some dumb animal."

"A white man from the U.S.A.," Gaborone said. He forced a smile. "If this one ran into the forest, he'll be lost by now."

"But going somewhere, all the same," Sharif replied. "We're wasting time."

"On the contrary. Even as some search the village, others are scouting the perimeter. They will discover any signs of recent passage."

Camacho shifted restlessly, hands clinched to fists inside his trouser pockets. "Tell us something more of this American you've lost. How do you know he's not a spy?"

"I know my people," Gaborone replied. "They're converts, gentlemen, not infiltrators. Each has sacrificed to demonstrate devotion. They have given up their lives and families to follow me."

"Still, if a spy wants to impress you," said Camacho, "he could do all that and more. I've been indicted in absentia by the government in Washington. For all I know, your arsonist is a narcotics agent and these fires were signals for a raid."

"In which case," Gaborone asked his uneasy guest, "where are the raiders? Do you hear the sound of aircraft circling overhead? The only landing strip within a hundred miles is guarded by my men, and they have radios as well as weapons. You are perfectly secure in Obike."

"Why don't I *feel* secure?" Camacho asked.

"Perhaps you've lived in fear too long," Gaborone said. "In fact, the young man whom we seek converted to the Process months ago. Before I had the pleasure of your company—or yours, Mr. Sharif. Could he predict that we would meet and come to terms on business matters, gentlemen? I doubt it very much."

"We have not come to terms," Sharif reminded him. "Not yet."

Gaborone was rapidly reaching the end of his patience. "Indeed," he replied, "have we not? Please pardon my presumption. I assumed that our discussions had some basis in reality. If you prefer to look elsewhere for what you seek, I won't detain you any further. I can halt the trivial pursuit of one young man and have you taken to the airstrip. Are your things in order? Is an hour soon enough?"

Camacho fanned the muggy air with an impatient hand. "No one said anything about leaving. I can't speak for Sharif, but *I* still want the merchandise, if we can strike a bargain on the price."

"And I!" Sharif confirmed. "I've come empowered to close a deal."

"Then, by all means," Gaborone said, "leave petty matters of internal discipline to me. I'll soon find out who set the fires and what possessed him to make such a grave mistake. Until then, gentlemen, please take advantage of our hospitality."

He left them less than satisfied, but they were staying. It was all that mattered at the moment.

That, and finding Patrick Quinn.

NICO MBARGA HAD INFORMED his men, at the beginning of the search, that all results should be reported directly to him, without troubling the master. His troops knew the drill well enough, but it did no harm to remind them, especially when there were strangers in the village who might form a bad impression of the Process if its guards ran willy-nilly, here and there, spreading false rumors to the populace.

In this case, though, Mbarga was concerned with truth, as much as lies.

He wanted to be confident of every detail the master received about what had transpired. He also meant to be the only messenger with access to the throne.

To that end, long ago, Mbarga had commanded that his men shouldn't address the master unless spoken to directly by His Eminence. If such a conversation should occur outside Mbarga's presence, they were tasked to find him afterward and faithfully report whatever had been said. And as insurance against crafty liars, Mbarga had decreed that his soldiers had to always work in pairs, thus providing a witness for any chance encounter with the master.

It was the best he could do, and now it seemed that his system might be shattered by a pasty-faced American of no account.

Mbarga knew Patrick Quinn as he knew everyone in Obike, as a sketchy printout from the personal computer in his head. Quinn was a white boy from America, apparently devoted to the Process if his former words and actions were a proper guide. He'd come from money but had been cut off from access by his parents. That occurred from time to time, and while the disappointment hadn't been enough for Gaborone to cut him loose, it ended any chance of Quinn's advancement to the master's inner circle. Quinn would be a cipher, toiling in the fields or begging handouts for the Process on some street corner until he either quit the sect or died.

This day, the latter exit seemed more probable.

Mbarga supervised the search, rather than rushing door-to-door himself and peering into cupboards, groping under cots. He left the grunt work to his men, as usual, and relegated to himself the task of asking questions where he thought they might be useful.

His knowledge of the white boy didn't extend to peripheral friendships, so Mbarga questioned first the other occupants of Quinn's barracks. Two-thirds of them were Africans, the other pair young Arabs, possibly Jordanian. In that mix, it was no surprise to find Quinn rated as a quiet loner who made few attempts at conversation. Probably, they wouldn't understand him if he spoke, and wouldn't care about the subject matter if they did. One failing of the master, Mbarga ruefully admitted to himself, had been the effort to dissolve racial and ethnic barriers between disciples of the Process. Sermons on the subject were absorbed, but never seemed to take.

The upshot of Mbarga's grilling was that he knew nothing more of Quinn than when he'd started. Did the young man have a special friend inside the village, either male or female? Master Gaborone himself controlled the coupling of his congregants, selecting mates based on criteria known to himself alone. Even the married people, though, were segregated into dorms by gender, granted conjugal relations at the master's pleasure, once per month on average.

Of course, that didn't stop some villagers from falling prey to whimsies of the flesh. Mbarga and his men caught them from time to time, rutting like animals inside a storage shed or in the forest, passion honed to razor sharpness by the danger of discovery. In such cases, Mbarga took names for Master Gaborone, and punishments were devised to fit the crime. Public humiliation was a common penalty, sometimes accompanied by corporal punishment.

And wayward girls were marked. The master liked to counsel them himself.

In fact, the young American named Quinn appeared to have no contacts of that kind within the village—which meant none at all, since he was never sent outside Obike on his own. It seemed unlikely, then, that passion would've led to fire setting, and since he'd fled alone, it couldn't be supposed that he'd eloped.

Mbarga still had more questions than answers when he carried his final report to the master, but at least one thing was settled. He knew where the white man had gone. More precisely, he knew how Patrick Quinn had left the village, though his destination still remained obscure.

He found the master standing with their foreign guests, and approached cautiously from fear of interrupting some important conversation. They had business to discuss, Mbarga knew, and it was not his place to meddle in such things.

"Nico, what news?" the master asked as he approached.

"Master, the white man is no longer in Obike, but I found the point where he departed from the village, heading south."

"Toward Brazzaville?" Gaborone asked.

"Master, the city is two hundred miles away."

"I know that!"

"My apologies, Master."

"You must go after him and bring him back at once."

"Of course, Master."

"A hunting party, is it?" the Colombian asked. "That sounds like fun. I'll join you."

The Arab standing to his left immediately looked suspicious. "I will also go," he said.

"You wish to interrupt negotiations?" Gaborone seemed more amused than curious.

"Why not?" the Colombian asked. "It won't take long."

"By all means, then, enjoy yourselves," Gaborone said. "But be aware of dangers in the jungle. Trust in Nico's judgment if you value life and limb. And, Nico?"

"Yes, Master?"

"I want the boy alive."

"WHO ARE YOU?" Patrick Quinn demanded when his eyes swam into focus on the stranger's face in front of him.

"A friend," Bolan replied, not altogether sure if that was true.

"I don't think so," the youth challenged. He tried to rise, but weakness and the residue of drugs still coursing through his system dropped him back against the tree trunk. "I was with my friends," he said, "before you grabbed me. You *kidnapped* me from Obike!"

Bolan didn't have the time or inclination to debate the point. "That's one way you could see it."

"It's the true way. But you didn't knock me out," Quinn said. He raised a slow hand to his neck, feeling the sore spot there. "What did you—? Did you drug me?"

"Nothing heavy," Bolan lied. "We didn't have the luxury of sitting down to tea and chatting. It was touch and go, you might say."

"You're a fool for choosing me," Quinn told him. "I

suppose you've heard my family's rich, but guess what? They've disowned me. I don't have a penny to my name, and they won't pay whatever ransom you're expecting." Quinn produced a woozy smile. "You're out of luck."

"It's not a ransom snatch," Bolan replied, and watched the humor vanish from his young companion's face, supplanted by confusion and a healthy dose of fear.

"You don't want money?"

"No."

"Then why...?"

Apparently, Quinn's mind was clear enough to think of several possibilities. The first one he came up with was a stretch, but it caused him to tremble, even though he tried to hide it.

"No ransom. That means you're working for the enemy!"

"I told you, I'm a friend."

"You would say that, of course. You're lying! Master Gaborone has warned us. But you're making a mistake."

"How's that?" Bolan asked.

"I don't have the information that you're looking for. Whatever you came after, I can't help you. I'm nobody, just a flunky in the village."

Bolan frowned. "I thought you all were equal in the master's sight?"

"Well, yes, but... See, that proves it! You've been studying the Process. That makes you—"

"A friend of Val Querente," Bolan interrupted him. "Do you remember her, or is your brain really as messed up as it sounds?"

"*Val* sent you?" Quinn considered it, then shook his head. "I don't believe it. No, you're lying. It's impossible. How could she—"

"Care enough to go the extra mile and help you?" Bolan shrugged. "Beats me. I only work here. Now, if you can make your legs work—"

"Wait! You think I'm going somewhere with you?"

"One way or another, that's exactly what I think."

"Well, guess again. You took me by surprise the first time, with your needle or whatever, but I see you now. I won't go quietly."

Bolan leaned closer, let the muzzle of his Steyr AUG rest lightly on Quinn's left kneecap. "I've carried you this far," he said, "and I can carry you to the LZ. You don't need kneecaps to ride piggyback, and consciousness is strictly optional."

Quinn didn't seem to register the threat. "LZ? What's that?" he asked.

"Your exit from the Process. Will you walk, or not?"

Quinn struggled to his feet, using the tree trunk for support. "Val wouldn't do this," he insisted. "I explained to her about my faith. I grant you that she wasn't happy, but she understands."

"You can discuss it with her soon," Bolan said.

"This is a mistake," Quinn said.

"It wouldn't be my first," the Executioner replied. Then he pointed through the trees and said, "That way."

GABORONE WATCHED as the hunting party vanished into jungle gloom, a tracker leading Nico and four of his men, Camacho and Sharif surrounded in the middle of the group. He craned his neck and tried to find the sky above the forest canopy, where daylight glimmered on the sea of leaves.

How long before nightfall?

Some hours yet, and maybe time enough for Mbarga's team to overtake the fugitive American. Mbarga was pledged to capture him alive, if possible, but there were other perils in the forest that might claim Quinn's life before he was discovered. If they found him dead, the fires and his escape would be a nagging mystery.

~~Or worse.~~

Gaborone had puzzled over the events, attempting to resolve them in his mind, but there were still too many missing pieces. It seemed inconceivable that Quinn had been corrupted by their enemies outside Obike, but if that wasn't the case, what had possessed him? Had his mind snapped in the jungle, as some others had before? Why else would he attempt to burn the village down, then flee into the forest?

It was too much to suppose that someone else had set the fires, and that Quinn coincidentally had chosen that precise moment to run away. That was preposterous. Unthinkable.

Or was it?

Gaborone began to worry that Mbarga's party might not find Quinn, even with the tracker's keen nose to guide them. If the American was fleeing southward toward Brazzaville, despite the near impossibility of a white man and a stranger to the jungle covering that distance on his own, Gaborone knew he should do anything within his power to cut that journey short. Quinn might find other settlements much closer to Obike, and who could predict what he would say about the Process or its master if he wasn't silenced?

Gaborone still had a few tricks up his sleeve, and there would never be a better time to use one.

Picking up the sermon megaphone, Gaborone faced toward the heart of the village and called out an amplified name. "Samburu! Samburu Changa, come to me!"

A moment later he saw Mbarga's first lieutenant running toward him from the eastern corner of the village. Changa wore a worried look, as if afraid that some new crisis had befallen them and he wouldn't be equal to the task awaiting him. He stopped short, several paces from the stoop of Gaborone's bungalow, breathing heavily and clutching his rifle tight to one side.

"Master, how may I serve you?"

"As you know," Gaborone said, "Nico has gone to find our missing sheep. The visitors are with him, and I fear that they may slow his pace."

Changa waited for more. He had the gift of silence.

"I've decided you should help him," Gaborone explained. "I want another team to hurry on ahead and intercept our wayward brother. Failing that, you may explore the nearer villages and satisfy yourself that he will find no shelter there."

"Master," Changa said, looking suddenly confused,

"the nearest village to Obike, southward, is still fifteen miles away. I cannot reach it before nightfall, even if I leave right now. To overtake Captain Mbarga—"

"Calm yourself, Samburu. I ask nothing human flesh and bone cannot achieve. Fetch Danso Beira and three soldiers you can trust. Drive to the airstrip. Use the bird!"

Changa smiled at that, now understanding the command. "Yes, Master! As you say, so let it be!"

"Go swiftly! Time is of the essence."

Bowing sharply from the waist, Changa turned and fled the royal presence, shouting names as he moved through the village. Gaborone smiled after him, convinced that his last-minute inspiration would resolve their problem nicely. He would catch Quinn in a pincers, capture him alive with any luck, and then squeeze him at leisure for the secrets of his flight.

Rapid resolution of the crisis would persuade his visitors that Gaborone was someone to be taken seriously. They would respect him as more than a conduit for the merchandise they craved, and having seen him act decisively, they might be less inclined to quibble over price.

Perhaps.

If not, thought Gaborone, he might be forced to wipe the slate clean and begin anew with different customers.

It was a seller's market, after all.

And Armageddon could afford to wait.

CHAPTER FIVE

The world seemed upside down to Patrick Quinn. His thoughts were jumbled, often contradictory, and he could only blame a part of that on the injection he'd received before the stranger snatched him from Obike. Truth be told, the hazy aftershock of being drugged was fading rapidly, but Quinn's mind still played tricks on him.

He knew what Master Gaborone would say and do if their positions were reversed, and yet another part of Quinn rebelled against indoctrination, whispering to him that he was safe now, better off than he had been in months.

But how could that be right?

If Master Gaborone was truly wise, a prophet of the Lord, then being separated from him was a loss no true believer should accept without a fight. And yet, the stranger who had kidnapped Quinn knew Val Querente—knew her name, at least, and Quinn's association with her in the States. He hadn't picked that information from thin air. And yet…

Quinn *had* discussed his newfound faith with Val, and while she'd clearly disapproved, she'd left the decision to him. Free will, and all that. Quinn's father hadn't been so understanding, tried to get his way, as usual, with bribery and threats. Quinn hadn't been surprised when he was cut off from his trust fund, and the master didn't seem to mind. There'd been no sudden exile from the Process, as Quinn's father had predicted. It was still his family, his home.

The move to Africa had seemed like an adventure, though it had plainly troubled Val. He'd seen her only once after the great transition was announced. She'd tried to talk him out of it, more earnest than he'd ever seen her, but Quinn had been resolute. A man should be decisive, as his father always said, and Quinn had made his choice.

"Another ten feet to your left," the man behind him said, "and hold that course until I tell you otherwise."

Quinn did as he was told without complaint, for now. He still didn't feel strong enough to fight the larger man, armed as he was, but he was fleet of foot and reckoned that he could outrun the stranger when he had an opening and had regained his strength.

How long until they reached the "exit," the mysterious LZ? Quinn didn't know, but he felt stronger with every stride along the twisting jungle trails.

At any other time, Quinn might've stopped and marveled at the forest, as he did sometimes when he was sent to gather firewood for the village or to clear a patch for planting. At such times, he understood why Master Gaborone had brought his faithful children to the Congo, far from everything that most of them had known in their abandoned lives. It was the closest thing to Eden Quinn had ever seen, and if he had to watch for serpents in the garden, separation from the gray, polluted world of men made up for any transient inconvenience.

Not that it was an easy life with Master Gaborone, by any means. The work assignments were precisely that, hard work, and meals were basic. Quinn knew that he'd been losing weight, but so had most of those around him. Mbarga's troop of bodyguards got more to eat and had contrived a crude gymnasium to keep themselves in shape, but labor served the other villagers as well. Obesity wasn't a problem in Obike, and while Quinn sometimes complained about their diet, its monotony and lack of flavor, he recalled that old-time prophets in the Bible had survived on bread and honey in the wilderness.

Honey. Now *that* would be a treat.

The man behind him moved so quietly that under other circumstances, Quinn might've forgotten he was there. He was a soldier—no, make that a *mercenary,* from the way he talked—and where would Val Querente ever meet a man like that? Did they still advertise their services in *Soldier of Fortune* or similar rags? Did the back pages of telephone directories carry coded ads?

Kidnapping seemed like something that his father would've tried, if he had cared enough. In fact, the old man hadn't raised a finger to prevent his leaving the United States, once he'd nailed down the trust fund and with an order of protection from a friendly judge. Quinn couldn't touch the money now until he'd satisfied the court that he was "competent," which doubtless meant agreeing to whatever Daddy said and jumping through a string of hoops designed to strip him of his dignity.

Quinn thought of Val, tried to imagine her discussing his abduction with this stranger, plotting it, but the pervasive sense of unreality left him confused.

He needed Master Gaborone's advice, but that meant breaking free, returning to Obike. Could he do it? Was he man enough?

Quinn walked and waited for the proper moment to find out.

THE FIRST EXPLOSION startled Jack Grimaldi from a muddled dream of rotor blades and treetops. He was flying somewhere, seeking someone, then his chopper took a hit and it was spinning, spinning, down and down.

A heartbeat later he was wide awake and on his feet, a pistol in his hand though he couldn't remember drawing it. A second blast outside, followed by popping sounds of gunfire, told Grimaldi that the first explosion hadn't been a dream.

He tucked the pistol out of sight beneath his dangling shirttail, left his little room and moved along a narrow corridor to reach the nearest exit. Once outside, he saw smoke rising from a hangar to his left. Grimaldi moved in that direction, heard more gunfire, then saw uniforms rushing pell-mell toward the explosive sounds of combat.

He'd known that there were scattered pockets of unrest throughout the country, areas where rebels fought to rule the countryside, but nothing had prepared him for a strike against the Brazzaville airport. Grimaldi hoped that he was wrong, but what else could the shooting mean? Explosions might be accidental, but the kind of concentrated gunfire he was hearing meant that battle had been joined.

Jesus! he thought. Why now?

His first thought, once again, was Bolan and the young man they were supposed to be extracting from the jungle. Conscious of the sat phone in his pocket, knowing it could ring at any moment now, Grimaldi cursed the timing of the airport strike. Even if it was quelled within the next few minutes, he knew how police and soldiers worked. They'd want to rope off the whole scene, lock down the airport, cancel all incoming and departing flights until they'd searched the place from top to bottom, satisfied themselves no further threat remained.

And then they'd start to analyze the mess, a process that could last for hours, days or even weeks. They wouldn't leave the airport closed that long, of course, but Grimaldi needed to fly this night, perhaps within the hour.

When the fight was over, when they started scouring the airport, soldiers would be checking out the grounded aircraft, making sure no rebels hid inside them.

Anything beyond a cursory examination of Grimaldi's rented helicopter would reveal the duffel bag he'd stowed inside it, and if it was opened....

Shit! Now he would have to fetch the guns, find someplace better to conceal them while avoiding troops and dodging bullets, and somehow avoid arrest before he answered Bolan's call.

A call for help that he might be unable to provide.

Grimaldi reached a corner, peered around it and saw soldiers rushing toward a hangar all in flames. Some of them fired short bursts from automatic weapons as they ran, while others waited for a target to reveal itself. Beyond his line of sight, more gunfire crackled and another blast—perhaps a detonating hand grenade— echoed across the tarmac.

That was close, Grimaldi thought.

"Oh, no," he muttered, breaking cover for a dash across the runway, toward the corner of the airport where he'd left the Hughes 500 whirlybird. Acoustics could be tricky in a firefight, but the last explosion sounded to Grimaldi as if it had emanated from the chopper's resting place.

Or too damned close for comfort, anyway.

Grimaldi checked his flanks and made another run for cover, drawing nearer to the helipad. He saw the black smoke rising well before he got there, knowing in his gut that it could only mean one thing. A few more loping strides, and his worst fears were realized.

Grenade or rocket, either way the chopper was a total loss. Flames hungrily devoured the cockpit, licking through its shattered windscreen, while the rotors sagged as if resigned to death. Its fuel tank blew just as Grimaldi reached the apron of the helipad, and in another second ammunition started cooking off inside, a minifirefight without living enemies on either side.

At least the soldiers wouldn't find his guns, Grimaldi thought, unless they stopped him on the way back to his room and shook him down. Reluctantly, he drew the pistol from his belt and pitched it overhand into the flaming wreckage of the whirlybird.

And then, as if on cue, the sat phone in his pocket rang.

THE TELEPHONE RANG twice before Grimaldi answered, "Yo."

"It's me," said Bolan. "Are you ready?"

Hesitation on the line told him something was wrong before Grimaldi answered, "Not exactly."

"What does that mean?"

"If you can believe this shit," Grimaldi said, "some rebels just attacked the airport. Can you hear the firing?"

Bolan listened, pictured Jack raising the phone to empty air, and heard the distant but familiar sounds of small-arms fire.

"I hear it," he admitted when Grimaldi came back on the line. "Are you locked down?"

"It's worse than that. One of the bastards nailed our chopper. It's a write-off, man. I'll have to start from scratch."

It was the worst news possible. Grimaldi had required the better part of a day to find the helicopter he had rented, leaving an extravagant deposit as insurance for its safe return. Bolan couldn't begin to guess how long he'd need to scare up a replacement, or if Jack had cash enough on hand to make the deal.

Despair was an emotion he couldn't afford. Inaction in the present case would more than likely get him killed.

"Okay," he said. "We'll use Plan B."

"Sounds good," Grimaldi said. "You want to fill me in on that one, when you get a second?"

Bolan couldn't help but smile at Jack's reaction. "You ever see the movie *March or Die?*" he asked.

"See it? I think I lived it," said Grimaldi replied.

"Well, we're living it again," Bolan replied. "I've got the package and we're heading your way, overland. Do what you can for transportation and I'll try to keep in touch."

"I hate this, man."

"So, fix it," Bolan said. "I need to save these batteries for when the good news comes."

"Okay. You're right. I'm on it."

"Good."

Bolan switched off the phone and met Quinn's troubled gaze. He'd kept the young man in full view throughout the brief exchange and hoped his poker face was still intact.

"What's going on?" Quinn asked.

"Air transport's been delayed. We have a longer walk ahead of us than I'd intended," Bolan said.

Quinn's turn to smile, as if some inner doubt had been resolved. "You must know that's a sign."

"Of what?"

"You're meant to let me go. I need to be with Master Gaborone. The Lord wills it."

"In that case," Bolan told him, "I'll be disappointing all of you."

"Are you so arrogant that you believe you have the power to contravene God's will?"

"The arrogance would be assuming I knew what that was," Bolan replied. "Now move out. Same direction as before."

"And if I don't?"

He raised the AUG. "We covered that."

"Would Val want you to cripple me? I don't think so."

"She wants you home alive. The means were left to my discretion."

"They'll have realized I'm gone by now," Quinn said. "And they'll be coming after me."

"I'm banking on it," Bolan answered. "What you need to ask yourself is, why?"

Quinn frowned at that, a puzzled look. "I don't know what you mean."

"They'll know that someone tried to torch the place, and you're the only person unaccounted for. I'm not sure how the Process does arithmetic, but two plus two still equals four."

"They won't blame *me* for that!" Quinn answered, defiantly.

"Who will they blame? The boogeyman?"

For the first time, it seemed that he had penetrated Quinn's stout wall of faith. Was that a victory? If it could get the young man moving, Bolan was prepared to call it one.

"When I explain—"

"There won't be any fireside chats," he interrupted. "I can gag you, bind your hands and leave you free to walk, or I can carry you. Your choice. But if they overtake us, men with guns, there'll be no conversation."

"So, you plan to kill them?"

"I intend for both of us to make it back alive. Get used to it."

"You're trifling with God's wrath!"

"I'll risk it," Bolan said. "Now move!"

Reluctantly, Quinn did as he was told. The forest had grown darker as they'd argued, warning Bolan that it would be dusk soon, followed by a moonless jungle night. They'd have to stop at nightfall, since he couldn't risk Quinn trying to escape on ground that Bolan hadn't charted for himself and couldn't clearly see. They'd make a cold camp, let the night conceal them if it would, and hope that any hunters from the village fared no better.

Until then—

Up ahead, Quinn shot a backward glance at Bolan, grimaced and rushed headlong through the jungle shadows, sprinting at a right angle from the narrow trail.

SAMBURU CHANGA WASN'T born to fly. In spite of his devotion to the Process and to Master Gaborone, he clung to certain myths and superstitions learned in childhood. One of those was that the jungle gods might punish humans who attempted to usurp their powers, such as flight.

Unfortunately, Changa had no choice that afternoon. The gods sometimes relaxed their vigilance, but Master Gaborone and Changa's captain never failed to punish disobedience. What penalty could he expect if he refused to help retrieve the white traitor?

Changa shuddered to think of it, and tried his best to concentrate on keeping down the lunch that roiled and grumbled in his stomach.

Master Gaborone's helicopter was an Aérospatiale SA-315B Lama, designed in France and built in the United States. It seated five inside its crowded, bubble-nosed cabin and featured old-time latticework in place of metal siding on its tail boom.

They were flying at three hundred feet, the helicopter droning more or less due south. Although they were a hundred feet above the forest canopy, Changa imagined that the chopper's struts would tangle in the branches and propel them through a screaming somersault before the fuel tank exploded and they all went up in flames. It stood to reason that the pilot, Danso Beira, harbored no such fears, but the soldiers packed into the rear seats of the cabin shamed Changa, pointing and giggling like children as they enjoyed the bird's-eye view.

"Silence!" Changa ordered. "We're on business for the master, not some foolish game."

They sobered instantly, exchanging glances that displayed embarrassment and fear in equal parts. Changa paid no attention to their feelings. He'd been taught that leaders—even mere lieutenants—were supposed to lead, not waste their time befriending various subordinates. Changa took orders from Nico Mbarga without question, and his men could do the same or face the consequences.

Watching for the white man was a waste of time. The treetops covered everything below them, and it would require a fluke of unimaginable luck for Changa or the pilot to see anything of human size in the deeply shaded jungle. Rather than a wasted pass over the forest, they were making for the nearest village, fifteen miles south of Obike. Master Gaborone commanded it, and Changa would obey.

For once, he understood the master's reasoning without an explanation from Mbarga. If the fugitive was headed for Brazzaville, he'd likely seek out food and shelter from any natives he encountered on the way. Changa doubted that the white American knew where another village was, after he left Obike, but there was a chance he'd stumble onto it by accident. In any case, if Master Gaborone commanded Changa to fly south and search the village for his prey, it would be done.

The village they were seeking, to the best of Changa's knowledge, had no name. Cities were named, of course, and towns above a certain size, but naming tiny rural villages was commonly regarded as a waste of time. In that sense, as in many others, Master Gaborone had cast aside tradition, naming his community Obike as a sign of strength and hope.

The villagers Changa was sent to question didn't know it yet, but hope was running out for them.

The master had provided no specific orders for his handling of the mission, and since Nico wasn't here to think for him, Changa had mapped a strategy himself. He was expected to retrieve the missing arsonist, or at the very least to satisfy himself that no one in the nameless village hid the white man or had knowledge of his whereabouts. Changa believed it would be easy to interrogate the villagers and search their homes, since he and all his men were armed with automatic weapons, but he also had to think about what happened afterward.

Feuds between villages weren't uncommon in the Congo, and he dared not risk retaliation on Obike by a mob of angry villagers. Likewise, it would be bad for Master Gaborone if word of the encounter reached authorities in Brazzaville. Changa had puzzled long and hard over his problem, and he had the answer now.

It would be bloody work, but blessed in the master's name.

QUINN KNEW HIS BREAK for freedom was a joke, but he was bound to try. He glanced back once and saw his nameless captor look up toward the treetops, following some sound, and then he bolted, taking off at top speed through the jungle.

Top speed wasn't much, unfortunately, in his present situation. Quinn had nearly shaken off the drugs, but he felt weak, as if his muscles had been starved for oxygen while he was traveling unconscious, slumped over the mercenary's shoulder. It was strange, that weakness, and he wondered whether part of it was fear, but Quinn pushed through it, sprinting now as if his life depended on it.

Knowing in a very real sense that it did.

He had to lose the kidnapper and find his way back to Obike soon, before the master and Nico Mbarga reached the false conclusions that his captor had predicted. Quinn could now explain the fires, his disappearance from the village, but the truth would have no value to him if he was a prisoner, unable to express himself.

And if the man who'd kidnapped him confronted Nico's guards, if one of them was killed, Quinn realized that there might be no going back. There was a decent chance the rest of them would shoot him then, and never mind the explanations.

Running with the best speed he could manage, hearing rapid footsteps on the forest floor behind him, Quinn immediately recognized another problem.

He was lost.

Unconscious when he'd left Obike, Quinn had no idea of the direction they had traveled while he slumbered. Even had he known the proper compass points, he wouldn't have been able to retrace his captor's steps with any accuracy. Even without the stranger chasing him, Quinn knew it would require a miracle for him to find Obike on his own.

He was a city boy at heart, if Casper qualified for city status, and the wild lands he was most familiar with were Rocky Mountain slopes and open plains. The jungle was a realm of mystery and lurking danger that both lured and frightened him. Even without a mercenary breathing down his neck, or Nico's gunmen hunting him, Quinn knew that he didn't possess the requisite survival skills to keep himself alive. He didn't know which native plants were safe to eat, and he was hopeless as a hunter. If his captor let him go, he'd likely wander aimlessly in circles while starvation wore him down, unless a leopard or a mamba stopped him first.

But there was no hope of the kidnapper releasing him. Quinn knew that from the sounds of ongoing pursuit, the other's footsteps gaining on him now. The hunter didn't call for him to stop, but rather saved his breath for running, long legs eating up the forest floor.

Quinn tried a zigzag course, then quickly realized it was a waste of vital breath and energy. He chose a straight line then, or hoped that it was straight, and poured his last reserves of strength into an all-or-nothing sprint.

Behind him, for the first time, the pursuing footsteps dwindled, growing fainter. Quinn exulted in his momentary triumph. He was younger than the kidnapper, unburdened by a pack and military hardware. It was only right that he should run the faster race.

Doubt nagged him, almost tripped him as his stride began to falter. Quinn knew that he had to check the trail behind him, see what kind of lead he'd taken from his enemy.

A quick look and he wouldn't even have to slow his

pace. Just turn his head and glance across one shoulder while he ran, the simplest thing. No trick to it at all.

Quinn slowed his pace a fraction, glanced back quickly to his right, saw nothing, and was turning to his left when he collided with a massive tree. The impact stunned him, spun him, sent him tumbling to the ground.

But there was no earth to receive him as he fell.

Instead, Quinn plummeted some ten or fifteen feet before he bounced once on a muddy slope, performed a sloppy cartwheel in midair and splashed down into murky water. It closed over him, surrounded him, filled his nose and mouth.

He came up gagging on the algae taste of it, chilled by the soaking even though he knew the water temperature was seventy degrees or more. Quinn couldn't find the bottom with his feet. Blinking his eyes, he dog-paddled in circles, searching for dry land.

And found it, as the first of several crocodiles pushed off the riverbank and came for him, dark water streaming from its armored dragon hide.

NICO MBARGA TRUSTED Master Gaborone in all things, but if he had dared, he would've criticized his leader's choice of visitors. He didn't trust Pablo Camacho or Adnan Ibn Sharif, and hated having them along when there was urgent work to do.

The foreigners were rude and condescending toward Mbarga's people. Worse, they slowed him and wouldn't shut their mouths. Mbarga had requested silence on the trail, yet the Colombian and Arab were obsessed with needling one another, framing not-so-subtle insults in the guise of small talk while they followed Mbarga's tracker through the jungle. Both were armed, another grave mistake, and Mbarga feared what might transpire if he should challenge them too forcefully.

The tracker, for his part, wasn't distracted by the patter behind his back. He worked by sight and sometimes seemed to sniff the trail they followed, but he didn't seem to count on their elusive quarry making any sounds.

Mbarga, frankly, was surprised that Quinn had come this far in a straight line after he fled the village. When they set out from Obike, he'd expected a meandering advance, with marks of stumbling and the like, perhaps circling by slow degrees back toward their starting point. Instead, the young American had struck a course and held to it, making surprisingly good time.

Or had he?

Twice, the tracker showed Mbarga footprints clearly outlined on the forest floor. It didn't take a trained eye to make out the tread of boot soles or to recognize that no such boots were worn by any member of the Process in Obike. Cheap athletic shoes or sandals were the village norm, and even Mbarga's soldiers didn't sport the kind of footwear that had made these tracks.

Mbarga would've bet his life that Patrick Quinn owned no such footwear. But whose were they, and why were no other tracks found with them in the mud?

He kept those questions to himself as they proceeded, following a trail that Mbarga wouldn't have discovered by himself. The tracker was a sorcerer of sorts, reading the forest signs most eyes would find inscrutable.

After another quarter mile, the point man stopped them, crouching and circling near the base of a giant mahogany tree. At length, just when Nico's patience was nearly exhausted, the tracker pointed out a range of random scuff marks on the soil.

"Two men, now," he declared.

"Two men?" Mbarga challenged. "How can that be?"

Bending closer to the earth, the tracker studied first one mark and then another. Nico watched him probe a partial footprint with one fingertip before the tracker rocked back on his haunches, smiling. Satisfied.

"The boot tracks not so deep now," he explained in French, which took some effort to translate. "One man carried the other from Obike. Dropped him here. From here, the two walk on together."

"What?"

Mbarga understood what he'd been told, but making proper sense of it was something else again. Before he had a chance to think it through, Camacho and Sharif were at his elbow, interrupting him.

"What does he say?" the Colombian asked. "Where is our man?"

"Two men," Nico informed him, taking care to keep his face deadpan.

"Two men?" Sharif echoed his own confusion. "So, another met the first one here?"

Mbarga shook his head, too busy with his own thoughts to reply. If he could trust the tracker—and he couldn't think of any reason why the man would lie—it meant that Patrick Quinn was taken from the village by another, possibly against his will. And from that piece of information, Mbarga could hypothesize that the intruder was their arsonist, the fires set as diversions for his kidnapping of Patrick Quinn.

Mbarga stopped himself before he went too far. He had no proof that Quinn was taken from the camp against his will, although it made no sense for the intruder to have carried Quinn this far, if they were allies. In that case, wouldn't Quinn have simply followed where the stranger led, thus sparing him a heavy burden on the trail?

But if it *was* a kidnapping, Mbarga asked himself, why choose a member of the sect who had no special value? Patrick Quinn was a nonentity within the Process, simply one of hundreds who adored the master and obeyed his every word. He held no office in the sect and was entrusted with no secrets. He knew next to nothing of the visitors, for instance, nothing whatsoever of their private talks with Master Gaborone.

Why Patrick Quinn?

Mbarga was puzzling over that and staring at the tracks in front of him, when a distant crack of gunfire drew his team's attention off to the southeast.

CHAPTER SIX

The nearest crocodile to Quinn was nearly twelve feet long, by Bolan's estimation. It was nowhere near the record, but it measured more than twice Quinn's height and could dispatch him with a single bite if Bolan didn't intervene. The three remaining crocs, just pushing off the muddy riverbank as the soldier reached the overhanging bluff, were in the six- to eight-foot range.

Quinn's thrashing in the water seemed to whet the largest reptile's appetite. The monster flicked its great tail almost casually, barely causing a ripple as it powered toward its hapless meal.

Quinn had to have seen the croc approaching, for he gave a little sputtering squeal and started paddling for the riverbank. He didn't swim with any stroke that Bolan recognized, beating the surface with his arms and kicking wildly underneath. His progress toward the shore was minimal.

Bolan peered through the Steyr's scope, fixing its crosshairs at a point between the big croc's eyes. He wasn't thrilled by the idea of firing shots that might attract pursuers, but he wasn't Tarzan, either. Bolan didn't plan to fight the crocodile bare-handed, even if he could've scrambled down the slope and hit the water soon enough to interpose himself between the reptile and its prey.

Bolan reviewed his knowledge of the crocodilians in a millisecond. Thick hide protected everything above the waterline. Only a clean shot to the brain or heart would guarantee a kill. He doubted if he could find the creature's heart in time to rescue Quinn, and while he had a fair fix on the brain, he also knew that it was smaller than a pack of cigarettes, protected by a bony skull.

Thanking the battle gods for armor-piercing ammunition, Bolan held his mark and gently squeezed the Steyr's trigger, rattling off a 3-round burst. The weapon's cyclic rate, 650 rounds per minute, made the three shots sound like one, no help for trackers who might try to take a fix on the report.

His 5.56 mm slugs struck home at 3,080 feet per second and began tumbling on impact, opening the big croc's skull. The reptile instantly convulsed, its last chaotic brainwaves sending messages its muscles couldn't translate or obey. Scanning behind it, Bolan saw the smaller crocodiles scent blood and home in on the splashing of their stricken leader.

Bolan found a place where he could scramble down the muddy slope without repeating Quinn's swan dive into the river. By the time he stood on level ground again, Quinn's awkward swimming style had brought him barely halfway to the bank. Behind him, three excited crocodiles were ripping chunks of pale flesh from the giant that had cowed them only moments earlier. The river's brackish water, green before the feeding frenzy started, had acquired a sickly reddish hue.

"Come on," Bolan urged, trying not to shout for fear of giving trackers yet another lead. "Those crocs may want you for dessert if you keep stalling."

"I...can't...swim!" Quinn sputtered, even as he thrashed and strained to reach the shore.

No kidding, Bolan thought, frowning. He made the choice and waded out from shore until the water reached midthigh. Keeping a close eye on the crocs that he could see, hoping no others were about to strike below the roiling surface, Bolan clutched the Steyr in his right hand, holding out the left to Quinn.

Their hands met, slipped apart, renewed contact. Bolan caught hold the second time and hauled Quinn from the water, letting go when he was stretched out on the bank.

"You lost a shoe," said Bolan, nodding toward Quinn's bare right foot. "Want to go back for it?"

Quinn shook his head, the effort costing him. "No, thanks."

"Okay, but we still need to move. Those crocs feed just as well on land, and I already sent a flare up for your buddies when I shot the first one."

"They can find us?" At the moment, Bolan couldn't

tell if Quinn was hopeful, worried or just winded from his brush with sudden death.

"From the one burst? Doubtful. But it may help narrow down the field. If you still want to spare them from a firefight, now's the time to prove it."

Panting, dripping wet, Quinn struggled to his feet. His drenched clothes added weight, and Bolan knew they'd chill him after nightfall, but there'd be no fire to keep him warm. The missing shoe made Quinn lopsided, put a limp into his walk.

"Where are we going?" he inquired.

"First thing, we need to lose the river and your scaly playmates," Bolan said. He eyed the bluff above them, scanning left and right until he saw a more negotiable slope a hundred yards down range. "That way, then climb," he ordered.

Hobbling down the riverbank ahead of Bolan, Quinn asked wearily, "Why don't you leave me? Light a fire to help the others find me and get out of here. I promise not to tell them where you've gone."

"You don't know where I'm going," Bolan countered, "and you're coming with me. I gave Val my word."

"You have no right to do this," Quinn replied. "Neither does she."

"I don't know why she thinks you're worth the trouble," Bolan said. "Maybe she's wrong. The two of you can work that out together. In the meantime, hit that slope. Let's hope you climb a damn sight better than you swim."

NICO MBARGA HUDDLED with his tracker, hoping that the gunfire would repeat itself, giving a more precise location for the shooter than a general southeasterly direction. It was something, granted, but Mbarga wanted more.

He didn't get it.

Cursing to himself, he turned and told the others, "They have gone off course, southeastward. Maybe they are lost. Maybe they're lost." He shrugged. "Or maybe not."

"Maybe?" Camacho spit. "Is that all you can say?"

Mbarga fought to keep his temper as he answered, "We don't know the second man, or why he took Quinn from the village. We don't know if Quinn's cooperating, or if he was kidnapped. We have no idea where they are going, and we don't know why those shots were fired. If you can read their minds, Mr. Camacho, please enlighten us."

That made the Arab laugh. Camacho scowled at him but offered no reply.

"Southeastward, then," Mbarga commanded, and the point man forged a new course through the trees ahead of them.

Why had the shots been fired? Mbarga recognized a short burst from an automatic weapon, and he had enough experience with the Kalashnikov to know the gun he'd heard was something else. Beyond that, though, the gunfire was another taunting mystery.

It might work out to his advantage, Nico thought, but pinning down the source of one brief sound was difficult, if not impossible. The tracker was their best hope, but he needed signs to work with, and a sound left no impression on the wind. If they got close enough for him to smell a trace of gunpowder, at least they'd know approximately where the shooting had occurred.

But by that time, where would their quarry be?

Mbarga hated failure, most particularly when it carried penalties. He dreaded going back to face the master without Patrick Quinn in tow—and now he owed *two* men to Master Gaborone. His task grew harder by the moment with no relief in sight.

What if the gunshots they had heard meant Quinn was dead? Suppose they found him murdered on the trail. Then, what?

Nico considered it, then dismissed the notion from his mind. It made no sense. Why take Quinn from the village, march him off two miles or more into the jungle, just to kill him? An intruder who could infiltrate Obike, set three fires and flee unseen with Quinn would find it easier to slit Quinn's throat and leave him where he fell.

Perhaps the prowler wanted information first, Mbarga thought. But what knowledge did Quinn possess, beyond that of five hundred other villagers? What made him special, if in fact he was?

Mbarga ran the short list in his mind, checking each point as he pursued the tracker, keeping sharp eyes on the trail they followed. Quinn was white, of course, but so were ninety or a hundred others in the village. They possessed no special rank or privileges, and Quinn didn't stand out among the other members of his race.

He was American, but so were twenty-odd percent

of Master Gaborone's disciples in Obike. Once again, their nationality had no fringe benefits. If anything, the Master favored Africans, although he took pains not to outwardly discriminate.

Mbarga thought that Quinn had been a rich man once, but he was cut off from the money now, some family dispute whose details presently eluded him. Was that the answer? Had his family decided that their errant offspring was worth saving after all? Had they perhaps employed someone to snatch him from the viper's nest?

If that was true, Mbarga had to ask himself again, Was Quinn a prisoner or an accomplice to his own abduction from Obike? Had he set the fires himself, or was he taken by surprise and carried off against his will?

And once again, in any case, who fired the gunshots? Why?

There were a hundred reasons, Mbarga realized, why someone with a weapon might discharge it in the jungle. There were snakes and leopards, plus a host of other predators. They might've stumbled onto bandits, but he doubted it, convinced there would've been more shooting in that case.

But what if Quinn *was* snatched against his will and then attempted to escape? Might a kidnapper hired to rescue him suffer a momentary lapse and gun him down, instead?

In that case, Nico reckoned that Quinn's corpse would be abandoned in the forest. Who would drag dead meat around the jungle, as an invitation to its feral scavengers? Unless, of course, they had a rendezvous with others to extract them from the wilderness.

Rich family. United States. Would they be satisfied with one employee on the job?

A sudden sense of urgency enveloped Mbarga. Hissing at the tracker to move faster, he pressed on as darkness crept around them through the trees and nightfall threatened to abort their search.

"*HOW* MUCH?"

The number was repeated with a wide smile. Grimaldi's hands made fists inside his trouser pockets, but he swallowed the impulse to pummel his companion's face.

The helicopter was a vintage Hiller UH-12, once designated Raven by the U.S. military. It was smaller than the airship he had lost, but faster—ninety miles per hour at top speed—and it still seated five. It wasn't new, by any stretch of the imagination, but he'd done a turn around the private helipad to check it out.

All systems go.

Except that now the chopper's owner wanted a deposit roughly twice what it was worth brand-new, and the Stony Man pilot was running short of cash. He could afford the fuel and basic rental fee with change enough left over for a burger, hold the cheese, but the deposit was light-years beyond his reach.

He'd lost three precious hours as it was, trying to find a another whirlybird, and now he couldn't spring for what he needed, since there'd definitely be no refund on the chopper that was toasted at the airport. It had been a touch-and-go experience for Grimaldi, just getting off the airport property without being detained for questioning, and now he'd hit another rude dead end.

"Look, I don't want to buy your bird," Grimaldi said, "just rent it. How about the rental fee up front, and I can leave my car with you. Collateral."

The Hiller's owner blinked twice at Grimaldi's aged rental car and shook his head. "Deposit first. In case you not come back."

Thanks for your confidence, Grimaldi thought. It was a possibility, but the reminder left a sour feeling in his gut. He couldn't even steal the damned thing, since he'd ditched his pistol at the airport and it would've caused more problems if and when he made it back to Brazzaville with passengers aboard.

It seemed to be the Hiller, now, or nothing. He could either find a way to pay the tab, or leave Bolan to do the rest alone. Two hundred miles of jungle, give or take, with hunters snapping at his heels.

"I need to make some calls," Grimaldi said. "An hour, maybe more."

"Deposit first." The African repeated his mantra, adding, "First come, first served."

Grimaldi turned a full three-sixty, checking out the heliport. They were alone, no other human beings close enough to shout at, much less lining up to rent the helicopter.

"You expecting someone else tonight?" he asked.

A shrug. "I busy man."

"I see that," Grimaldi said.

There was only one thing for it. He would have to make the call.

Grimaldi walked back to his car and drove around the block. Making the call was bad enough, without the chopper's owner grinning at him while he pleaded his case.

He used the sat phone, tapped the number out from memory and waited for the link to be completed. Two rings into it, a male voice answered on the private, scrambled line.

"Identify."

"Granite, 1196."

Ten seconds passed before the voice replied, "Confirmed. May I direct your call?"

"I'm looking for the Bear."

"One moment, please."

It was a bit longer than that before Aaron Kurtzman's voice came on the line. Scrambled or not, he played it by the book.

"Granite, what can I do for you?"

"We've hit a snag. That is, *I* have. My transportation for the pickup's totaled, and I can't replace it with the funds I have available. If there's some way to float a loan," Grimaldi told him, "it'd be a lifesaver."

"How much?" Kurtzman asked.

Grimaldi repeated the number, almost wincing as he said it. "A deposit, that would be," he added. "Most of it's refundable when I return the bird."

Kurtzman was silent for a moment, but the background noises of a keyboard told Grimaldi he was working. When his voice came back, Kurtzman said, "We can do that, Granite, but we'll need your firstborn for collateral."

"Sure thing," Grimaldi said through his relief. "I'll get a start on that as soon as we wrap up this job."

"I guess you'll need a wire transfer."

"How long will that take?"

"Well, you've got no Amex office and no Western Union there in Brazzaville. That means we'll have to use a bank."

Grimaldi's spirits fell. "Tomorrow morning, then."

"Looks like it. Sorry. No way we can make them open in the middle of the night."

"Maybe the embassy—?"

"Sorry," Kurtzman repeated, and he sounded it. "They don't have the facility for deals like this. Even the banks are dicey, but I've got one here that ought to have the capital on hand." He waited for Grimaldi to produce a pen and scrap of paper, then read off the name and address of a major downtown bank.

"Okay," Grimaldi said in parting. "Thanks."

He killed the sat phone, cursed his luck and focused on the job of getting through the night.

ANOTHER HOUR PASSED, by Quinn's best estimate, before his kidnapper allowed a rest stop. It was nearly dark now, and a new wave of mosquitoes would be out in force at sundown. Quinn sat miserable in his sodden clothes, imagining their buzz around his ears, their stinging bites. It made him itch to think of them, and when he scratched Quinn felt some pulpy object underneath his shirt, stuck to his flesh.

"What the—?"

He rose and started tearing at his buttons, heard his captor ask what he was doing but ignored it, peeling off his wet and clinging shirt.

Oh, God!

Quinn saw the first leech fastened to his stomach, sleek and black against his own pale flesh. There was another one beneath his left arm, looking for a better place to feed after he'd nearly scratched it loose. And if there were two leeches he could see—

Frantic, Quinn started clawing at the bloodsuckers, vaguely embarrassed by the whining sound that issued from his throat, but too disgusted with the sight of leeches on his flesh to really care. The first one clung tenaciously, its razor remaining anchored in his stomach even after Quinn had crushed its slimy body flat and wrung it dry.

The blood that stained his fingers was his own. He nearly fainted from the sight of it, reeling until his kidnapper provided a supporting arm.

"Sit down," the mercenary ordered. Seconds later, he pressed a cheap disposable cigarette lighter into Quinn's hand, saying, "It's easier to burn them off."

Quinn nodded, flicking at the lighter with his thumb, but there was something wrong with it or wrong with him. No matter how he tried, the gift of fire eluded him.

"All right, let me."

His keeper took back the lighter and thumbed it once, producing instant flame. Quinn closed his eyes as the tongue of fire moved toward the remnants of leech on his stomach. The heat made him flinch, but it never quite burned him. He sat deathly still as the camou-clad soldier burned leeches away from his left side and back.

Quinn stopped counting at five.

When the lighter snapped shut, Quinn reluctantly opened his eyes. "That was bad," he confessed. "Listen, thank you—"

"Not yet. Better take off your pants. Just in case," the soldier added.

Quinn rose. Trembling fingers attacked his rope belt, but it took him three tries to untie it. He dropped his wet and filthy trousers in a heap around his ankles, but he didn't dare to check his legs for leeches. If he saw them feeding there, Quinn thought he might start to scream.

"This could take a while," his captor warned.

Quinn braced his hands against the nearest tree and let them take his weight, as if submitting to a frisk by the police. He closed his mind as far as possible to what was happening below his waist. The moving flame became his friend, no matter how it made him cringe and grimace on the verge of weeping.

"Finished," the soldier said sometime later. "You should check your clothes before you dress."

"All right." Quinn barely recognized his own parched voice.

"There's no real harm done."

"No."

"But you should hurry up. We're losing daylight."

Quinn obeyed like an automaton. He found no leeches in his clothing, but the shirt and trousers still repulsed him with their clammy touch against his violated flesh. His bare right foot was bruised and felt as if it might be swelling, but he had to walk on it regardless.

He was in the middle of a living nightmare, with no end in sight.

"Thank you," Quinn repeated as he finished dressing.

"Never mind."

"I feel like I should know your name."

"Why's that?" the soldier asked.

"Because we can't escape each other."

After a stall, his captor said, "It's Cooper. Now move out. We're wasting time."

BOLAN WONDERED whether Quinn was slipping into Stockholm Syndrome, or if he was simply worn down after a traumatic afternoon. The syndrome drew its name from an incident in Stockholm, Sweden, where bandits had taken a group of bank employees hostage and attempted to negotiate favors from the police. They'd failed, but several of the captives had emerged as outspoken defenders of their kidnappers. Two of the female hostages even professed love for the men who'd held them prisoner.

It hadn't gone *that* far with Quinn and never would, even if Bolan had to kick his ass, but his reaction to the whole leech incident suggested that his nerves were frayed and on the verge of snapping. Bolan didn't think

Quinn would turn violent in his present state. It seemed that fear, depression and fatigue had sapped Quinn's anger—for the moment, anyway—and left him feeling beaten down.

That worked for Bolan to a point, unless Quinn fell apart and ceased to function altogether. He was strong enough to carry Quinn, despite their hours on the trail, but with no word from Jack Grimaldi and no end in sight, the prospect was a daunting one.

Nightfall would give Quinn time to rest, and Bolan, too. He didn't want to stop, but had decided it would be too risky marching his charge ahead of him through jungle darkness. In another hour or so, Bolan would start to look for places where he could restrain Quinn without harming him, a place that gave him cover to defend.

In case his enemies marched through the night.

Bolan had no proof yet that anyone was trailing them, but instinct told him Gaborone's security detail should be coming. He had no way of knowing when they'd started or how fast they'd travel through the forest. Vehicles were out, but if they had a decent tracker and were willing to exert themselves—

The sound of helicopter rotor blades arrested Bolan in midstride. He called for Quinn to halt and saw the young man wobble, zombielike, on his last step. The sky sounds made him think first of Grimaldi, but there'd been no time for Jack to find another whirlybird and make the flight from Brazzaville.

Besides, he realized, the chopper was approaching from behind them, from the general direction of Obike.

Bolan stood and waited for the whirlybird to pass above them and a hundred yards or so off to their left. When it was gone, sounds of its passage fading off southward, he considered what it meant.

One thing was obvious: the helicopter either came from Gaborone or it didn't. If not, then Bolan could dismiss it from his mind. But if the Process had a whirlybird available, then, what?

A pilot couldn't track his progress through the jungle without infrared technology or something similar, and Bolan knew that would be stretching it, no matter how many trust funds Ahmadou Gaborone had tapped to build his African community. The place Bolan had seen wasn't high tech, by any means. Indeed, it had seemed primitive.

Bolan had seen no chopper in the village, but he knew there was an airstrip five miles farther east. He had assumed it was for flights delivering supplies or visitors, maybe a charter hop to Brazzaville from time to time, but what if he had underestimated Gaborone?

Assume he had the chopper, then. What could he do with it? Searching a jungle from the sky was fruitless, in the absence of advanced technology. Air sweeps for fugitives on foot worked best in open country. Even if the helicopter carried spotlights, they'd accomplish nothing through the looming jungle canopy.

But with a chopper, Gaborone could drop a team in front of Bolan, certainly. The guru might not know exactly where his quarry was, but he could put men on the ground and have them backtrack toward Obike, hoping they could intercept the runners.

Did they know Quinn wasn't alone?

That was the question nagging Bolan worst of all. If Gaborone believed that Quinn had set fire to the village and escaped unaided, then his hunters would be unprepared for armed resistance. Bolan had a better chance in that case to surprise them, and to stay alive.

"Go on now," he told Quinn when there was no sign of the chopper coming back.

Was that a hopeful sign, meaning that some official or civilian flight had passed en route to Brazzaville? Or did it mean the helicopter had set down somewhere in front of them to lay a trap?

Whichever, Bolan's instinct told him that he wouldn't know the answer until he was face-to-face with enemies who meant to spill his blood.

CHAPTER SEVEN

Just when Samburu Changa was convinced that he could stand no more, Danso Beira turned from his controls and said, "Here is the village."

Changa craned his neck, fighting a sudden rush of vertigo, and bit his tongue to keep from crying out as Beira tipped the helicopter somehow toward his side, thereby improving his view of the green abyss. Below him, through a small break in the canopy, Changa glimpsed several thatched rooftops already swathed in dusky shadows.

"Can you land here?" he asked Beira.

"No. Our rotor blades would clip the trees. I'll try to find the nearest open space."

"Don't try," Changa replied. "Do it."

They began to circle, moving outward from the village in a spiral pattern. Beira brought the helicopter closer to the treetops, making Changa curl his toes involuntarily. No matter how he tried to loosen his death grip on the Kalashnikov between his knees, Changa squeezed the barrel till his fingers cramped.

"I see a place!" Beira announced excitedly after they'd circled for ten minutes. "There!"

He pointed to a broad gap in the forest canopy, some sixty feet across, by Changa's reckoning. He hovered briefly over it, then shifted his controls somehow, so that the helicopter settled slowly, vertically, into the shadows. Changa watched in something close to awe as treetops closed around them, then receded overhead. The great trunks stood like pillars fore and aft, to either side, surrounding them.

"Watch out for branches here," Beira advised. "We can't afford to break a rotor blade."

The warning nearly panicked Changa, but he clenched his thighs around the AK-47 while he ground his teeth together. Wide-eyed, he turned this and that way, frightened that a branch might thrust into his line of sight from nowhere, foul the rotors whirling overhead and send them plunging to their deaths.

In fact, they landed safely, settling in a glade where fanlike ferns grew waist high to a man of average height. Changa was first out of the cabin, jogging several steps away and crouching underneath the rotors, every muscle in his body clenched to keep from trembling visibly. His three men followed, seeming more relaxed, although they eyed the forest shadows warily. Beira switched off the Lama's motor but he made no move to leave the pilot's seat.

Changa walked back to him and said, "You're coming with us, Danso."

"What?" The man sounded horrified. "And leave the bird for anyone to come along and tamper with?"

"I see no one," Changa replied.

"But still—"

"How many people are there in the village, Danso?"

Beira made a puzzled face. "How many? How should I know?"

"More than twenty? Thirty?"

"Probably."

"Then I need every man and gun available. You're coming with us. Bring the keys."

"There are no keys."

"So much the better. Come!"

Beira didn't have a Kalashnikov, but he had brought an Uzi submachine gun that he now clutched nervously against his chest, standing among the others with the forest giants towering above them. It was nearly dusk, and night would fall swiftly beneath the jungle canopy. There was no time to waste.

"How far to the village?" Changa asked his pilot. "And which way?"

Beira removed a compass from his pocket and consulted it. "That way," he said at last, pointing. "Perhaps a kilometer eastward."

"You lead," Changa commanded.

Beira blinked. "Why me?"

"You have the compass."

"I will give it to—"

"And none of us can read it," Changa added. "Go!"

They followed Danso Beira through the forest, keeping up a steady pace except where obstacles delayed them. Once, they encountered a fallen mahogany tree, its slowly rotting trunk some twenty-five feet in diameter. Rather than clamber over it, they hiked around, veering a hundred feet off course, then waiting while Beira found their direction again. Two hundred yards on, they had to ford a rushing stream that left their trousers drenched, feet slimy in their off-brand jogging shoes.

When they had traveled twenty minutes from the helicopter, Changa smelled the village. They were cooking supper, and it made his mouth water. His stomach rumbled as he signaled for his men to stop. They closed in as he beckoned them, craning to hear his whispered orders.

"Remember," he instructed them, "we're looking for a white man from Obike. If he's here, we take him back with us. If not, we search and question everyone to find out if they've seen him. They may lie, but we must have the truth for Master Gaborone. He trusts us to protect Obike and the Process. Any questions?"

Danso Beira, ever practical, asked, "What if they report us later? The police—"

"Don't worry," Changa told him. "There'll be no report."

"But how can—"

"We will see to it," Changa said. "Are there any other questions?"

There was none. Hungry and anxious to repay

someone for the discomfort he had lately suffered, Changa led his soldiers through the dusk into the nameless village.

IT SEEMED TO QUINN that night had nearly overtaken them. Back in Obike, he supposed, the evening meal would be prepared. Some kind of stew with stringy meat if they were lucky, no one quite prepared to ask where it had come from, what it was. Still, any food at all was better than the present growling in his stomach, loud enough that he supposed his kidnapper—the stoic Cooper—had to be hearing by now.

Cooper.

The name was common. It meant nothing to him. Once again he tried to puzzle out how Val Querente, living in Wyoming, could've met a man like this, much less persuaded him to risk his life in Africa. Quinn knew she wasn't rich. He'd been inside her home, and while the place was comfortable, it wasn't the home of a woman who pulled strings with mercenaries, sending them halfway around the world to rescue friends in need.

I don't need rescuing, Quinn told himself again. This Cooper wasn't saving him from anything. Rather, he was abducting Quinn from the community and fellowship he'd chosen of his own free will.

Obike wasn't much to look at, granted, but it was evolving day by day. Quinn had some difficulties with communication, but he'd made good progress with his French in recent weeks. Some of the Africans still looked at him askance, but who could blame them, with the white man's racist legacy in Africa? Quinn was convinced that most of them would come around in time, as some already had—but now they had to believe he hadn't set the fires that threatened their community, then fled into the jungle like a madman.

Rage at Cooper sparked a sour burning in his stomach, nearly canceling the hunger that had nagged him. Nearly, but not quite. The combination of sensations simply made Quinn more uncomfortable as he plodded through the forest, chilled from his wet clothing, right foot raw and throbbing in the absence of its shoe. At least the leech bites had quit stinging, until Quinn remembered them and cringed anew at the fresh memory of wormlike creatures feasting on his blood.

Green Hell, he thought. Somebody got it right.

But only hours earlier, Quinn had been happy in Obike, cheerfully surrounded by the same jungle, the same insects and predators. He'd been content to spend his life there, serving Master Gaborone.

Or had he?

If a little hardship shook his faith this much, Quinn had to question whether he was ready for a pilgrim's dedicated life. Suppose the master sent him on a mission by himself, as Gaborone had done with others? Was he equal to the task, or would it leave him whining for support from others in the Process?

I'm dedicated, damn it! Quinn assured himself. I don't break down the first time things go.wrong.

But he was getting pretty close to it, the way he felt

right now. Fatigue, pain, weakness, fear of the unknown—they all combined to challenge his devotion to the Process and to Master Gaborone. That unexpected doubt enraged him, not only against his kidnapper but also against Val Querente.

Who was she to undermine his faith this way? He'd trusted her, said things to her in confidence that he had never shared with anybody else on Earth. She knew him better than his parents did, in some ways. Better than the one lover he'd briefly had in college, though he never thought of Val that way.

He stepped down on a hidden stone and gasped in pain. Quinn staggered, nearly lost his balance. Cooper was about to catch him by one arm, before he wrenched away and staggered in the opposite direction.

"I'm all right!" he snapped. "Leave me alone."

"Not likely," Bolan said. "But if you're fit to walk, then do it."

"I'm sorry if I'm slowing down your getaway," Quinn answered, "but I'm barefoot here."

"Bad luck, but now you've got to deal with it."

"Is that what they teach you in kidnapper's school?"

"It's what you learn in life, if you survive."

"You said we'd stop when it got dark."

"It's not dark yet," Bolan informed him. "Walk. I'll let you know when you can stop."

BOLAN WAS BUSY watching Quinn and nearly lost him in the process. He was fairly sure that Quinn wouldn't attempt another break, after his last experience and having lost one shoe, but fairly sure and certain were two very different things. As dusk descended on the Congo jungle, trailing night behind it like a shroud, he started watching for places they could stop to rest.

He didn't look for running water, since he'd have to boil it anyway and they would have no fire. Instead he sought a place that was defensible, while offering an opportunity to physically restrain his prisoner while Bolan slept. He'd come equipped with duct tape and a number of the flexible restraints police use when they're running short of handcuffs. It would do, but only if he found the proper place.

A place where trackers couldn't take him by surprise.

He thought about Grimaldi, back in Brazzaville, and wondered how the search for wings was going. Bolan could've called him, but he'd waited, knowing that the sat phone worked both ways. When Jack had something to report, he'd call and set new rendezvous coordinates.

Assuming that he found another helicopter.

And assuming Bolan was alive to take the call.

Whatever happened, Bolan knew his old friend wouldn't let him down for lack of trying. Jack would move heaven and Earth if that was what it took to hold up his end of the bargain. But he couldn't build a whirlybird from scratch, and there was nothing he could do from Brazzaville to keep hunters off Bolan's track.

There was no sign of them so far, unless the chopper flyby counted, and his mind was still divided on that score. If Gaborone *had* sent the helicopter winging southward, then it meant he'd found their trail, or at the very least surmised which way they'd run. And if he knew that, Bolan had to think there would be trackers coming on behind him, doing what they could to shave his lead.

And what was that, exactly?

If their woodcraft was superior, they'd find him, given time. He hadn't taken time to mask the trail and would've found it difficult, if not impossible, to hide Quinn's tracks while covering his own. By this time, if they were pursued, Bolan assumed the hunters knew that they were looking for two persons.

But they wouldn't know that they were dealing with the Executioner.

If he assumed the worst, a mobile firing squad prepared to kill on sight, the enemy still couldn't know that he was armed, much less that Bolan had survived jungle engagements where he was outnumbered and outgunned by true professionals. If Gaborone was using triggermen accustomed to game hunting or to facing unarmed, unskilled humans, they were in for a surprise.

That said, Bolan would rather flee than fight if given half a chance. He still clung to the altered version of his first plan, calling for extraction without conflict, if Grimaldi could find wings and make it back from Brazzaville.

If not, then Bolan had a long hot walk in front of him, and he'd be babysitting Patrick Quinn until they reached their destination or were stopped dead in their tracks.

Without Grimaldi, Bolan had a long hot walk in front of him, but not to Brazzaville. It was pure fantasy to think that he could shepherd Patrick Quinn across two hundred miles of savage jungle. Rather, he had hatched a backup plan, in case they were deprived of air support.

A river, the Banguelu, lay some twenty miles due east of their trail overland. Its course ran north to south, and it would take them close enough to Brazzaville for Bolan and his captive to complete the trip on foot within a day or two, if they were forced to make that choice. Of course, they'd need some kind of boat to navigate the river, but obtaining a canoe would be the least of Bolan's problems if it came to that.

Plan A was still his first choice, and he kept his fingers crossed that Brazzaville would yield another helicopter for Grimaldi.

And that adversaries wouldn't overtake them first.

"CLOSE NOW," the tracker told Mbarga.

"Are you sure?"

His point man sniffed the air, so still it wrapped around Mbarga like a damp and cloying blanket. "Smell that?" the tracker asked.

Mbarga closed his eyes and took a whiff. Nothing. He shook his head.

"Cordite," the tracker said. "They shoot 'round here, for sure."

Camacho made a snorting sound behind him, whether out of mirth or sheer contempt, Mbarga couldn't tell. He didn't trust himself to look at the Colombian just then, for fear he might struck the man or worse, and thus earn Master Gaborone's enduring wrath.

"How far?" he asked the tracker, fearing it was hopeless. "Where?"

"This way."

The point man led them several yards off course, until they stood atop a bluff, staring into a jungle river dark below them. Once again the sniffing ritual, before the tracker pointed toward the muddy bank below and told Mbarga, "There."

Mbarga scanned the riverbank as far as he could see in both directions, but he saw no trace of Patrick Quinn or his anonymous companion. Maybe he was blind, because the tracker pointed once again, grunting before he set off, following the bluff southward. Five minutes later they stood looking at a portion of the hillside scuffed by climbing hands and feet.

"Went down back there," the tracker said, thumbing the air across one shoulder. "Came up here. Go off…that way."

He waited for Mbarga's nod, then got back on the trail. Mbarga, trailing, heard Camacho tell Sharif, "We're on a wild-duck chase, I think."

Mbarga rounded on him, smiling fit to burst. "Sir may be right," he said. "Sir should feel free to go back now."

"Go back?" Camacho blinked at him uncertainly. "Go where?"

"You will be welcome in Obike, where a meal has doubtless been prepared by now," Mbarga said. The smile felt carved into his face.

"I don't know how to find your village," Camacho said. "How in hell do *I* know where we are?"

Mbarga shrugged. "Alas, Master Gaborone has given us a mission to complete. You weren't ordered to attend, of course, but made the choice yourself. My soldiers need to hurry now. I must ask you respectfully to keep up with the group and to be quiet while we hunt."

Without waiting for a reply, Mbarga turned, snapped at his men to double-time, and led them by example, jogging rapidly behind the tracker who was almost out of sight. If the Colombian or Arab muttered anything behind his back, Mbarga didn't hear them and he didn't care.

Their path led southward once again, in the direction of the village nearest to Obike. He had no idea if Quinn knew where the village was, or if his nameless guide might know the way. The helicopter that had passed over their heads a short time earlier was headed in the same direction, and Mbarga wondered now if Master Gaborone had sent more men to aid them as an afterthought.

Who would he choose to lead the second team? Perhaps Samburu Changa, Nico's first lieutenant, though his fear of flying would present an obstacle. Would Changa hesitate if Master Gaborone told him to fly?

If so, Mbarga guessed that he would have to find himself a new right hand.

In any case, he couldn't take for granted that the overflight meant reinforcements waiting somewhere on the trail ahead. Mbarga had his work to do, and he wouldn't permit the foreigners to slow him, much less treat him with disrespect in front of his men. Better that one of them should have an accident while tramping through the jungle. That could always be explained, and it would leave the other customer to deal with Master Gaborone on favorable terms.

The prospect made Mbarga smile, but the expression swiftly fled his face. Somewhere ahead of him were two men he had sworn to capture. He owed two lives to the master, and he did not mean for one of them to be his own.

THE VILLAGERS WERE roasting wild pig from the forest, gathered for a feast of sorts, when Changa's hunting party burst upon them from the shadows. Conversation halted instantly, as if some unseen hand had drawn a blade across their vocal cords. All eyes followed the new arrivals as they strode into the village, automatic weapons carried at the ready.

Changa tried them first in French, asking the chief or headman to identify himself, but stony silence greeted his command. The villagers examined him as if he represented some life-form unknown to them. He tried Lingala next, without result. Beira addressed them in Kikongo, but the forest people simply stared, a few of them exchanging puzzled looks.

"Enough," Changa said. Breaking from his little group, he picked a young girl from the crowd, no more than six or eight years old, and dragged her to a point beside the fire and spitted pig. The muzzle of his AK-47 nudged her skull as he declared, "Last chance!"

A tattooed man of sixty years or so, clad in a loincloth made from leopard skin, stepped forward. "Wait," he said in French. "I am the headman."

"So, you're playing games with me," Changa said. "Shall we let the little one play, too?"

"The fault is only mine."

Changa made a decision, nodded once and roughly shoved the girl back toward her mother's side. "You know my face, old man?"

The village leader shook his head.

"But you know where we've come from, yes?"

The elder shrugged.

"You know Obike?"

"We don't go there," the chief said.

"But you know where it is."

A solemn nod.

"We're looking for a white man," Changa said. "He set fire to Obike earlier today and ran in this direction. Have you seen him?"

"No," the headman answered.

"No? Why don't you ask your people?"

"There is no need to ask. A white man would be noticed and reported."

"Ah. To you?"

The elder hesitated, then replied, "To me. Yes."

"And you'd surely tell me if the man we're seeking had passed through your village, yes? Even if you were promised money for your silence?"

"Money?" The old man smiled at that. "It has no value here."

"Or goods, perhaps? Trinkets?"

"We've seen no white men."

Half turning toward his soldiers, Changa asked them, "Should I trust him? Does he seem an honest man to you?"

The pilot, Danso Beira, answered first. "We should make sure."

"A good idea," Changa agreed, as if his course of action wasn't planned out in advance. "We can't go back to Master Gaborone and say we took a stranger's word for something so important. Search the village. Turn it inside out, if need be. Do it now!"

His soldiers fanned out warily, clutching their weapons, Beira slowest of them all. They were outnumbered, but the villagers appeared to have no weapons. They weren't expecting company, much less invaders, and whatever arms they might possess would be inside their huts.

"Be careful!" Changa called after his men. "Search closely. Anything you find, bring here to me."

He waited with the headman and the other villagers, suddenly conscious that they could rush forward, overpower him and crush him to the earth. But something in their eyes told Changa that they wouldn't risk it. He could feel them studying his AK-47, fearing it and its proximity to the old man who led them. If they charged, the elder would be first to die, and others would fall with him. Changa might be torn apart bare-handed, but his men would hear the shots and finish what he'd started, blasting everyone in sight.

Would they, in turn, be slaughtered?

Changa wasn't sure, but something in the headman's eyes and his defeated attitude told Changa that he didn't have to worry. These were people long accustomed to abuse. They would absorb it in the knowledge that this trial would pass, and that in time they would be left alone.

They were half right, at least.

Whether his men found any trace of Patrick Quinn or not, Changa would leave the villagers in peace.

But he would leave no living witnesses.

CHAPTER EIGHT

Voices and odors told Bolan that they were drawing closer to some kind of jungle settlement. The smells included smoke and meat left too long on the fire; the voices, raised in angry shouting, told him that they could've picked a better time to drop by unannounced.

Bolan was ready to bypass the village, leave its people to their argument and hope they never knew that he and Quinn were in the neighborhood. He hadn't counted on assistance from the natives, and in fact wasn't convinced that he could trust Obike's neighbors. It was possible that Gaborone had swayed their minds and mood in his direction, maybe courted them with gifts, and Bolan reckoned he had ample problems as it was, without inviting more.

The first gunshots changed that.

It was a short burst from an AK-47, no mistaking it for anyone who'd ever been on the receiving end. A high-pitched scream immediately followed, probably a female voice, then further shouting, a man.

Before encroaching further, Bolan gripped Quinn by the arm and leaned close, whisper-hissing in his ear. "I need to see what's happening, find out if it affects us. We don't know who's shooting, but it wouldn't be a smart idea to jump out of the trees and take them by surprise. You understand?"

Quinn nodded. The expression on his sweat-streaked face was mingled curiosity and worry.

Bolan led the way this time, to keep it stealthy. If Quinn bolted, he would have to run the youngster down, subdue him, bind him tight before he checked out what was happening ahead. Unless, of course, the ruckus brought a swarm of armed and battle-ready villagers down on their heads. He hoped Quinn would be smart enough to think about his own welfare, at least, as they pushed through the final layers of greenery to find a clutch of huts built in between the boles of looming trees.

The village layout had required some planning, to erect more than a dozen homes without clearing the ground, but Bolan had no time to study native architecture at the moment. He was focused on the scene unfolding, four men armed with automatic weapons facing down perhaps three dozen empty-handed villagers. Between the two groups, near a fire pit with a small pig on a spit, a man lay sprawled and motionless.

"Changa," Quinn whispered, as if talking to himself.

"You know them?" Bolan asked, barely breathing it out loud.

Quinn nodded. "They're the master's guards. Samburu Changa's speaking, but I don't—"

"Is he their leader?" Bolan interrupted.

"Second in command, after Nico Mbarga. Well, third after Master Gaborone. They shouldn't be here."

Not unless they're hunting, Bolan thought, and gripped his AUG, ready to strike Quinn down if the young man tried to alert his friends.

Except he didn't sound that friendly toward them at the moment. More confused, troubled about their presence in the village and the grim sight of a stranger dead or dying on the ground.

Bolan decided that he couldn't help the man who'd just been shot. His first responsibility was Patrick Quinn, keeping the young man with him and alive until Grimaldi picked them up or they could find another means of transportation back to Brazzaville. He hadn't signed on for another jungle rescue mission on the side and hoped he would be spared any peripheral involvements.

Still, he waited, watching. Just in case.

Changa was raging at the villagers again, waving his AK-47 like a mad conductor trying to direct a silent orchestra. He had the full attention of his audience, but still received no answers to his shouted questions.

"What's he saying?" Bolan asked.

Quinn squinted, shook his head. "Not sure. He's switching back and forth from French to native dialect, maybe Kikongo or Lingala, I don't know. The part I get, something about a white man."

"Singular?" Bolan asked.

"Yes, I think so. *Man*, not *men*."

The inference sank as soon as Quinn had finished speaking. He blinked rapidly and licked his lips, mouth working without sound as if his tongue had gone Sahara dry.

"Makes sense," Bolan whispered. "They're after you."

Quinn found his voice, a breathless, choked-off sound. "Like this? Why would they shoot that man?"

"My guess," Bolan replied, "he wouldn't tell them where you were."

"He didn't know!"

"I'd bet he told them that."

"Oh, God!"

Changa and his three men were shouting all together now, herding the villagers off toward the tree line on their left. Some of the women wept and wailed, unheeded by the gunmen. A boy of ten or twelve broke from the pack, running full tilt, until one of the gunners fired a wild burst from the hip and brought him tumbling down.

Bolan's left hand covered Quinn's mouth before he could cry out. He whispered into Quinn's ear, "I have to stop this. If you make me run you down, it won't be pretty."

Short of clubbing Quinn unconscious, it was all that he could do. Bolan left him and started moving swiftly through the trees to intercept the firing squad.

THE RUNNING BOY had startled Changa, but he hadn't gotten far. The other villagers were muttering or sobbing now, depending on their gender. Native men were often stoic in the face of death, though breakdowns weren't unknown. If anyone believed tears would dissuade him from his course, they had mistaken Changa for a man who cared.

His master's orders would be carried out, regardless of the price in blood.

Changa now realized the villagers were ignorant of Patrick Quinn, yet having listened to his questions they were living, breathing liabilities.

But not for long.

There would be questions when the slaughter was discovered, but that might not be for weeks or even months. The jungle was voracious. By this time tomorrow, scavengers and insects would've rendered Changa's victims something less than human. Three days hence, only their scattered bones would tell the tale. Whoever found them, finally, might summon the authorities, but their response would take more time. And what would they discover, in the end?

Changa assumed that Master Gaborone would blame the massacre on rebels, and corrupt authorities in Brazzaville would probably agree. They were bedeviled by guerrillas in the countryside. Why question one who spoke with God and paid top dollar for his privacy?

Perhaps they could test bullets from the bodies, whatever remained of them, but Changa doubted that the effort would be made. Life was a cheap commodity in the Republic of Congo. And who would miss these peasants, after all?

Danso Beira seemed nervous, almost trembling, as they drove the villagers toward what would be their final resting place. The pilot kept his Uzi leveled at the targets right enough, but his wide eyes betrayed unseemly fear.

It was embarrassing to work with such a man. If Changa hadn't needed Beira for their flight back to Obike, he would have been tempted to—

Another child broke from the huddled group of villagers, running for cover. Changa saw one of his soldiers, Liban Jatta, aiming his Kalashnikov. He waited for a burst to bring the little runner down, but when it came, the sound of it was wrong and Jatta fell, twitching, with fresh blood on his face and chest.

It took a second, maybe less, for Changa to assess the situation. In that time, a second burst of automatic fire came from the dark tree line. Another of his men, Hosea Youlou, crumpled in his tracks, triggering half a magazine from his AK as he collapsed.

"Take cover!" Changa shouted at his two survivors. "Sniper in the trees!"

He almost ran inside a hut, but instantly thought better of it and ducked low behind one of the structure's crude thatched walls. It might not stop a bullet, but for now it would conceal him from the shooter. On the second burst he'd glimpsed a muzzle-flash and judged the shooter couldn't see him where he'd gone to ground.

Unless he moved, that was. Or had companions in the jungle, waiting to unleash more deadly fire.

Changa wondered where Danso Beira was, if he could find the pilot and escape back to the waiting helicopter. In the process, if he found his other man—

Jarari Dacko—that would be a bonus, but it wasn't necessary to survival. Getting out was all that mattered
now, and never mind that he had failed to silence all the
village witnesses.

Perhaps he could return and murder them some other
time, before they spoke to the police. And if worse
came to worst, they didn't know his name. Changa
could flee the district, find a place to hide until—

The thought of leaving Master Gaborone was
suddenly more frightening than any prospect of arrest,
but it would be irrelevant unless he managed to survive
the next few minutes. Listening as gunfire crackled
through the village, Changa struggled to identify the
weapons. There was Dacko's AK-47, by the sound of
it, and Beira's lightweight Uzi. When a weapon
answered from the tree line, Changa knew it was a rifle,
but of smaller caliber than his and Dacko's.

And he glimpsed a ray of hope.

If only one weapon opposed them, perhaps they
could flush out the shooter and kill him, or take him
alive and find out who he was. Either way, they'd be free
to proceed with their cleanup around the village, as the
master ordained.

The prospect brought a wary smile to Changa's lips
as he began to crawl.

QUINN WATCHED the master's bodyguards go down, first
one and then another. Both had been familiar to him,
faces he had seen around Obike, but he didn't know
their names. He thought it should've saddened him or

made him furious to see them killed, but after what they'd done he only felt a sickly queasiness.

He didn't understand why Changa's men would kill the helpless villagers. Was it because of him, as Cooper said? And if so, why? Even if Master Gaborone thought Quinn had set the fires around Obike, why would he send men to raid a village Quinn had never seen?

It made no sense in any scheme of logic Quinn could fathom, unless Master Gaborone believed he was a traitor who might share some precious secret with the outside world. In that case, he supposed the full might of the Process would be turned against him to protect the faith, safeguard the prophet's master plan.

Quinn felt a sudden chill, winced as more gunfire echoed through the forest. Shadows blanketed most of the village now, but firelight from the cooking pit illuminated portions of the battleground. Quinn marked the movement of combatants by their muzzle-flashes as night fell.

Cooper had killed two of the master's men, which still left three against him. Changa had escaped to cover with two others whom Quinn didn't know by name. The odds were still in Changa's favor. With his men, he might surround Cooper and finish him.

And what would happen then?

Did Changa know Cooper had snatched Quinn from Obike? Did the master think they were allies? Had that belief somehow provoked the village murders?

If it had—or even if it hadn't—Quinn now realized he dared not show himself to Changa and the others.

Having dealt with Cooper, they might shoot Quinn down on sight. He'd have no chance to plead his case, assuming that the master or his men were predisposed to listen.

Quinn felt sickened, doubled over where he crouched behind a screen of ferns. Watching the murder of a child was bad enough, but now he felt a numbing sense of private loss. It was as if his faith, his future, had been stripped away from him in one fell swoop, without warning. If Master Gaborone had turned against him, what was left?

Tears stung Quinn's eyes. He felt abandoned and betrayed, through no fault of his own. He couldn't blame the master's bodyguards for hunting him, if those had been their orders, but Gaborone should certainly have trusted him enough to let Quinn speak before he had unleashed the dogs.

Quinn rose without conscious volition, caught himself after his first step toward the jungle village. Walking into Cooper's battle as he was, unarmed and unprepared, was tantamount to suicide. Still, Quinn felt driven to assist the villagers somehow, if he could only find a way.

Scanning the battlefield, he saw that most of them had run to sanctuary in the forest, fifty yards or so off to his left. Encroaching darkness sheltered them, but Quinn could pick them out because he'd seen them running to their hiding place. Instead of fleeing for their lives, the villagers had lingered close enough to watch the fight and see which way it went, in case they had a chance to save their homes.

It struck Quinn as naive, the villagers believing Master Gaborone would give up and forget them if his first small team of raiders was defeated. Quinn had never pictured anything like this occurring, but he knew the master well enough to realize that he never surrendered. It was something in the prophet's makeup—dedication, zeal, fanaticism, pick your term of choice—but Gaborone had simply never learned to lose.

No, that was wrong. He had to have lost something, at sometime in the past, but he couldn't accept it. If the villagers or Cooper wiped out Changa's men, another team would be dispatched, and yet another after that.

In fact, for all Quinn knew, the reinforcements were already on their way.

He swallowed hard and started creeping through the forest, toward the shadowed figures of the huddled villagers.

BOLAN SQUEEZED OFF another short burst from his AUG, then left his sniper's nest and started moving counterclockwise, circling the village at a swift, ground-eating pace. Erratic gunfire from the huts covered whatever sounds he made while passing through the trees and undergrowth.

Three men remained, and they weren't the best he'd ever faced by any means, but neither were they total fools. He reckoned they were natives or the next best thing, with knowledge of the local rain forest surpassing Bolan's own. He didn't take them lightly, but they didn't frighten him.

Barring an evil stroke of luck or the arrival of support troops from the Process, Bolan meant to kill them all.

It was a purely practical decision. He required no new intelligence about the cult, and thus needed no prisoners. If any of the raiders managed to escape, they'd either dog him through the forest for revenge, or worse yet, flee to Gaborone with a report of Bolan's whereabouts, his progress. Either way, the threat could be eliminated by eradicating those who'd come to massacre the hapless villagers.

It was a simple choice, and Bolan didn't hesitate.

When he'd completed half a circuit of the village, he picked out a vantage point and waited for the next barrage of firing to erupt. The shooters had no target, but it seemed to make them feel better if they fired off a few rounds every ten or fifteen seconds. They were wasting ammunition, but he'd seen the bandoliers some of them wore and couldn't wait for their supply to be exhausted.

Bolan had to move, and soon, to finish it.

The muzzle-flashes winked again, as if in chain reaction, one after the other. Bolan marked their places, noting that all three were firing toward the north and northwest quadrants of the tree line where he'd first cut loose with interdicting fire. They obviously didn't know he'd moved, and Bolan was prepared to take advantage of that lapse.

He left the tree line's cover, moving in a silent crouch that brought him in behind the nearest shooter, from the target's blind side. Bolan didn't know if it was Changa, the commander, or one of his troops, but they were all the same in Bolan's eyes.

He held the assault rifle ready, pointed at his man, but hoped he wouldn't have to use it this time. If he managed to get closer, close the killing range to six or seven feet without alarming his intended prey, Bolan was confident that he could make a quiet kill and move on toward the others without triggering alarms.

At twenty feet he let the weapon dangle from its shoulder strap and drew his Swiss survival knife. In theory, it was meant for cutting food and firewood, whittling tent stakes and the like, but it could also be a killing tool. The satin finish on its eight-inch blade wouldn't reflect moonlight, but it would penetrate tough hide, Kevlar, even sheet metal if the arm behind it had sufficient power.

Bolan's did.

He crept up on his adversary from behind, taking his time although he worried about gunfire in the jungle night and other hunters hurrying to reach the village. He was seven feet behind his target when the gunman leaned around the tree he used for cover, triggering another burst from his Kalashnikov into the night.

Bolan leaped forward, struck the rifle down with his left arm before it clamped around his victim's neck. His blade drove deep and true between the struggling gunman's ribs, slid out and back, then twisted brutally.

In his adversary's grip, the dying shooter twitched and trembled, thrashed against him briefly, but with fading strength. No cry escaped his lips, since Bolan had his throat pinched off, strangling and silencing his enemy at the same time. Heels thumped against the tree trunk in a final spasm as the nearly dead man tried to free himself one hopeless final time, and then went limp.

Bolan held him another thirty seconds, making sure. When he was confident no stubborn trace of life remained, he crouched and eased his burden to the ground. Short bursts from two more weapons told him that the others hadn't marked their comrade's passing.

Three down, two to go.

The Executioner bent low and wiped his slick blade on the dead man's pants, then sheathed it. Taking up the AUG again, he peered around the tree in time to see another muzzle-flash some twenty feet in front of him and slightly to his right.

The shadows cloaked him as he moved in for another kill.

IT TOOK CHANGA a moment to discover that he'd lost another of his men. One moment he was firing into darkness, praying for a target, and the next he heard the sound of Beira's Uzi from the next hut over, on his left.

But what about Jarari Dacko's AK-47?

Changa tried to think when he had heard it last, but he was damnably confused. With all the ducking, hiding, firing at shadows, he had lost track of Dacko. Now, when his Kalashnikov appeared to be the only one still active in the village, Changa wondered what had happened to his man.

He didn't think Dacko would run away, though anything was possible if fear took hold of him. He *knew* Dacko hadn't run out of ammunition, since he wore a bandolier across his chest with eight or ten spare magazines. But if his silent soldier still had ammo and he hadn't run, where was he?

Dead, a small voice whispered in the back of Changa's mind, but he dismissed the warning. He remembered Dacko firing moments earlier, and there'd been no more gunshots from the dark tree line since then. If Dacko had been killed since then, it meant...

His killer was inside the village, creeping silently among the huts!

Changa spun swiftly, nearly toppled over in his haste, but caught himself before he fell. He stopped short of firing a wild burst at nothing, then swallowed a cry of surprise as Beira rattled off another Uzi burst behind him. If the enemy hadn't discovered his location yet, Changa didn't wish to reveal himself.

Changa began to calculate his chances of escaping to the helicopter. He imagined he could make it back to the airship, but it would be a useless trek if he abandoned Danso Beira in the village. If the two of them could make it...

How would he explain his failure to the master? How explain the loss of men with nothing to show for it?

Changa supposed he could take a leaf from Master Gaborone's own book. The master talked about a world of enemies encroaching on their small community from every side. After the trouble at Obike, how could anyone deny they were besieged? Changa could blame the enemy for his misfortune, and he wouldn't even need to offer names.

But would it be enough?

Changa would only know that when he laid out the story for Master Gaborone. And to accomplish that, he had to save himself, along with Beira, from their unseen enemies.

The scream almost returned to Changa's throat as someone called his name, a reedy whisper in the darkness. Biting back the yelp of fear, he realized it had to be Danso Beira. Who else in the village knew his name?

Changa crawled closer to the southeast corner of the hut that sheltered him, straining his ears for any further words. When Beira didn't speak again and didn't fire his weapon, Changa took a chance and softly called the pilot's name.

"Danso! Can you hear me?"

No answer.

A scowl carved furrows into Changa's face. Why would Beira call to him one moment and refuse to answer him the next? Was it a trick of his imagination, or had something happened in the fleeting interval between the call and his response?

Changa knew where the pilot was, or had been, when he fired his submachine gun last. Some thirty feet away, behind another hut, Beira should have been relatively safe from snipers or a face-on charge, but if there was a creeping enemy among them…

"Danso! Answer me!"

Nothing.

Changa decided that he had to find out for himself. A large tree stood off center in the open space between his hiding place and Beira's. It would give him cover on his run, someplace to stop and hide if bullets started flying while he was exposed.

Changa delayed another moment, marshaling his nerve. He was embarrassed by his trembling hands and clutched his rifle all the more tightly to make it stop. He was about to move when he heard Beira's voice again.

"Changa!"

He heard pain in that voice, or maybe just imagined it. If Beira had been wounded, could he still fly the machine? A bright new flare of panic lit up Changa's mind.

"I'm coming!" he called to Beira, scarcely bothering to whisper. Breaking from the hut's cover, he sprinted toward the spot where Danso Beira should've been. A few more yards. No more than five or six long strides.

The shadow rose in front of him, stepping into view around the tree trunk in his path, a hulking shape he didn't recognize. Changa had no time to react before the long knife pierced his solar plexus, angling upward toward his heart, and straining muscles lifted him six inches off the ground.

Samburu Changa died suspended in midair, surprised and disappointed that he couldn't recognize his killer's face.

"ALL DONE," said Bolan, speaking to the darkness, knowing that his voice would carry in the stillness of the killing ground.

At first, he wasn't altogether sure that Patrick Quinn had stayed to watch the battle. The young man could've run while Bolan fought the others, and there was a decent chance he wouldn't find Quinn's trail before sunrise, assuming he could stick around that long. If there were hunters coming overland from Obike, the firefight would've given them the best fix they could hope for on their quarry. Ten full minutes of sporadic firing was enough for any decent scout to plot a course, by day or night.

But when would they arrive?

A solitary figure hobbled toward him from the darkness, empty-handed. Firelight from the cooking pit revealed half of Quinn's face, leaving the other half in shadow. He moved sluggishly, almost a zombie's pace.

"You killed them all."

It hadn't been a question, thus required no answer. "You should try to find a pair of shoes that fit," Bolan said.

"Dead man's shoes?"

"They aren't contaminated yet," Bolan replied. "We still have miles to go, but if you'd rather do it barefoot, that's your call."

"I'll look around," Quinn said, but didn't move at once. Instead he asked, "Why were they killing villagers?"

"I didn't know them," Bolan answered. "I don't

know the man who sent them. I don't know if the kills were ordered, or if they were improvising."

Quinn's voice was dull as he responded. "Changa wouldn't do it on his own."

"In that case," Bolan said, "I'd have to guess they were eliminating witnesses."

"To what?"

"Maybe their presence here," Bolan said, "or the fact that they were hunting us. It's hard to say, but after Rathbun's party disappeared—"

"Is that the congressman?" Quinn asked.

"That's right."

Quinn slumped, legs folding until he was crouching, shoulders bent, with elbows braced upon his knees. He kept his eyes averted as he said, "They didn't disappear, those people. They were neutralized."

Despite his sense of urgency, Bolan made time to say, "Explain."

"They came as enemies into Obike," Quinn replied. The hard edge of defiance in his voice was dulled now. "Master Gaborone was forced to deal with them, in order to protect us."

"Did you see it?"

"No." Quinn shook his head, still staring at the earth. "He told us, though. After."

"What did you think about it?"

"Think? It wasn't my decision, but if they were enemies who wanted to destroy us, well…"

"You didn't think that getting rid of them might bring more enemies?"

"It's not my place to question Master Gaborone. He speaks to God, *for* God."

"And if he calls for war…"

"It's not *his* call," Quinn said, raising his eyes for the first time. "Go back and read your Bible. Armageddon's coming. It's the last great struggle between good and evil. Only the true believers will survive."

"Here in the Congo?"

"That's the beauty of the master's plan," Quinn said. "When the final battle comes, it's between East and West. The signs are all in place. Whether the first spark comes from Eastern Europe or the Holy Land, wherever, the result is preordained. The faithful *have* to win. It's written down!"

"Dewey beats Truman," Bolan said.

Quinn blinked at him, befuddled. "What?"

"It's history. Forget it. If you want those shoes, you've got five minutes. Then we're leaving, either way."

"But what about the others?"

"Who?"

"The villagers."

The thought had been on Bolan's mind. "You want to tell them it's all right? We're leaving bodies in their village that we don't have time to bury. Someone will come looking for them soon. They may ask questions, or they may just finish what your buddies started."

"Changa wasn't—"

"Either way," Bolan said, interrupting him, "we don't have time to stay and talk about it with them. I doubt we could even find them in the jungle, if they didn't want us to."

"So, we just leave?"

"That's right."

"But we—"

"You're wasting time for them, as well as us."

Quinn rose and went to check the dead for footwear. Luck was with him on the second corpse, a man with feet approximately his same size. Quinn grimaced as he unlaced and removed the muddy joggers, but they fit him fairly well. While he was tying them, Bolan saw Quinn glance toward the dead man's rifle.

"Only if you're ready for what happens next," he warned.

Quinn rose and left the weapon where it lay.

CHAPTER NINE

"Smell it!" the point man said after he stopped and called Nico Mbarga to his side.

Mbarga stood and sniffed the night, immediately conscious of a roast-meat smell and wood smoke, with an undertone of something else.

"More cordite?"

Smiling by moonlight, the tracker nodded. "And the rest?"

Mbarga told him, but the young man shook his head. "There's blood," he answered.

"Show me."

"This way."

Mbarga paced the tracker, let the others keep up as they might. At least an hour had passed with no more gunfire, but he sensed that they were headed in the right direction. Toward the village, he supposed, though how or why his quarry should've tried to reach it was a mystery Mbarga couldn't crack.

It bothered him a bit, the tracker smelling blood, but maybe that was simple showmanship. They'd find out soon, if they were close enough to smell meat cooking in the village.

Meat. Cooking.

Mbarga felt his stomach tighten, trying to imagine the worst-case scenario. It didn't help on this day of surprises, when it seemed that nothing in the world ran true to form.

Some twenty minutes after stopping on the trail, Mbarga caught a glimpse of firelight through the trees. It wasn't much, a flame almost reduced to embers, but it helped the tracker guide him to their target. Slowing into the approach, the hunters held their weapons ready for whatever happened next.

It took only a moment for Mbarga to determine that the nameless village was deserted. Its inhabitants had fled—or most of them, at least. From where he stood, flanked by his tracker and Adnan Ibn Sharif, Mbarga could see bodies lying on the ground. Their attitude and stillness told him they were dead.

He counted three and wondered whether they'd find more as they moved through the village. Was Patrick Quinn among them, or was he responsible for this? It seemed unlikely, but Mbarga didn't know the man who had accompanied Quinn, much less his fighting skills.

They entered the dead village cautiously, fanned out in a broad skirmish line with enough space between them that no single gunner could cut them all down before most went to ground. Camacho and Sharif hung back, letting Mbarga's men precede them, and they offered no suggestions now on how the search should be conducted.

The first corpse Nico encountered was a boy's. He didn't bother guessing at the age. Shot in the back while running, by the look of it, and he had fallen twisted to the earth.

The next dead man was one of his own, a young soldier named Rono Maskini. Mbarga crouched beside him, used a pocket flashlight to dispel the shadows, counting three wounds in Maskini's neck, chest and side. He'd been shot from the right flank and dropped where he stood. Mbarga looked for his Kalashnikov and couldn't find it. On Maskini's belt, an empty holster yawned.

Someone had stripped the dead man of his weapons, and those guns might even now be aiming at Mbarga's party from the jungle darkness. Thinking of it made his flesh creep, but Mbarga knew he couldn't search the whole damned forest. He had a specific mission to accomplish and he wouldn't be distracted.

The third corpse lay facedown, arms slack against the sides. One of Mbarga's soldiers rolled it over to reveal the lifeless features of Gedi Cocody, yet another of the master's bodyguards. Again, three shots had done the job, drilling his forehead, cheek and throat. And once again, the body had been stripped of weapons.

Mbarga assumed the thieves were villagers. Where were they, otherwise? Watching from shadows on the outskirts of the village with their newfound toys? If they were looking for revenge, when would they open fire?

"Another one," the tracker said.

They hadn't seen this body from the tree line. Mbarga stood above it, realizing that his men had killed at least two villagers before they'd started taking hits. But who had led the raiding party? Were there others to be found?

"Another," called the point man, with an eager tone that made Mbarga want to slap him.

Seconds later, Mbarga stood above the body of Jarari Dacko. Like the other soldiers, he was now unarmed, but Dacko hadn't died from gunshot wounds. Someone had drawn a blade across his throat and had also plunged the knife at least twice into Dacko's rib cage.

Mbarga heard Camacho and Sharif whispering urgently to each other, several yards off to his left. He didn't bother eavesdropping, for he no longer cared what they were thinking, what they had to say. His men had fought and died here, slaughtered by an unknown hand. Spent cartridges scattered around Jarari Dacko's corpse told him that the man had used his AK-47, but the piece was nowhere to be seen.

"Two more!" the tracker called from the middle of the village.

Samburu Changa was the next, curled shrimplike in a fetal ball. The blade had only pierced him once, but that had been enough. Changa was drenched in blood, perhaps from the heart.

Mbarga turned to see the final body, only half a dozen paces distant, and at last he understood how Changa's party had outrun him. Danso Beira had been stabbed at least three times by someone who had thrown him to the ground and crouched above him, cutting deep. As with the rest, he was unarmed, though pistol cartridges littered the turf around his body.

"This one was a pilot," Mbarga told Camacho and Sharif. "The master must have sent them on ahead to block the way."

"It didn't work," Camacho said.

Mbarga fought the urge to kill him. "They could only use a helicopter to set down here," he went on. "And since we have the pilot here, it can't have gone away. We need to find it now, quickly, before it falls into the wrong hands and is lost."

ALL THOUGHTS of camping for the night were banished. Bolan concentrated on the trail in front of him, leading the way now with his GPS device and years of personal experience surviving in the wild. He'd hear if Quinn took off again, or tried to rush him from behind, but both ideas struck Bolan as improbable.

The village massacre had taken something out of Quinn, diminished him somehow. His old defiance had been wiped away like chalk marks from a slate, leaving him beaten and fatigued.

Broken?

Bolan wouldn't have bet his life on that, but for the moment he was satisfied if Quinn could keep up with his pace.

The news about Lee Rathbun's party was hardly a shock, though it had come as a surprise to learn that

Gaborone discussed such matters with his flock. That meant there could be witnesses to testify against him if the Congolese authorities filed charges, but securing indictments wasn't part of Bolan's job.

He'd come to extricate one youth from Gaborone's clutches, and that was still the task at hand. It wasn't finished, by a long shot, and the outcome would be touch-and-go until they had reached Brazzaville.

If they reached Brazzaville.

Gaborone had surprised him by airlifting troops to interdict his line of march. That revealed clear strategic thinking and warned Bolan that the prophet had a repertoire of unexpected of tricks on hand.

The whirlybird, for one. Where was it now? Had it gone home, or was it sitting somewhere in the jungle, within reach? Was there a pilot waiting with it, or had Bolan killed him in the village?

If they found it sitting empty, it was useless to him. Bolan's skills were many, but he was only minimally qualified to fly a helicopter and he couldn't chance it in the middle of the rain forest.

If they got lucky, found the chopper on their eastward march toward the Banguelu River, he would play the rest by ear. A pilot in the cockpit meant a lift at gunpoint from the jungle, back to something that resembled safety. If the helicopter sat alone, he would disable it, prevent his enemies from using it against him in the future.

When an hour passed with no sign of the airship, Bolan knew he'd missed his chance. They might've passed within a dozen yards of it, sheltered by darkness, and he would be none the wiser.

Pilot or not, the bird wouldn't be carrying the village raiding party into any further battles. They were done, and their murder of innocent civilians had inspired Bolan to nurse a deep, abiding rage against the so-called prophet who commanded them.

Ahmadou Gaborone was more than a huckster and swindler. He wasn't just a jungle Elmer Gantry with a messianic complex. He had supervised and ordered murders—eight that Bolan knew of, now—and there was no doubt he would kill again in order to achieve his goals.

And what were they, beyond preparing for some vague apocalypse?

Bolan decided he would try to squeeze more information out of Quinn at their next rest stop. In the meantime, though, he let his young companion focus on the march, putting one foot in front of the other, keeping up the pace.

To survive they had to outrun their enemies.

The rest, Bolan sincerely hoped, would take care of itself.

THE RUNNER FOUND Gaborone in his quarters, sipping herbal tea and striving toward a meditative state. The blessed sense of peace was at his fingertips, almost within his reach, when eager rapping on his door shattered the spell.

"Master! Master!"

Instead of raging at the runner, Gaborone said softly, "Enter."

He couldn't recall the young man's name. There were so many now that names and faces ran together for him. They were sheep, albeit his, and Gaborone had trouble telling them apart. Perhaps he should require name tags, or give them numbers like the cattle in a feed lot.

"Master?"

The runner stood hunched over on the threshold, bowing from the waist. Perhaps he had grown dizzy in that posture while his lord and master daydreamed.

"What is it, my son?"

"A message, Master. On the radio."

"What message?"

"Captain Mbarga's calling. He will speak only to you, Master."

Bad news? There was but one way to find out.

"In that case," the prophet said, "let us go."

The runner went ahead of him, as if to clear the way. It was a short walk from his quarters to the communications hut. Inside, another member of his congregation sat in front of the shortwave set, bolting upright at his first glimpse of Gaborone.

"Master!"

"There is a message for me, I believe?"

"Yes, sir!"

The operator took off his headset, wiped at the earphones with a tissue from his pocket and presented them to Gaborone.

"You may sit here, Master. Or stand. Or—"

"I know how to use the radio."

"Of course, Master! I must apologize for—"

"Leave me," Gaborone instructed. "Both of you."

The sheep departed, closed the door behind them. He slipped on the earphones, sat down, leaned closer to the microphone and keyed it for transmission.

"Prophet calling Pilgrim. Can you hear me, Pilgrim? Over."

"Pilgrim calling Prophet. Yes, sir. Over."

"You have something to report? Over."

"We're at the village, sir," Mbarga told him. "There were others here before us. Over."

Easy now, Gaborone thought. The night has ears.

"Were they of any help?" he asked. "Over?"

Mbarga hesitated, letting static fill the void, then said, "No, sir. They won't be coming back. Over."

"What happened?" In his haste to learn the details, Gaborone forgot his wireless etiquette. "Over!" he blurted finally, when there was no reply.

"It seems they met resistance, sir. I'd best explain in person, when I see you. Over."

"Yes, I understand. What of their transportation? Over."

"We're about to look for it. Over."

"Do not forget the other matter," Gaborone reminded him. "Over."

"No, sir. I think both problems are related. Over."

"You must bring back our lost sheep, Pilgrim. Over."

"We're after two sheep now, sir. Over."

"Please explain, Pilgrim. Over."

"We followed two sheep to the village, sir. They aren't here now. Over."

A sour churning in the prophet's stomach made him wince. "I need to see them both, Pilgrim. It is imperative. Over."

"We hope to find them soon, sir. Over."

"If you find the bird and send it back, I can provide more help. Over."

There was another moment's hesitation before Mbarga said, "We've lost the pilot, sir. Over."

The churning in his gut became a needle lance of pain. "I see. Do what you can, in that case, Pilgrim. Over."

"Sir, we will. Over and out."

Gaborone switched off the microphone, removed the headset, damp with perspiration now, and left the hut. Outside, the runner and the radio's attendant watched him go, their conversation falling silent as he passed.

His cryptic dialogue with Mbarga didn't tell him what had happened in the village, but his men were dead. They'd "met resistance" and were gone forever. Five less mouths to feed, but one of them had been his pilot, slaughtered with the others.

And by whom?

Mbarga said he had followed *two* men from Obike to the village. Gaborone would have to trust him and their tracker on that score. He had no evidence to contradict them, no reason to think that Patrick Quinn could have eluded—much less killed—Samburu Changa's airborne hunting party.

Still, *someone* had killed them. Mbarga was constrained in how much information he could broadcast, but the possibilities were limited. If Quinn and his unknown companion hadn't done the killing, only three firm candidates remained.

The villagers might be responsible, but Mbarga hadn't hinted at a general slaughter, and he would've been compelled to punish those who'd murdered Changa and his men.

If the authorities had interrupted Changa's raid against the village, if they'd killed his people in a fire-fight, they would still be at the scene. Such clashes were recorded, charted on a map, with body counts and paperwork in triplicate. Mbarga and his companions would've been warned off, or else arrested at the scene, if it had been a military kill.

The third and final possibility involved bandits or rebels. Lawless elements abounded in the Congo, some of them political, while others served only themselves, their greed. Obike had been spared from their marauding, but perhaps Changa's men had met a raiding party in the night.

Gaborone knew that he would have to wait to hear what Nico had to say when he returned. Meanwhile, he rued the softness that had let Camacho and Sharif go on the jungle hunt. If they were killed, it meant starting all over with his plan.

No matter.

There would always be more customers.

He might not light the spark of Armageddon this week, or the next, but it would come. The prophet was convinced of that.

It was an article of faith.

QUINN MOVED LIKE A ROBOT through the jungle night, placing one foot in front of the other with dogged precision, while his mind took flight and sped beyond the cloying, hostile world he occupied. The stolen shoes were loose enough to chafe his heels, but they were still a relief after hobbling for miles with one foot bare. After he stopped and stuffed them with dead leaves, Quinn would've rated them as comfortable, on a par with a celebrity's designer kicks.

The numbness that pervaded him had little or nothing to do with fatigue or the physical beating he'd taken since he was abducted that morning. Rather, he was stricken with a numbness of the spirit while his mind ran on without him, seeking desperately for a solution.

Patrick Quinn knew things. Some had been shared with him as a devoted member of the Process, and he'd picked up others quite by chance. A snatch of conversation overheard by accident, an observation of activities that should've been concealed. And knowing things, he couldn't always stop his mind from drawing links, playing connect-the-dots. Sometimes it interrupted his devotions and embarrassed him, but Quinn trusted the master to forgive his shortcomings.

Unless he told.

There would be no forgiveness for a traitor. He was sure of that. It had been drilled into his head as if it were a catechism. Enemies conspired against the Process day and night. Any adherent who assisted them was damned, struck from the Book of Life and all rewards in paradise. It was the one sin neither Master Gaborone nor God Himself could pardon.

But, the small voice nagged him: What if it's a lie?

What did it mean to Quinn's salvation if the master had deceived him, if he'd let himself be led astray despite the earnest warnings from his family and Val Querente? He would never have believed it, but for the events of recent days. First came the congressman and his companions, seemingly concerned about some of Obike's residents, silenced forever on the master's order. Quinn had been disturbed by that, but he'd accepted Gaborone's account of why the act was necessary.

Now he'd seen what happened in the jungle village, innocents who offered no threat to the Process gunned down by the master's bodyguards, and Quinn knew they'd have all been slaughtered if the man called Cooper hadn't intervened.

How many others had been murdered that Quinn didn't know about?

How many more would die if Master Gaborone proceeded with his plan for bringing on the Final Days?

Quinn didn't want to think about it, but he couldn't stop himself. His mind was running on automatic pilot, while his body slogged through jungle muck with all the animation of a zombie. Cooper glanced at him from time to time, to make sure he was keeping up, and something in his eyes told Quinn that he was well aware of something brewing in Quinn's head.

What would the soldier do if Quinn told everything?

What could he do?

There's one way to find out, Quinn thought.

When they had traveled roughly two miles from the village slaughter ground, he spoke softly to Cooper's back.

"We need to talk," Quinn said.

"COME!" THE TRACKER CALLED. "Come quick!"

Nico Mbarga dashed to join him, almost tripping on a vine that seemed to have a crude mind of its own. Even before he reached the tracker, Mbarga saw what had excited him.

The helicopter occupied a forest clearing, squatting like some giant prehistoric dragonfly, surrounded by the dark columns of ancient trees. Mbarga knew it had to have settled vertically, descending through a rupture in the jungle canopy to reach this landing site. He gave credit to Danso Beira for the feat and wondered how on earth they'd ever get the airship out again.

The others joined him moments later, circling wide around the chopper, probing every shadow until they had satisfied themselves that no ambush awaited them. If their fleeing enemies had found the helicopter first, they'd unaccountably decided to leave it intact.

Or had they?

Mbarga peered inside the chopper's cabin, eyes scanning the controls and instrument panel, detecting no obvious damage. He had half expected to find shattered gauges, wires stripped from the console, dangling like a nest of anorexic snakes. Instead, the ship sat as if waiting for its pilot to return and take it home.

Mbarga had flown in the aircraft a half dozen times, but he didn't understand the intricate mechanics of it. He supposed there had to be ways to sabotage a helicopter that weren't apparent from a quick exterior inspection. Dirt or other foreign matter in the fuel tank, for example. Subtle damage to assorted wires or cables, loosened bolts or screws, and so on. If they had a pilot, maybe they could lift off in the bird, but then would come the screaming plunge to fiery death.

Of course, they had no pilot, so the problem solved itself. Eventually, someone else could take the risk. If Mbarga had a choice, he would be busy elsewhere when the bird took its next flight.

He waited for the all-clear from his soldiers, pleased and irritated all at once that there was no sign of their quarry. He had no desire to wage a jungle firefight in the dark, but failure to connect with those he sought meant that the hunt had to still go on.

How long?

Until his master's quest for information and revenge was satisfied.

Reluctantly, Mbarga palmed the two-way radio he carried, raised it to his lips and keyed the button to transmit. "Pilgrim to Prophet. Pilgrim calling Prophet. Do you read? Over."

After a brief delay, the tinny voice came back to him, riding a wave of atmospheric sibilance. "Prophet to Pilgrim. Read you clearly. Over."

"Prophet, we have found the bird. It seems undamaged, but I can't be sure. Over."

"That's good news, Pilgrim. Prophet will be pleased. Can you return it? Over."

Mbarga almost shook his head, then realized the commo operator in Obike couldn't see him. "Negative," he said. "We have no pilot with us. O—"

A firm hand on his shoulder stopped Mbarga in midsyllable. He spun, prepared to lash out at the soldier who had interrupted him, and found himself facing Adnan Ibn Sharif.

"You have a pilot," the Arab said.

"Who?" Mbarga asked, eyes narrowed with suspicion.

"I can fly this bird."

Mbarga frowned and told the radio, "Wait one, Prophet."

Then to Sharif, he said, "Where did you learn?"

The Arab shrugged. "What does it matter? I was trained to fly the Russian Hind. It is more complicated than this model, I suppose. Your helicopter has no weapons systems. Still, I think that I can manage it."

"Be sure," Mbarga warned Sharif. "We all suffer if you destroy the master's airship."

"I suppose you'll have to trust me," Sharif said.

Mbarga didn't like it, but he didn't fancy the alternatives, either. He might be ordered to remain and guard the helicopter while his quarry got away, or else to split his team, leave guards behind, and push on with a force too small to guarantee survival or success.

At last, he raised the radio again and told home base,

"Prophet, it seems we have a pilot after all. Advise the master. We await instructions. Over."

"Stand by, Pilgrim. We'll respond ASAP. Over and out."

Mbarga left the radio turned on, waiting. Whatever happened next, he had a feeling that he wouldn't like it, but the choice would not be his. On one thing only was his mind decided, the decision carved in stone.

If Sharif should be approved to fly the master's helicopter, Mbarga meant to watch his first flight from the ground.

"SO, TALK," Bolan replied when they had halted on the trail. "But make it quick."

"There's something you should know," Quinn said.

"I'm waiting."

"Master Gaborone believes in Armageddon, but that's only part of it. He's working night and day to bring it on. The Final Days are real to him. They're real to all of us, okay, but he intends to bring them on."

"That's no small order," Bolan answered. He made no attempt to mask his skepticism. "What's he have in mind? A plague of locusts? Forty days of rain? Earthquakes? Volcanoes?"

"Atom bombs." Quinn spoke so softly that his words were barely audible. "Or one, at least."

"Say what?"

"A few months back, we had a visitor from somewhere in the old USSR. I didn't catch his name, but he had military bearing, like he used to be an officer."

"He visited Obike?" Bolan asked.

Quinn nodded. "Yes. He stayed about ten days and spent a lot of time with Master Gaborone in private. When he'd gone, I heard one of Mbarga's soldiers saying that he'd taken half the master's treasure with him. I assumed he was exaggerating."

"Treasure?"

"It's no secret," Quinn replied, "that members of the congregation donate all their worldly goods to help support the Process. It's a choice we make. My father calls it communism."

"And this Russian took it with him?"

"Some of it, apparently. He wouldn't have to carry it himself, of course. The master has a bank account, you know. Or maybe several. But he keeps cash and other valuables in Obike, for emergencies."

"What was the Russian selling?" Bolan asked.

"Two weeks after he left, I was assigned to join a work party. They bussed us to the airstrip, five miles from the village. Have you seen it?"

"Just in photographs."

Quinn shrugged. "No matter. We arrived just as a plane was taking off. They'd left two wooden crates, one roughly six feet long by three feet tall and wide, the other half that size. We had to load them on the bus, then walk back to Obike since we couldn't fit inside the bus."

"Did either of these crates have labels?"

"Nothing I could read," said Quinn. "I found out later what they were, by eavesdropping on Nico's men and snooping when I had the opportunity."

"Okay." Bolan already knew where Quinn was going with his story, but he had to ask. "What were they?"

"The components for an A-bomb, or whatever people call them nowadays. From what I heard, I worked out that they ship the detonator separately, in case of accidents."

"And when was this?" Bolan asked.

"Four, five months ago."

The warrior frowned. "It didn't give you any second thoughts, having a nuke in camp? What did you think they planned to do with it?"

"I knew exactly why they wanted it," Quinn said. "Or thought I did, at least. It was for self-defense against our enemies."

"Makes perfect sense," Bolan replied. "Someone invades your house, you set off nukes. That's logic for you."

"Maybe not," Quinn said, defensively, "but bear in mind what we've been taught, what we believe. The world is in its last days, winding down. Our challenge is to spread that message, showcase the corruption that's infested so-called civilized society, and that breeds enemies. We can't resist them if they come for us in strength, but we can take them with us. And if that sparks Armageddon, then we've done the human race a favor, speeding up the Final Days."

Bolan recalled the topsy-turvy logic of an Army officer who'd once explained the shelling of a major city in South Vietnam. *We destroyed the city in order to save it.*

"So, what's changed?" he asked Quinn. "If you still believe that line, why share with me?"

"Let's say what happened back there in the village shook my faith a little."

"Just a little?"

"And there's something else."

"Still listening," Bolan replied.

"I'm ninety-five percent convinced that Master Gaborone intends to sell his bomb."

A knot began to form in Bolan's gut. "What makes you think so?" he inquired.

"We've got more visitors. You missed them during the siesta, but they're in Obike as we speak. An Arab named Sharif and some guy called Camacho. He's Latino. One of Nico's people claims he's from Colombia."

"Just two? No backup?"

"Maybe they trust Master Gaborone," Quinn said. "Maybe he wouldn't let them bring supporters if they want to bid."

"Bid for the bomb."

Quinn nodded once again, emphatically. "I'm sure of it," he said. "That's why they're here."

CHAPTER TEN

"I know it sounds fantastic, but—"

"Not necessarily," Bolan said. He was studying Quinn's face by filtered moonlight, eyes moving over every feature as if he were mapping not only the face but the skull underneath it.

"You've heard of things like this before?" Quinn asked, surprised.

"When the Soviet Union collapsed in 1991 most of its former republics were left destitute. They couldn't pay soldiers, technicians, whatever. Most governments agreed to destroy their nuclear stockpiles. Some did it, while others claimed the job was done and sold their warheads on the sly. Other materials were stolen for black market sale by military personnel, ex-KGBs, the Russian *mafiya,* whatever. If you're being straight with me—"

"I am," Quinn said.

"Okay. It sounds like Gaborone hooked up somehow

and bought himself a nuke. They don't come cheap, think tens of millions, but if he could raise the cash, it's doable."

Quinn thought about the money. *Tens of millions.* His own trust fund would've paid two million dollars on his twenty-first birthday. He guessed there had to be other bonus babies in the Process, maybe fat cats in the background. Add it to the income Master Gaborone received from sundry business operations handled by his rank and file, donations from new members, possibly some sly investments…

"He could swing it," Quinn told Bolan. "Definitely."

Bolan nodded, as if he had seen the answer coming. "It's a seller's market. No one's sure how many outlaw nukes there were to start with, much less how many remain in circulation. Washington and London have a standing buyback offer and they've nailed a few. Some others have been taken off the street by MI-6, the CIA and FBI."

"But none have made it to the States, so far?"

"That's obviously one concern. Who knows? You're sure about those names?"

"Camacho and Sharif. I'm sure. No first names, though."

"It may not matter." Bolan seemed distracted for a moment, then he asked, "Why do you figure Gaborone's selling the bomb?"

"You have to understand what he believes—or what he says, at least. After tonight, I'm not sure whether he's been straight with us on anything."

"Just tell it," Bolan urged.

"It's simple, really. You know how the Bible says that

God helps those who help themselves? Well, for Master Gaborone, that carries over into prophecy. Let's say some great event's supposed to be preceded by specific signs and wonders, right? And let's say one of them's a fire in Paris or in London. Take your pick. The master might suggest that we can help matters along. If you research the prophecy, make sure you have the details right, then maybe set the fire yourself."

"Isn't that cheating?" Bolan asked him.

"Who's to say? We know that God works in mysterious ways. Maybe scripture was written back in olden times to *make* us set that fire. But not just any fire, okay? Without the research, prayer and revelation, it would be a waste of time. Maybe a sin."

"And by that logic, there's a chance that you could jump-start Armageddon, bringing on—"

"The Final Days," Quinn finished for him, nodding. "Yes. Why not?"

"It's been a while since Sunday school," Bolan replied, "but I recall that Armageddon is supposed to be a battle."

"Revelation 16:16," Quinn informed him. "Two great armies, East and West."

"That's not some headcase setting off a suitcase nuke in Washington or New York City."

"Every war requires a trigger incident," Quinn said. "I read my share of history in college, Mr. Cooper. Spain and England went to war because a Briton lost his ear to Spanish coast guards. When the smoke cleared, London had a claim on Panama and half of Florida. An A-bomb could be plenty if it went off in the right place."

"And the right people were blamed," Bolan said.

"There you go."

The soldier stepped in close, so swiftly that it took Quinn's breath away. He gathered Quinn's damp shirt in one hard fist and lifted Quinn until he stood on tiptoe.

"Listen up," he said, his voice lowered and more ominous for that. "I don't know if I trust your sudden change of heart or not, but you can take this to the bank. If it's a scam you're running, just to get back with your friends, it *will* come back to bite you in the ass."

"Get back? No, wait! That isn't what I want."

Quinn was amazed to hear the words come from his lips and realize that they were true. A few short hours earlier, returning to Obike was his only goal. Now, considering the village slaughter and the rest of it, the very thought filled him with dread.

What happened to my faith? Quinn asked himself.

And got no answer from inside.

Bolan released him, causing Quinn to stagger slightly as he rocked back on his heels. "We're not, are we?" he asked. "Not going back?"

"Sit tight," Bolan said, fishing in one of his pockets for a compact telephone. "I need to make a call."

"PROPHET TO PILGRIM. Do you read me? Over, Pilgrim."

Gaborone tried meditating while he waited for an answer, but there wasn't time. The small voice came back after only half a dozen heartbeats, reed thin, static-ridden from its journey through the night.

"Pilgrim to Prophet. Read you five-by-five, sir."

"I believe you have the bird. Over?"

"Yes, sir. Over."

"And I've been told that one of your companions has the skills to fly it. Over."

"So he claims. The Palestinian. I'm not convinced, sir. Over."

Gaborone tried to imagine why Adnan Sharif would lie about a thing so easily disproved. If he was asked to fly the helicopter and couldn't, he was disgraced. More to the point, if he was airborne when his luck ran out, the Arab might be killed.

His death would be a small thing, but the helicopter's loss would seriously hamper Gaborone. Aside from the expense, it would reduce his personal mobility just when he had begun to think it might be necessary for him to escape on short notice. He had no other pilot readily available, but if Sharif could fly…

"Pilgrim to Prophet. Are you there, sir? Over."

"Permit him to attempt the flight, Pilgrim. But watch him closely. Do you understand? Over."

The words came back reluctantly. "Yes, sir. Over."

"A test flight first, to prove himself. Stay with him, for security. Make sure your other guest is not on board. If he succeeds, call back and I'll have further orders. Over."

Dead air whispered through his earphones. Gaborone could picture Mbarga digesting his orders, fearing what might happen if he went aloft with Sharif in the chopper. This could be a major test of faith, of Gaborone's control over his troops. If Mbarga balked, defied him openly, the virus of dissatisfaction might spread swiftly, fatally.

At length Mbarga replied, "I understand. Yes, sir. Over."

"Be careful, Pilgrim. Stay alert. Our prayers are with you. Over."

"Thank you, sir. Prayers couldn't hurt. Over and out."

There came a time when even prophets had to trust in God or Fate. Gaborone had hedged his bet by making sure Luis Camacho wasn't on the helicopter's test flight. That way, if Sharif was lying or his skills were somehow proved inadequate, one buyer for his merchandise would still remain. He'd have to hike back through the jungle as he'd come, but that would simply make Camacho grateful for the master's hospitality.

And if Sharif *could* fly, so much the better. In that case, Mbarga could resume the search for Patrick Quinn and the unknown stranger who had lifted him from Obike. Only then, Gaborone thought, would they learn who had ambushed Samburu Changa's party in the forest.

What about the villagers? That nagging inner voice.

Gaborone wasn't overly worried. Survivors of the village raid were still more than a hundred miles from Brazzaville and help, if that was where they chose to go. More likely, they would linger in the jungle, either come back to their homes—in which case he would have them—or start over at another site. If they sent runners out to spread the story, it was still a long, perilous road. And Gaborone could have his say in Brazzaville before the peasants made their voices heard.

No problem, then. Except their accusations would come hard upon the heels of dark suspicions surrounding the disappearance of Lee Rathbun and his companions. Too many alarms raised in too short a time might undo Gaborone's work with pliant officials. It could jeopardize all he'd achieved so far.

But soon that wouldn't matter. Soon his problem would be solved by the unfolding of events. And Gaborone could say with pride that he had done his part to make the last days a reality.

If one of his imported customers survived the night.

JACK GRIMALDI WAS waiting on the sidewalk when the bank opened for business. He wasn't the first through the doors, even so, but he came in third and walked directly to the information desk. The young receptionist spoke English fluently. She steered Grimaldi to an office cubicle of frosted glass, located in the lobby's northwest corner.

There, Grimaldi was compelled to take a seat, identify himself and sketch the outlines of a bogus story for the bank's assistant managing director. When he'd run down details of the nonexistent real-estate transaction and declined an offer of the bank's assistance in negotiating lower mortgage rates, the suit checked his computer and confirmed that a wire transfer had come in overnight. A short-term account had been opened in the name of Joseph Grant, and the funds were available for withdrawal—less the bank's commission—upon presentation of proper ID.

Grimaldi showed a passport with the proper name, signed half a dozen documents and was presented with a cashier's check. The suit's eyebrows did tense gymnastics when Grimaldi told him that he needed cash, and further documents were hastily produced for signing. Finally, after the better part of half an hour, Grimaldi filled his briefcase to the brim with bundled, multicolored notes and left the bank.

The Browning autoloader tucked beneath his belt, in back, felt reassuring on his short walk to the rental car. He didn't know the first thing about crime rates in the Congo, but it wouldn't take a mastermind to target a white foreigner emerging with a briefcase from a major downtown bank. Some thieves might go for the valise alone, empty or full. Pawn it for cash enough to buy a small luxury item—or food. The Congo was a poor country.

Grimaldi reached his car without a hitch, got in and locked the doors. He drove through snail-pace morning traffic toward the heliport outside town, where he would trade the cash for wings. If there were no snags at that point, he would be ready to complete his mission, fetch Bolan and Patrick Quinn from whatever LZ they'd managed to discover overnight.

Assuming they were still alive.

The thought was rattling around inside his head, haunting him. A night without contact, and anything could happen in the jungle.

Grimaldi started thinking that he ought to call ahead, before he claimed the whirlybird. It couldn't hurt—unless, of course, the bird's proprietor had screwed him, rented it to someone else after accepting his deposit. Telling Bolan he was on his way, then calling back to cancel it a second time, would be the worst scenario.

He would pick up the helicopter first.

Grimaldi pushed his rental to the posted limit. The sat phone in his pocket seemed to weigh a ton, dragging the right side of his body down as if some gremlin had replaced it with an anvil. And Grimaldi didn't need a crash course in psychology to know what *that* meant.

He was nervous, damn it, and the only cure was touching base with Bolan. Soon.

Grimaldi had a hand inside his pocket when he stopped himself. Not yet. He had another two miles, maybe three to go, and then the chopper would be his. As soon as Mr. Greedy signed off on the deal, he would call Bolan, put his seething mind at ease and take off for their rendezvous.

Simple.

Grimaldi drove on toward his destination, cursing every sluggish vehicle that blocked his path.

SOMETIMES IT FELT like Fate.

Grimaldi had the sat phone in his hand and was about to key in Bolan's number when it rang, a high-pitched trilling sound. He flinched, came close to dropping it, as startled as he was, then saved it.

The pilot mashed one of the buttons and said, "Hello?"

"What's up?" the deep, familiar voice inquired.

Relief sped through Grimaldi's veins like an endorphin rush. It was a lucky break that he was sitting down.

"I got the bird," he answered. "Tell me where and when. I'm there."

"We've had a change of plans," Bolan informed him.

"Oh?" Just mildly curious. "How's that?"

"Turns out the job's more complicated than I thought," Bolan replied. "It isn't just a pickup anymore."

"I see," Grimaldi lied.

"There's something back in town I have to fix before the wrong hands get hold of it," said Bolan.

"I'm not sure I read you," he admitted.

Bolan wasn't taking any chances on the sat line. Cryptically, he answered, "It turns out that Elmer Gantry's got a sideline selling party crackers. He's picked up a Russian model and it's going to the highest bidder pretty soon."

Grimaldi felt the bone-deep chill set in. He didn't need a code book to understand what Bolan was talking about. The Russian "party cracker" had to be a nuke, and Gaborone had put it on the auction block.

But why?

"That a religious thing?" he asked. "Or did we peg him wrong?"

"Could be a bit of both. He's got two buyers in the house right now. I only have last names, but maybe you could check them out."

"I'll find out what I can," Grimaldi promised.

"Okay. One's called Camacho. Maybe a Colombian,

but that's not positive. The other is Sharif. Some kind of Arab. I'm not sure about the spelling."

"I can work that out. You want deep background if it's there?"

"Whatever you can find out in the next few hours," Bolan said. "Meanwhile, we're heading back."

"To town?" He'd picked up Bolan's code for the Obike compound.

"Right," the soldier replied.

"Can't say I love the odds."

"I don't like thinking what could happen if the merchandise went public. Motive won't make any difference if that happens."

"Right, I hear you. I'll get on it and call back ASAP," Grimaldi told him.

"Let *me* call *you*," Bolan suggested. "I don't want to wake the neighbors if I can avoid it."

"That's better, sure."

Grimaldi cursed himself for not considering the risk. A ringing phone in downtown Brazzaville was one thing. In then middle of the jungle it would be a target hung on Bolan's chest.

"Don't let the bird go," Bolan added, sounding almost cheerful for a moment. "We'll still need you when its done."

"I'm standing by," he said. "Just give a shout with the coordinates, and I'll be there."

"I'll be in touch," Bolan told him, and the line went dead.

Kurtzman might blow a fuse, but there was no way

Jack could check with Hal Brognola first. Brognola didn't have a sat line in his home or office, so the plea for intel had to go straight to Stony Man.

What were the odds, Grimaldi wondered, that they'd wind up leaning on the Farm this much, the one time Bolan took a private job for old times' sake?

All things considered, he'd call it one hundred percent.

And it was time to bite the bullet. Bolan needed whatever information Stony Man could offer on the two bidders for Gaborone's hot merchandise. Grimaldi knew his old friend didn't want the intel strictly for himself. He could take down the buyers regardless, without pedigrees, even names. The information might be helpful, but it wasn't critical.

Unless he failed.

Bolan was thinking down the road, in case something went wrong. In that case, Jack and Stony Man would know who he'd been tracking, who they had to cover if Bolan couldn't scotch the deal.

It was a possibility that Jack Grimaldi didn't like to think about, but that was the reality. Bolan *might* fail to intercept the merchandise. He might not make it back. The hasty plan might go to hell.

But not if Jack had anything to say about it.

Not this time.

He keyed another number on the sat phone and sat waiting for the storm.

NICO MBARGA HAD his orders. He might not appreciate those orders, but he would obey them.

Even if it killed him.

He faced Adnan Ibn Sharif and told the Arab, "Master Gaborone is pleased to learn of your experience with helicopters. He appreciates your willingness to give a demonstration, on which I'm instructed to accompany you."

"More can come with us, if they like," Sharif replied.

"Two are enough for now," Mbarga said. "In case the aircraft has been sabotaged."

He'd tossed that in, hoping Sharif would back down from his offer, but the Arab merely nodded understanding. "Certainly. I can proceed alone, if you prefer."

"My orders call for me to join you."

"As you wish. Shall we begin?"

Mbarga took one of his men aside and placed him in command while Nico and Sharif were airborne. "If there's any trouble with the helicopter," he instructed, glossing over details, "take the rest back to Obike. Watch Camacho carefully. You understand?"

The soldier nodded. "Yes, Nico."

That done, the rough equivalent of putting his affairs in order, Mbarga walked with Sharif to the Lama. One of them got in on each side of the bubble-nosed cockpit, with Sharif in the pilot's seat. Mbarga found his safety harness, making sure to cinch it tight across his chest and lap.

Whatever happened in the next few moments, he wouldn't fall out and plummet to his death without the aircraft. Whatever befell the Lama would befall Nico Mbarga in his turn.

Sharif switched on the engine, flipped some switches, studied various gauges on the instrument panel. He frowned at one, leaned in to tap it with a forefinger, then sat back with a satisfied expression on his swarthy face.

"Ready?" he asked.

"My readiness is not the question," Mbarga said. He kept both hands tightly wrapped around the upright barrel of his AK-47. If Sharif attempted to escape, it was Mbarga's suicidal task to see that he did not go far.

Mbarga closed his eyes for just a moment, offering up a prayer, as Sharif took the controls. He clenched his teeth at the accelerating rotor noise above them, but that only made the sound vibrate inside his head, until he finally relaxed his jaw.

Liftoff was gentle, though a seesaw rocking back and forth curdled Mbarga's stomach. He held on to the Kalashnikov and watched the Arab's hands. He had no idea what Sharif was doing or should do, but he preferred the view of hands and levers to the sight of massive tree trunks looming all around them as they rose.

It wouldn't take much drift, one way or another, for the thirty-six-foot rotor blades to strike a tree and snap like chopsticks in a woodchipper. If that happened, and they were somehow spared from flying shrapnel, then the bird would fall.

But now it seemed the Arab truly knew what he was doing. Glancing left and right, ahead of them and in his two side-mounted mirrors, Sharif caused the Lama to levitate. They rose by inches, then by feet, then yards. It wasn't textbook perfect, but he held the chopper steady enough that Mbarga could have sipped coffee without spilling it.

When they were halfway to the sky, roughly a hundred feet above the forest clearing and their comrades, Mbarga grudgingly admitted to himself that Sharif had impressed him.

"I've surprised you, yes?" the Arab asked.

"Perhaps a little."

"You judged me by my reputation solely," Sharif said, then raised a hand from the controls as if to ward off glib denials.

Mbarga caught his breath, hoping Sharif could fly the bird one-handed, but he somehow found his voice. "I do not know your reputation," he replied.

Sharif blinked at him, either in surprise or disbelief, perhaps a mixture of the two. "Some call me terrorist," he said. "Killer of children in their classrooms, women in the marketplace."

"I don't—"

"It's true, of course," Sharif continued, almost cheerfully. "In war, we use whatever weapons we possess and strike the enemy where he is vulnerable, yes?"

They were approaching midnight-velvet sky, fringed by the ragged edges of a wide hole in the jungle canopy. It suddenly didn't seem wide at all.

"I'm satisfied that you can fly the helicopter," Mbarga said. "As for the rest, it has nothing to do with me. Please land."

"You wouldn't like to see the leaves by moonlight?" Sharif asked.

"Another time."

The Arab smiled, relaxing. "As you wish."

QUINN TRIED TO SORT OUT his emotions and make sense of them, as he and Cooper turned back toward Obike. He had made a choice that set him in defiance of the master, but it didn't bother him as much as he'd expected.

As much as it should.

What did it mean, if he could cast off months of heartfelt devotion in less than a day? Were his feelings and hopes mere illusions? Was he so shallow that what should've been a crushing loss now struck him merely as a kind of puzzlement?

Quinn understood that he wasn't simply leaving the Process and Master Gaborone. Rather, he'd set himself in grim defiance of them, marching now on a collision course that might spell death.

Cooper had briefed him on the risks, in case they weren't all clear enough. He had picked a slightly different course of travel with the GPS device, meaning to skirt the village where the killings had occurred, but there was still a chance—and quite a good one, Cooper said—of meeting "opposition" on the trail.

Quinn knew that he meant Process members, probably more of the master's bodyguards. That minimized the chance that they'd be friends of Quinn, since Master Gaborone's elite soldiers kept to themselves for the most part, thereby enhancing and preserving their mystique.

If they met opposition, Cooper said, Quinn was to keep his head down, stay out of the way. And stay alive.

Cooper was clearly troubled. He had spoken on his tiny telephone to someone, but he didn't share the substance of that conversation. Quinn initially believed that it was dealing with an A-bomb that had turned his escort grimly silent, but he'd changed his mind after a mile or so.

Cooper was certainly concerned about the bomb, but there was also something else. It took Quinn half a mile to figure out what was bothering the grim-faced soldier.

Val.

Whether for money or some other reason, Cooper had agreed to bring Quinn home from Africa, against his will if that was what it took. Now that the task was halfway done, or nearly so, he felt compelled to turn around and do another job instead.

The very fact that he would risk his mission, take Quinn back toward Master Gaborone and all the danger waiting for them there, told Quinn that Cooper wasn't on the clock. A mercenary simply would've done the job that he'd been paid to do, and never mind whatever else was happening in the vicinity.

Some shady characters shopping for nukes? So, what?

A threat to global peace and countless lives? Who cares, as long as I get paid?

But Cooper had been cut from different cloth. He saw the danger to himself and to his primary assignment, but it didn't change his mind.

Because he cared.

And why do I? Quinn asked himself.

The master taught that Armageddon was a good thing, for it ushered in the Final Days and brought true believers that much closer to eternity in Paradise. What did it matter if a thousand or a million people died? God knew His own and He would sort them out.

Something had changed, and while Quinn couldn't put his finger on it, he could put a name to the sensation that had overridden all his others.

It was called relief.

Quinn knew he should be shamed and saddened by his separation from Obike and the Process, but with every step he took it felt as if another ounce of weight was lifted from his shoulders. Quinn wasn't blind to the irony that every step now brought him closer to his former master and a team of gunmen who would likely view him as a traitor only fit for killing.

Maybe that was what it cost to be redeemed.

Or maybe, if he kept an eye on Cooper, he might still come out of it alive.

CHAPTER ELEVEN

The sudden change in Bolan's task disturbed him. He had come to Africa as Val Querente's friend, vowing to help her save a young man if he could. But now that he'd accomplished that, or nearly so, the Universe had pitched a curve across home plate, forcing the Executioner either to swing with all his might or to quit the game.

And he had never learned to quit.

The shift disturbed him on three levels. First, he had a sense of cheating Val, breaking his promise and betraying her. She wanted Patrick Quinn alive, wanted to see him standing in the U.S.A., and Bolan likely could accomplish that if he arranged the pickup with Grimaldi and left someone else to deal with Gaborone's experiment in nuclear proliferation. He could simply let it go and walk away.

But who would grab the ball if Bolan dropped it?

On another level, Bolan wondered if he was betraying Quinn. His young companion was escaping from the Process, shaking off the cult's indoctrination and accepting his own errors, but he needed time to soldier through it and get well. He'd have that chance at home, with Val and others who still cared for him—but not if Bolan led him back into the viper's nest and got him killed.

The final level of uneasiness was more abstract, but it plagued Bolan all the same. If he proceeded with the job he'd pledged to Val and focused all his thoughts on Quinn, taking him home, there was a fair chance that he'd be condemning thousands more to death. He didn't buy the Armageddon mumbo jumbo, though a well-placed nuclear explosion in the Middle East might well ignite another war, but the religious trappings were superfluous.

The threat of nuclear blackmail or worse was now a day-to-day reality of modern life. A suitcase nuke in New York or New Delhi would produce carnage that made the 9/11 raids look like a minor skirmish in the age-old war for hearts and minds. The warrior couldn't turn his back on that. He had to stop it if he could, but did that goal jibe with reality?

Was there a bomb at all?

Bolan believed himself a decent judge of character, but he'd been fooled on prior occasions and despite Quinn's personal appearance of sincerity, there was a chance Val's protégé was lying through his teeth about the nuke, the sale, the whole damned thing.

Take it another way. Suppose Quinn meant what he

was saying, but he had his facts wrong. Had he been duped by rumors? Misinterpreted snatches of conversation overheard in passing? With the several languages spoken in Gaborone's encampment, was he even qualified as an interpreter?

The only way to answer those and other questions was to go back, penetrate the village one more time and have another look around. Bolan needed to find the nuke or to prove to his own satisfaction that it wasn't there.

And what will that prove? asked an inner voice of nagging doubt.

By the time they reached Obike, the better part of a full day would've passed since he'd extracted Quinn. If Gaborone was worried by the incident, or if his buyers had a sudden case of nerves, there had been ample time to close a deal and start the deadly package on its way to Bogotá, Beirut, wherever.

That was the problem with negative proof. Not seeing something didn't mean the object that he sought didn't exist.

Which raised the ante for the next hand of his game.

It wouldn't be enough to simply penetrate Obike, scout the place, and say he'd done his best if he found nothing there. If Bolan couldn't find the crates Quinn had described and judge their contents for himself, he'd have to question someone who could solve the mystery.

And who would that be? Gaborone himself? One of the prophet's foreign visitors? All three?

It almost sounded simple, until Bolan thought about

the seven-hundred-plus disciples Gaborone had quartered in the village, ready to defend him with their lives if necessary. Throw in bodyguards with automatic weapons and he had the makings of another Jonestown massacre. However it went down, the loss of life, including innocents, could be substantial.

If he triggered that reaction, then discovered there'd been no bomb in the first place, Bolan wasn't sure how he would live with it.

Or even if he'd make it out alive.

But he was bound to try. He simply had no choice.

Along with quitting, he had never learned to look the other way.

THE SPONGY JUNGLE SOIL felt good beneath Nico Mbarga's feet. It might cling to his boots, even produce foul odors now and then, but it still beat hovering fifty yards above the forest floor with someone whom he barely knew at the controls of Master Gaborone's airship.

His orders from Obike were explicit. Master Gaborone commanded that Sharif and one or two others should search the jungle from above, watching for Quinn and his mysterious companion, while they still had ample fuel. The rest of Mbarga's party would proceed on foot, follow the bird as best they could, and try to strike the runners' trail.

Mbarga chose one of his men at random to accompany Sharif. Pablo Camacho sought to join them, but Mbarga drew the line, insisting that his master couldn't risk two valued friends. Besides, Mbarga lied,

Camacho's reputation as a gunman made him much more valuable on the ground. Machismo won out in the end, and the Colombian remained with Mbarge's infantry.

They'd waited for sunrise, camped out around the helicopter with no fire to keep them warm or to hold the jungle predators at bay. When the two foreigners craved light and heat, Mbarga had reminded them of his dead soldiers in the village and the shooters who might still be lurking in the forest, close at hand.

Daybreak was welcome, but the first full hour of daylight brought no revelation of their enemy. Mbarga listened to the helicopter circling, ranging farther out with every pass, and wondered how much fuel Sharif had left. He knew the Lama's cruising speed but had only a vague idea of how far it could travel before dropping from the sky with bone-dry tanks.

How long before Sharif was forced to land or to fly back to Obike?

There were eight men in their party, and the Lama seated only five. Mbarga wouldn't leave three of his soldiers in the jungle, miles from home, and he most certainly wouldn't remain behind with only two for company. Knowing the helicopter had to return and that only Sharif could fly it, he would soon be forced to make another choice.

Slogging through fitful, drizzling rain, he reckoned it was best to send Camacho with Sharif, be rid of both at once, and never mind the risk that he'd dreamed up to keep them separated on the hunt. Another problem then arose, since Mbarga wasn't sure if either one could find Obike from the air. The same was true of his men, no great navigators in the lot. Even their tracker was a down-to-earth man who, as far as Mbarga knew, had no experience directing aircraft.

He could fly back with Camacho and Sharif, but that would leave his men behind. Mbarga wouldn't favor one or two over the rest, and since they all held the same rank—mere grunts, despite their status as "elite" within the Process—none was seasoned at command. The tracker could be trusted to convey them home, but if they met some enemy along the way, whatever losses they sustained would be Mbarga's fault.

His only trusted officer, Samburu Changa, was already dead. Mbarga had two sergeants in Obike, but he couldn't radio for them to meet him in the jungle. It would leave the master with no ranking soldiers to command his bodyguards, and it would take too long for reinforcements to arrive, assuming they could find him in the first place, based on vague verbal directions.

No. The choice was his, and he would have to make it soon.

The one thing that he couldn't do was leave the master's helicopter sitting in the jungle while they all marched back. Even guarded, with a trail blazed to let them retrace their steps and claim it, he knew Master Gaborone wouldn't allow Mbarga to risk his flying chariot. For that matter, Sharif might not agree to make the march a second time, simply to fly the chopper home. If he refused for any reason, then the airship would be stranded where it was.

Mbarga tried to push the problem from his mind and concentrate on tracking Patrick Quinn, but that implied that they had found a trail to follow. Somehow, as they left the village killing ground, his scout had lost the scent. They kept on pushing southward, since the fugitives had gone that way so far, but now Mbarga had begun to worry that they might be wrong.

There was a river somewhere to the east, Nico recalled. What was it? The Banguelu, yes. Quinn wouldn't know it, since he'd never traveled this far from Obike overland, but what of his companion? If the unknown second man was native, or if he had taken time to study the terrain, might he be making for the river even now?

And if he got there, did he have some method of escape prepared?

Mbarga stopped dead in his tracks and took the walkie-talkie from his belt. He didn't call Obike this time, rather dialing to the helicopter's frequency.

"Walker to Flyer. Come in Flyer. Do you read me? Over."

Sharif's voice came back a moment later. "Yes, I hear you. Over."

Circled by his soldiers and Camacho, he commanded, "Shift your search eastward. You'll find a river there. We're changing course. Over and out."

QUINN WAS beyond exhaustion, but he wouldn't call for rest. When Cooper finally suggested a ten-minute break, after two hours on the trail, he had reluctantly agreed. Half frightened that his weary muscles would desert him if he sat, Quinn stayed upright and leaned against a tree to rest. As tired as he was, he hated wasting any time that could've brought them closer to the village and the master's weapon of destruction.

Thinking of it made Quinn feel absurd. Until a few short hours earlier, he'd swallowed any doubts he had about the bomb, accepting Gaborone's strange rationale without objection. Even now, convinced that he'd been wrong, Quinn realized that he was simply excess baggage on the journey, maybe worse than useless to the man who guided him.

Despite the months he'd spent with Gaborone and other members of the Process in Obike, he still couldn't find his way around the jungle if he strayed too far from town. Quinn wasn't leading Cooper to their destination. If he'd tried, they would be lost. And when they got there, he'd be useless when it came to handling the bomb.

He ought to leave me, Quinn decided. If the shoe were on the other foot...

Speaking before he had a chance to change his mind, Quinn said, "I think I'm in your way."

"Let me judge that," Bolan replied.

"I would, except you won't."

"Is that some kind of Process logic?"

"Simple fact. You're on the clock for Val and you don't want to let her down."

"Too late," the soldier said. "I did that when we turned around."

"You'd travel faster on your own, fight better if you have to. Why not just admit it? I'm your ball and chain."

Cooper seemed to consider it, then asked, "What would you do alone?"

"Wait here, what else? We both know I can't find my way around the corner, if there was a corner. Just wait here till you come back."

"And if I don't come back, what then?"

"Why wouldn't y—?"

It hit him, then. The prospect of his kidnapper-turned-escort dying in Obike or somewhere along the way, while Quinn sat waiting for him in the jungle, no idea of where he was or where to go from there.

"Well, shit."

"Is that allowed?" Bolan asked, smiling. "Does the Process go for swearing?"

"I'm about as far off program as it's possible to be," Quinn said. "To hell with it."

"And how's that working for you?"

"At the moment, not too bad."

"No second thoughts?"

"I've half forgotten what thoughts are," Quinn confessed ruefully. "I don't recall the last time that I had one of my own."

"Some people like it that way," Cooper said.

"I thought I did. Maybe a part of me still does, but there's no going back."

"In fact," Bolan said, glancing at his watch, "there is."

Quinn pushed off from the tree, relieved to feel no cramping in his legs. "We'd better get it done, then."

He was smiling, weariness be damned. It felt strange

on his face, but good at the same time. Quinn thought he could get used to it.

He stepped off with his left foot, then stopped dead. In front of him, no more than fifty feet away, an African wearing a faded khaki shirt and blue jeans gaped at Quinn and Bolan with an unmistakable expression of surprise.

Quinn felt as though he ought to recognize that face, but he was focused chiefly on the AK-47 in the new arrival's hands. A weapon that was rising now, bracing against the gunman's shoulder as he aimed and fired.

IT SEEMED to Bolan that a nervous spasm saved Quinn's life. He glimpsed the rifleman ahead of them, weapon upraised and aimed at Quinn since he was in the lead just then. At once, Quinn twitched and staggered backward, nearly falling as the stranger rattled off a burst of six or seven rounds.

There wasn't time to check on Quinn before Bolan reacted, firing from the hip at twenty yards or so. He pressed the Steyr's trigger twice, two 3-round bursts, and that left twenty-four in the clear plastic magazine.

He couldn't count the hits at that range, in the dappled shadows, but his target shuddered, danced an awkward little two-step and went down. Dying, the African triggered another burst skyward, his bullets peppering the forest canopy impossibly beyond his reach.

Those shots still echoed through the night, and Quinn was struggling to maintain his balance, one arm braced against the nearest tree, when other automatic weapons blazed in front of them. Bolan hit the deck and yelled for Quinn to do the same as bullets swarmed around them.

Bolan didn't know how many enemies were firing at them, but the racket made him think it had to be five or six, at least. They could be bandits or guerrillas, a chance encounter on the trail, but Bolan didn't think so. If he'd had a farm to bet, he would've wagered that these gunmen had been sent by Gaborone to find and finish them.

Huddled behind a giant mahogany tree, Bolan thought that in the prophet's place he would've had some questions that he wanted answered first, before the death sentence was passed, but maybe Gaborone felt differently. Or maybe his selected hunters had been on the trail all night, pursuing shadows, and they simply weren't in any mood to chat.

Whatever, they were laying down a screen of fire that precluded all negotiation, even if the Executioner had been inclined to deal. He wasn't, concentrating on the odds and angles while the angry hornet swarm surrounded him.

He risked a glance at Quinn, some twenty feet off to his left, and found the young man lying facedown in the shadow of another massive tree. He was alive, moving, with no wounds visible. If he could stay that way, they would be points ahead.

But that would only happen if the threat was neutralized, and that meant taking out the gunners who had pinned them down.

Bolan began to work on that, seeking position while a hail of slugs flew overhead. After a few blistering seconds, as their magazines ran dry, the unseen shooters had a chance to stop to catch their breath, reloading, taking stock of what they'd seen or hadn't seen so far. The hostile fire grew more sporadic then, as Bolan's enemies decided not to waste their precious ammo on a target that remained invisible.

By slow degrees he crept from cover, staying low, using the ferns and other knee-high undergrowth for flimsy cover. None of it would stop a bullet, aimed or wild, but if the flora helped conceal his movements that would be enough. He needed to improve his field of fire, his angle of attack, if he and Quinn were going to survive.

Somewhere ahead of him and to his left a male voice shouted orders. Bolan recognized that it was speaking French, and while he didn't understand the rapid-fire dialect, the sound served as a beacon, giving him direction in the worm's-eye world he presently inhabited.

The shouted order had to have been a cease-fire, based on the effect it had. Dead silence settled on the forest, nothing in the way of birdsong or the sounds of insects where the guns had blazed a moment earlier. The normal noises would return, he knew, but gradually, as the forest denizens consoled themselves and cautiously returned to their routines.

But not for long.

Bolan was planning to disrupt their world again, as soon as he could find a solid target in the ever-twilight of the jungle floor. As soon as he could mark an adversary and frame one of them in his sights.

He lay dead still and listened for the sounds of small, involuntary movements that were difficult to stop without supreme determination and long practice. Tension built up in a soldier's nerves and muscles on the firing line. Action relieved that pressure, for the most part. It remained, lurking, and when the soldier wasn't allowed to move—when he had to watch and wait for creeping shadows to advance and take his life—it twitched. Some men could control it. Some didn't even notice.

They're the ones who died with a surprised expression on their faces.

If he could only find a twitchy shooter hiding in the jungle spread in front of him. One or two of them who—

There!

He had one, craning forward, cast in profile, like a disembodied head in camouflage fatigues against the mottled greenery.

So slowly, barely breathing, Bolan raised the AUG and found his mark.

NICO MBARGA CURSED the tracker for his hasty firing on the trail. They'd had a chance, however slim, to take Quinn and the other man alive, but that was almost surely lost now. If the tracker wasn't lying dead in front of him, Mbarga might've done the job himself.

The words of Master Gaborone echoed in Nico's

head. *I need to see them both. It is imperative.* He wanted the two men alive, to question them, but now he'd have to stare at corpses.

Whose?

That silent question hit uncomfortably close to home. Mbarga had lost six men so far, and while the loss of Changa's team wasn't his fault, it still reflected on his worth as a commander. Master Gaborone would likely dump the full responsibility on him, but that would only matter if Mbarga made it back alive to face his punishment.

Right now, the issue was in doubt.

They'd wasted too much ammunition without scoring any hits, as far as he could tell from where he crouched beside a great mahogany, only his head exposed by the surrounding ferns. The men were following his order for a cease-fire, but he knew that wouldn't hold if their opponent showed himself or fired another round.

Could he control them, then? He didn't know.

In truth, Mbarga wasn't sure he could control himself.

A short burst hammered from the forest to his left, wringing a cry of mortal pain from yet another of his men. The others started firing instantly, spraying the trees and shadows, trusting random fire to stop their enemy, or at the very least to pin him down.

Mbarga waited, held his fire, found nothing to entice him. If he found another vantage point, perhaps his view would be improved. With that in mind, he started crawling to his right, digging with knees and elbows while he clutched his AK-47 in both hands, ready to fire at once if he was threatened.

Creeping, he wondered whether Quinn was armed now, if he'd seized a gun and extra magazines from one of Changa's men. Mbarga didn't think the young American was trained to fight, but fear and desperation could be great incentives.

Listening, he heard only one weapon that was strange, a lighter sound than the Kalashnikovs his people carried. That was one opponent, but he thought Quinn might've walked off with an AK-47 from the village massacre.

If so, the odds had changed. The danger had increased.

Nico Mbarga was no coward, but he had no immediate desire to die. The odds at five to one were adequate, in his opinion. But at five to two, life suddenly became more difficult.

He tried to crawl in the direction of the one strange weapon he could hear. Unfortunately, it was moving— or the hammering of friendly rifles and the jungle's echoes had deceived him. Either way, pinning down the shooter was proving difficult.

One of his own men loomed in front of him, back turned to Mbarga as he rose and fired a long burst to the west. Bright cartridges cascaded from his weapon, pattering among the broad-leafed ferns. Mbarga hoped he had a target, wasn't merely firing for the sake of noise to make himself feel better.

He was almost close enough to touch the soldier's boot, when suddenly the man pitched backward, uttering a strangled cry of shock or pain. Blood spattered Mbarga's upturned face, stinging one eye before he flinched. The dying soldier fell beside him, arms outflung. His rifle struck the back of his commander's legs, its barrel burning through the fabric of his trousers.

Gasping, Mbarga rolled away from him, and struggled to all fours. He made a better target kneeling, but he didn't care. Something inside his head had snapped, and he was shouting at his team before he even recognized the words that issued from his mouth.

"Attack!" Almost hysterically repeating it. "Attack! *Attack!*"

THE CHARGE, if he could call it that, began in chaos. Someone started shouting in the midst of random fire, one word repeated frantically like a defensive mantra, and the rest surged to their feet, springing from cover, firing as they came.

It was a desperate tactic, charging unseen enemies, but still it might've worked if anyone had made an effort to coordinate the rush. Instead, the shouted order simply set men running off in all directions, spraying bullets toward whatever goal they set themselves, with no coordination whatsoever.

One leaped out from cover twenty feet in front of Bolan, rushing toward him more by chance than any conscious plan. The runner's AK-47 cut a swath ahead of him, but his aim was chest high on an upright man of his own size, the bullets wasted on tree trunks and smoky air.

Bolan fired from the ground and gutted him, a rising burst that ripped his man from groin to sternum, plucked him off his feet and slammed him onto his back. Stone dead before he hit the turf, the shooter barely twitched.

To Bolan's right, another camo-clad attacker saw his buddy fall and veered in that direction, bellowing a wordless battle cry that matched the thunder of his weapon. Bolan rolled to save himself, while AK bullets clipped the ferns and churned the soil around him.

Firing as he went, with barely time to aim, he cut the shooter's legs from under him and dropped him on his backside. Pain short-circuited his adversary's brain just long enough to take his finger off the AK-47's trigger when it mattered. Wounded as he was, the gunman still might've had time to save himself, but shock stalled his response. Instead of emptying his magazine at Bolan, he blinked twice and mouthed a silent note of agony.

And that was all it took.

Bolan's next burst ripped through the wounded shooter's chest and finished him. Sweeping on, he marked another nearby rifleman and brought the AUG to bear on target number four.

Before he had a chance to squeeze the trigger, someone beat him to it. From the undergrowth and shadows at his back, gunfire erupted, found the runner he had singled out and knocked him sprawling in the weeds. It didn't have the feel of a clean kill, but it would do for now.

Bolan hadn't expected friendly fire to help him, but he'd take whatever aid was thrown his way and pay the careless shooter back in kind, as soon as possible. Just now, he had another enemy advancing toward him at a dead run through the trees, no doubt about his destination or the bloody murder in his eyes.

Bolan half rose to meet him, didn't bother with the Steyr's built-in scope. He fired at something close to point-blank range, muzzle velocity and the momentum of his target amplifying impact of his 5.56 mm tumbling projectiles, and they tore through fabric, flesh and bone.

The shooter jerked, spun, staggered, taking hits in front and back before he flopped facedown into a bed of multicolored fungus. Bolan heard the Steyr's slide lock open on an empty chamber and he dropped the empty magazine, reaching for a replacement at his waist.

The first shot from behind should probably have killed him, but the shooter rushed it, jerked his trigger in a rage and scored a hit on Bolan's pack instead. The blow still pitched him sideways, falling heavily, and nearly made him drop the loaded magazine. Two other shots sang overhead, one of them close enough for him to feel its hot wind on his face.

He tried to seat the magazine, but then a shadow loomed above him. Glancing up, he was surprised to see a relatively pale face staring down the AK-47's barrel. Not an African, perhaps Latino. He registered surprise and saw his killer smile across the weapon pointed at his head. It was a smile of triumph, mocking him.

The burst of AK fire was loud, up close. Bolan had braced himself to meet the rain of death with open eyes, but it was blood that showered him. The shooter's chest exploded, spewing scarlet, and his smile was twisted into something else as he collapsed, his deadweight pinning Bolan's legs.

Behind him, Patrick Quinn stood with a smoking rifle braced against his shoulder, wide eyes gaping from a mask of sweat and mud.

"Sorry I took so long," he said. "Are you okay?"

CHAPTER TWELVE

"I haven't been in touch with him myself, you under-stand," Hal Brognola said.

He was hedging. Johnny Gray could hear it in the big Fed's gruff voice. He didn't have to see Brognola's face. Shifting to stretch his leg and ease the pressure on his walking cast, he said, "I know."

"The information comes back to me from the Farm," Brognola said. "It's secondhand, but I trust their account. We all do, every day. We trust them with our lives."

"Of course," Johnny replied.

"Okay, then. What I'm hearing is that Striker made the pickup right on time, no problem, but they've hit a snag concerning extrication." He was being cagey, even on the scrambled phone line.

"What does that mean?" Johnny pressed him.

"Well, the fact is," Brognola replied, "they've had two problems. One was pure logistics. Something happened to the pickup chopper and they had to find a new one. One thing and another in a Third World country, that created some delays."

"And what's the other thing."

"Ah, right. On that, now, Striker has decided that he needs to stay and deal with certain peripheral matters that came up unexpectedly."

"Such as?"

Brognola cleared his throat. "I can't go into that right now."

"Excuse me?"

"It's been classified as need-to-know."

"Okay. My brother's in the shit. I put him there. I need to know."

Johnny could almost see the scrunched expression on Brognola's face, as if he felt an ulcer's bite deep down. A moment's silence stretched to nearly two before he spoke again.

"Turns out the guru's holding certain items that he's not supposed to have. He's offered them for sale to high-risk individuals, and Striker wants to nip it in the bud. I really can't say any more."

"Okay, then. What about the package?" Johnny could play cryptic, too.

"The last I heard, it was intact," Brognola said. "Of course, the shipment's been delayed while Striker deals with those peripheral concerns."

"Of course. But they have wings now, when they need them?"

"That's my understanding, yes."

"Wings, but no ETA."

"Unfortunately, no."

"I guess there's nothing more to say," Johnny conceded.

"Not right now." Brognola's tone was buoyed by relief. "I'll get in touch, you know, the minute I hear anything."

"Assuming you can share it," Johnny said.

"Uh, right. You know the drill."

"Too well. I'll pass it on."

"How is she?" Brognola inquired.

"How do you think?"

After he cradled the receiver, Johnny rose and left the den, using one crutch to navigate the turn, a hallway lined with family photos, entering the living room where Jack and Val sat close together on a sofa, holding hands and whispering. He knew they hadn't been eavesdropping. Johnny had invited both of them to listen in, ask anything they wanted to, and they'd declined. He was their chosen filter, their interpreter.

Jack watched him hobble to a nearby easy chair and settle down. Rubbing his right knee, shattered by a bullet years ago, the former G-man forced a smile and told him, "We make quite a pair."

"We do all right," Johnny replied.

"We do." Jack glanced at Val, received her nod. "So, what's the word?" he asked.

"Hal couldn't tell me much. From what he *did* say, Mack collected Patrick from Obike without opposition. Something happened to the chopper, though, and scrubbed the pickup."

"What?" There was an edge to Val's voice that he'd rarely heard before.

"Hang on," Johnny said. "I don't have the details, but it sounds like something technical. Renting a helicopter in the Congo, anything could happen. Engine problems, fuel, whatever."

"So, they're stranded?" Val was leaning forward, clutching Jack's hand hard enough to make him wince.

"No, no. They found another chopper," Johnny reassured her. "But they haven't been picked up yet."

"I don't understand. Why not?"

"Mack put it off."

Val blinked at him, confused.

"Why would he do that, son?" Jack asked.

"I don't have any details," Johnny said. "Broad strokes, it seems he found out Gaborone is peddling some kind of high-risk contraband. I took that to mean weapons, but I couldn't say what kind. Mack's staying on the ground to clean it up."

"And Pat?" Val asked him.

"They're together."

"I don't understand this. He was just supposed to go get Pat and come right back. Why would he do this other thing?"

"I guess he saw a need."

"He's putting both their lives in jeopardy!"

"That happened when he took the job," Johnny replied. "Now we just have to wait it out."

"What have I done?" she asked through tears.

"The best you could. We all have," Johnny answered, hoping it was true.

"I'M FINE," Bolan said. "Thanks to you."

"Just luck," Quinn told him. "I'm no good with guns."

"You did all right." Bolan heaved once and rolled the leaking, lifeless body off his legs. "There still may be another shooter here," he warned.

"No, this is it." Quinn sounded confident.

"One of their people over there got hit from that direction," Bolan said, pointing.

Quinn nodded. "That was me."

Rising, Bolan regarded him with new eyes. "You bagged two of them?"

A shrug. "There didn't seem to be much choice. Except...I feel a little... Can you take this for a minute?"

Bolan took the AK-47, eyes averted as the young man stumble-jogged behind a nearby tree. The retching sounds he made told Bolan sudden death was catching up with him.

"Sorry," Quinn said when he returned a moment later, hollow-eyed.

"No need."

"I ought to suck it up, I know. Get tough and all."

"It's not for everybody," Bolan said.

"Still, if we're going for the bomb, they won't just hand it to us, will they?"

"No," the Executioner replied. "I wouldn't think so."

"Well, then, I'll be ready."

"We can talk about that later." Toeing the Latino corpse, he asked Quinn, "Can you tell me who this is?"

"It *was* Camacho. What he's doing out here in the sticks, I couldn't tell you."

"He was hunting us."

"Okay. But why?"

"Something to do?" Bolan suggested as he knelt to search Camacho's pockets. He retrieved nothing of value—a half-empty box of small cigars, a folding knife, a money clip, a lighter. There was no passport, visa, driver's license. Zip.

"What are you looking for?" asked Quinn.

"ID. He must've left it back in camp."

"The mast— Er, Gaborone won't like losing a moneyman." He turned and scanned the field of death. "Oh, man. He'll like this even less."

"What is it?" Bolan, rising, asked him.

"It's Nico." Quinn was pointing at another corpse. "Nico Mbarga. He's chief of security."

"Not anymore."

"It makes me wonder."

"What?" Bolan asked.

"Well, we've got Mbarga and Camacho, right? But where's Sharif?"

"Maybe he doesn't like the jungle. Maybe he's no good at hunting. Maybe anything," Bolan asked.

"I guess. Seems funny, though."

"You want this back?"

Quinn nodded, took the AK-47 from his outstretched hand. "I'll likely need it, where we're going."

"Then you'd better pack more ammunition, too."

"I'm not sure what to take," Quinn said.

"They're all the same. Pick out a bandolier or two, whatever you can carry. Check the magazines before you choose. Make sure they're loaded."

"Right. Okay."

Quinn bypassed Gaborone's security chief, whose blood had soaked through the bandolier spanning his ruined chest, and stripped another body of its ammo belts. He came back looking queasy, but he kept the bile inside.

"I was just thinking," he told Bolan.

"What?"

"Well, I'm no expert, but we've seen too many bodies now to fit inside that helicopter."

Bolan nodded. "This lot followed us on foot. They tracked us from the village."

"So, while this bunch came along behind us, Changa's team flew up ahead?"

"That's how I read it."

"Ten, eleven guys?"

"About that."

"All for me," Quinn said. "I find that hard to swallow."

"Why?"

"I told you, man. I'm nobody inside the Process. If the prophet gave a thought to me at all—leaving, I mean—he'd let the jungle do me in."

"Well," Bolan said, "there were the fires."

"Okay, but still. A chopper and a dozen soldiers, give or take. Why do I rate?"

"Maybe he's worried that you'll give up what you know, or what he *thinks* you know."

"Guess he was right."

"We haven't solved the problem yet," Bolan reminded him. "And you can still stand down."

"No, thanks. I've killed two men. Whatever that does to the soul, I can't just cut and run."

The face beneath Quinn's mop of hair had aged, not only from the photographs in Val Querente's file, but in the hours he had spent with Bolan. Growing up could be a bitch, but Bolan had a hunch that Quinn would be a decent man one day.

If he survived that long.

"Well, if we're going," Bolan said, "let's do it. All that noise could draw more hunters, and I'd rather not be standing here when they show up."

Quinn nodded. They had only taken half a dozen steps when suddenly, behind them, Bolan heard one of the dead begin to squawk.

"WE'RE RUNNING LOW ON FUEL," Adnan Ibn Sharif observed. He knew the African could understand him, had insisted on it when Mbarga chose his traveling companion, but the man made no reply.

He tried the radio, preset before liftoff to the same frequency as the two-way carried by Gaborone's chief of security. "Mbarga, can you hear me? Answer if you do!"

"Call him 'Pilgrim,' sir," the African suggested. "No names on the radio."

"What should I call myself?"

A silent shrug.

Sharif tried once again. "Pilgrim, respond. If you can hear me, Pilgrim, answer. Over!"

Sharif spoke English, hadn't mastered French and had no inkling of the local dialects. Mbarga spoke English well enough to answer him, that much he knew.

"Pilgrim, here. I read you. Over?"

Sharif frowned at the voice. It didn't sound even remotely like Nico Mbarga. Did the radio distort voices that much? He hesitated, glancing at the African beside him, but the blank face told him nothing.

"Pilgrim, is it you? Over."

"Pilgrim. Affirmative. Over."

Sharif was stymied. He could either break off the connection or explain his problem. Finally he said, "Pilgrim, we have less than half a tank of fuel remaining. We cannot go on much longer searching. Please advise. Over."

The *please* rankled Sharif, but it wasn't the time for arrogance. He waited through another hesitation from the ground before the unfamiliar voice came back.

"Suggest you circle back to our position and continue searching. Over."

What? He'd told them that the helicopter would be running out of fuel, and still they wanted him to circle aimlessly above the jungle, seeking tiny figures on the ground he couldn't hope to glimpse?

"Pilgrim, I say again—my fuel is low. I must return to base while we still have enough to make the trip."

And that could be a problem, Sharif realized. He wasn't sure exactly where Obike was, much less the airstrip where Gaborone kept his helicopter. Sharif could navigate by instruments, but first he'd need coordinates for his prospective destination.

"Further search would be most helpful," came his answer from the ground. "Over."

Fuming, Sharif snapped, "Negative! I have no fuel to waste. Supply coordinates for the return flight, if you please. Over!"

"One minute," the voice said. "Over."

It soon turned into two, then three and four. Sharif was just about to key the microphone again when Pilgrim's voice emerged from speakers mounted in the cockpit.

"Are you ready to transcribe coordinates? Over."

"I'm ready, yes. Over."

The voice he couldn't place began dictating numbers, with degrees and minutes, north and west. Sharif repeated them, to lock them firmly in his mind. The rifleman in the copilot's seat observed him with a vaguely curious expression.

Idiot!

"All right, Pilgrim," Sharif replied, when he had memorized the flight coordinates. "I'll tell them back at camp that you've continued searching, shall I? Over?"

"Searching, yes. Good luck! Over and out."

Sharif wasn't unhappy to be giving up the hunt. It hadn't been the great adventure he'd expected, and he'd gladly leave Camacho to it. Tramping through the jungle was a pleasure better left to slaves and masochists.

Besides, he thought, this gives me more time with the so-called master, to negotiate a decent price.

That sparked a smile, aborted when the African began to speak.

"Sir, I believe there is an error, please."

"What are you saying?"

"I believe—"

"What error? Tell me what you mean!"

"Please, sir, Obike should be north."

"I know that. What's your point?"

"Are we not traveling northwest, sir? I perhaps misunderstood the message."

"Wait." Sharif reeled off the flight coordinates from memory. "That's it, I'm sure," he said. "Northwest."

"Is wrong, I think."

"Why would Mbarga give the wrong coordinates?"

"I did not recognize Captain Mbarga's voice, sir."

"Well, someone else, then. Aren't they all the same?"

A measure of contempt was now reflected in the African's expression. "Sir, I did not recognize the voice at all."

"Well, why in God's name didn't you say so?"

"Sir, you are the pilot. It is not for me to say."

"But now you speak. Incredible!" Sharif again picked up the microphone and spoke into the ether. "Pilgrim! Can you hear me, Pilgrim? Please confirm coordinates immediately. Over!"

Dead air crackled from the speakers all around him,

hissing with a sibilance that eerily reminded him of muffled laughter over some grim joke.

"Pilgrim! Respond at once! Over!"

Nothing.

Angry and frightened, Sharif put the microphone back on its hook and backhanded a film of perspiration from his brow.

How could he tell if the coordinates were wrong, before it was too late? And if they *were* wrong, where could he set down the helicopter without dying in the process?

Close to panic for the first time in more years than he could count, Adnan Ibn Sharif flew on above the jungle canopy, searching the blue sky for an answer that would save his life.

"WHAT WAS THAT all about?"

Bolan finished clipping Mbarga's two-way radio onto his web belt, then replied, "I want them off our case ASAP. If I can't keep them circling here while we run out from under them, the best thing is to send them home."

"Okay," Quinn said. "But how'd you know the longitude and whatnot for Obike?"

Bolan met his level gaze. "I don't," he said, "without checking the GPS."

"But you just—" Quinn stopped short. "Where are they going, then?"

"Beats me. With any luck, they're flying on fumes right now."

"You wanted them to crash?"

The soldier shrugged. "I don't mind if they find a

clearing and set down. The main thing is mobility without a fear of aerial surveillance. I'll be happy if we've managed that, regardless of the means."

"And two more dead."

"If they were here, attacking us, I would've shot them. What's the difference?"

Quinn's turn to shrug, uncertain whether Cooper saw it as they moved along the northbound trail. "I guess I hoped we'd seen the last of it. Killing, I mean."

Bolan stopped short and turned to face him in the jungle gloom. "You're heading in the wrong direction for a peaceful holiday. I don't know what all Gaborone has waiting for us in the village, but I guarantee he won't give up his golden nuke without a fight."

"So I was stupid. Sue me."

"Stupid's one thing, hopeful is another. Where we're going," Bolan told him, "either one can get you killed."

"I understand."

"Do you?"

"I said—"

"Because you won't be walking down the village avenue with firewood or a basketful of fruit this time. They won't be smiling at you, saying, 'Welcome home.' If you weren't marked before, you are by now. Remember that and keep your weapon ready. When the moment comes to save yourself, don't hesitate."

"Or you," Quinn said.

"How's that?" Bolan asked.

"When the moment comes to save myself or you. How quickly we forget."

"I'm not forgetting anything. I owe you one, and this is it—the best advice you'll ever get. The last time may have been a fluke. If you have any doubts concerning your ability to use that piece again—maybe on people you've had dinner with, sitting around the fire and telling stories—you should turn around right now."

"We've done this conversation," Quinn reminded him. "I can't just turn around. I don't know where in hell we are, and I don't have the global thingy. Anyway, I helped create this problem, didn't I?"

"Who says?"

"I do. Like everybody else who follows Gaborone, supports him, fills his pockets. Each and every one of us will be responsible if he goes through with this. I don't want Armageddon on my head, okay? I can't deal with the ghosts."

"All right, then," Bolan answered, turning north again. "Let's get it done."

Bolan had talked Quinn through the basics of the AK-47. How to load and cock it, how to clear a jam or switch the safety on and off. He knew about selective fire, full-auto versus semiautomatic for conserving ammunition. He could also load a magazine, although the odds of him discovering loose ammo were approximately slim to none.

He didn't know how far it was back to Obike, but the weariness had settled into every part of him, muscle and bone. Quinn wanted rest, suspected that he could've slept for two days straight, but he would not allow fatigue to beat him down. He'd come too far for that already, seen and done too much, surrendered everything that he'd believed was vital in his life.

A snatch of old song lyrics played inside his head, something about what a difference a day made.

The songwriter no doubt had something else in mind, but he or she was right. Sometimes a day made all the difference in the world. And if this day should prove to be his last, Quinn would at least know that he'd spent it well.

For once, thinking of someone other than himself.

GABORONE'S WORLD was closing in on him, constricting to the point where he felt stifled, trapped. It was a feeling that he'd thought to leave behind when he began communing with the Infinite, but here it was again to haunt him

What was happening?

He'd been *that* close to making a sweet deal, advancing Armageddon's timetable and bringing on the Final Days. His private payoff, to a fat bank in the Cayman Islands, had been frosting on the cake. If something happened and he didn't get to sample it, at least he knew that a reward awaited him in paradise.

Unless he failed in his primary goal.

No matter how he puzzled over it, Ahmadou Gaborone could make no sense of Patrick Quinn's rebellion. Several other Process members had been driven mad by Gaborone's demands and jungle living, but they'd always turned the bitter wrath against themselves. Two suicides and two more runners, both presumed dead in the forest. None of them had tried to burn the village down or to kill his bodyguards. More to the point, none of them had the benefit of outside help.

That was the most disturbing thing of all for Gaborone. The knowledge that he had been right, that outsiders not only schemed against him night and day, but that their plans had been translated into action. Now, perhaps too late, he feared that he might come out second best in any contest with his enemies.

Would God allow it? Did He even really care?

A rapping on his door disrupted Gaborone's dark introspection. It was locked this time, forcing the prophet to stand up and cross the room, unlatch it to reveal the nervous-looking runner on his threshold.

"Master, quickly, please. A message from Mr. Sharif!"

"Sharif? What do you mean?"

"Master, the radio! Please hurry! *Please!*"

He crossed the compound with long strides, refusing to be hurried further. Dignity was critical. If his disciples saw him running, what might they conclude? Panic could spark a blind stampede.

Inside the commo hut, he took the earphones once again and slipped them on, then gripped the microphone. Before he had a chance to speak, the Arab's crackling voice was in his ears.

"Base camp, come in! Emergency! Over!"

He had no code name for the Palestinian, so Gaborone simply replied, "I'm here. Over."

"Praise God! We are nearly out of fuel. I need proper coordinates to reach the airstrip. Over!"

Proper coordinates? "Where are you now?" Gaborone asked. "Over."

Sharif replied with gibberish, presumably the numbers from a map or chart. Since Gaborone had never learned to read one, they meant nothing to him. Finally he asked, "Who gave you those coordinates? Over."

"Pilgrim! Or someone, I'm not sure. Are they correct? Over."

Gaborone turned toward the runner and the communications operator. "Do you know the camp's coordinates?" he asked them. "Either of you?"

"No, Master."

"No, no, Master."

He keyed the microphone again. "In which direction are you flying? Over."

"North by northwest," came the answer. "Hurry, please. Over!"

"Be patient. I must find someone who knows the answer. Over."

"Hurry, please!" the Arab's voice repeated, with no sign-off this time.

Facing his two devotees, Gaborone commanded, "Find someone who knows the village's coordinates. The latitude and longitude. Go now!"

They fled, wide-eyed, and left him wondering if anyone around him had the answer. It was something that he might've asked Nico Mbarga.

Why not?

Sharif implied that Mbarga had supplied him with

the wrong coordinates, but that made no sense what-soever. Mbarga had his orders and had never disobeyed them in the past. He might not like Camacho or Sharif, but Gaborone couldn't believe that he would try to sabotage the helicopter, knowing that exposure of such treachery would cost his life.

It had to be some kind of a misunderstanding. If Sharif couldn't communicate with Mbarga for whatever reason, Gaborone would do it for him. He would solve this problem as he always had before, with diligence and faith.

"Prophet to Pilgrim. Calling Pilgrim. Do you read me? Over."

How could silence whisper like the hiss of reptiles? It was simply static, but it chilled him, raised the short hairs on his nape. He tried again, repeating the short message, waiting for an answer.

Nothing.

Where was Nico? What was happening?

Fighting the lethal parasite of doubt, he hunched over the microphone, unwilling to admit defeat, and cast his pleading words into the void.

BOLAN HEARD NONE of the transmissions from Obike or the helicopter. He'd switched off the radio after feeding Gaborone's pilot bogus coordinates, and he would leave it off until there was a need to eavesdrop on the enemy. Meanwhile, an active squawk box on his hip would be a hazard, telling anyone within earshot exactly where they were.

He used the GPS instead, consulting it at frequent intervals, correcting their direction when he went astray. Bolan had learned his woodcraft at a time before eyes in the sky could guide a foot soldier to battle, and he still had faith in his ability to find the target without gadgetry, but if the GPS could speed things up or hone his aim to pinpoint accuracy, he would take advantage of it.

Absolutely.

They were on track, so far, and Quinn had dammed the flow of questions that his first kills had unleashed. More accurately, he had given up on asking Bolan and was trying to work out the answers for himself.

Or maybe he was simply too dog-tired to think beyond the simple act of walking, staying upright while he put one foot in front of the other, slogging onward through the jungle's heat and mud and intermittent rain.

He gave the young man points for lasting this long, keeping up so far. Quinn's pitch-in at the firefight had surprised Bolan and saved his life, but he still had to ask himself if second thoughts would make Quinn freeze next time he had to pull the trigger. He'd been brave enough or scared enough to kill in self-defense, but it could be a different story when they crept into the village he'd called home a short day previously. He might choke if called upon to fire on coreligionists and friends.

Bolan cut off that train of thought, already well aware of their potential for a lethal foul-up. He replaced defeatist thinking with the facts he knew about Obike and its master.

Gaborone had roughly seven hundred followers collected in the village, most of them unarmed but dedicated to the Process and its leader, maybe to the point of laying down their lives to stop invaders. Riding herd on those disciples was a team of forty-odd gunmen, less those who had already been eliminated. Call it thirty, then, well armed and hampered by no squeamishness where killing was concerned.

And somewhere in the camp, perhaps, a weapon that could set the world on fire.

Not literally, but he knew that damage from a nuclear explosion in a modern city would extend beyond the finite blast zone and the lurking plague of radiation poisoning. Depending on the circumstances, there would be investigations, accusations and retaliations dwarfing the reactions to 9/11. Wars had been fought for much, much less, and if the fireball was accompanied by "evidence" suggesting some specific nation was to blame for the assault, payback might mean another mushroom cloud, and then another…

He didn't want to go there, didn't even want to glimpse a world of smoking rubble and nuclear winter. Could a handful of fanatics light the fuse that blew the world apart?

Why not?

It would've been unthinkable before the bomb, when even killing kings and presidents was something personal, a one-on-one event in most cases, with shock waves limited in scope. It was an altogether different ball game now.

One strike, and maybe everyone was out.

A part of Bolan hoped that Quinn was wrong, hoped they would find no bomb. If it meant dying in a wasted effort while the world dreamed on, oblivious, it might be worth the price.

But if Quinn wasn't wrong, then they were running out of time.

And if they failed, there would be hell to pay.

CHAPTER THIRTEEN

Adnan Ibn Sharif was on the verge of panic. He had been airborne for the better part of three hours now, and if the helicopter's gauge could be trusted, he was running dangerously low on fuel.

The Rolex watch on his left wrist told Sharif that fourteen minutes had elapsed since Gaborone last spoke to him over the radio. Each moment took him farther from his destination, while he waited for coordinates to help him find the village airstrip.

Damn it! What was wrong with Gaborone? Why didn't he respond?

Sharif wondered if this was part of some bizarre plan to eliminate him, but he couldn't see how that would be to Gaborone's advantage. Had Camacho offered such a high price for the package that its seller had capitulated without further bidding? Was the so-called prophet certain that Sharif wouldn't outbid the brash Colombian?

It made no sense, yet here he was, skimming above the jungle treetops, waiting for directions to the nearest landing strip, stonewalled by silence from the helicopter's owner.

Could it be that Gaborone would sacrifice the aircraft just to kill Sharif? Granted, the price that he was asking for his merchandise could buy a fleet of choppers, but it still seemed wasteful, verging on insane. He could have killed Sharif a hundred times already, in Obike, with a nod or finger-snap to the gorillas he called bodyguards.

One of them sat beside Sharif right now, apparently relaxed, as if he didn't understand the peril they were facing. Did he realize that sometime in the next half hour or less they would be plummeting to the earth, controls dead in the pilot's hands? If so, the bland face revealed nothing.

Sharif couldn't have said if that was courage or a form of idiocy. And just now, he didn't care.

His patience was exhausted. Snatching up the microphone, he barked, "Prophet! We have sufficient fuel for twenty minutes' flight or less. Demand coordinates for landing *now!* Over!"

More static, then a weary-sounding voice came back. He barely recognized it now. "Angel? I read you, Angel. Over."

Angel? If that was supposed to be a joke, Sharif found it to be in miserable taste. Still, this was not the time to squabble over code names, when his time was running out.

"Prophet, I hear you! Please relay coordinates. Over!"

"Angel," the beaten voice came back, "we're canvassing the village now. So far, no one has the coordinates. It may require some time. Over."

"We have no time!" Sharif raged at the microphone. "In fifteen minutes we will drop out of the fucking sky! Give me coordinates for landing now! Over!"

"I'm sorry, Angel. We will transmit the coordinates as soon as possible. Until then—"

Sharif didn't know he was about to scream. It was spontaneous, erupting from his throat with force enough to strain his vocal cords and leave him gasping when the wave of crimson fury passed. The helicopter dipped and yawed while he was in that dark place, then recovered as his vision cleared, hands steadied on the sensitive controls.

The African was trembling now, as if the full extent of their predicament had finally hit home. He stuttered something in a dialect the Arab didn't understand, then switched to English.

"We are in danger, yes?"

"Thanks to your master," Sharif answered, sneering, "we're in bloody mortal danger. Yes."

When was the last time Gaborone had fueled the helicopter? Had it started from the airstrip yesterday with a full tank?

"Go lower, please," the African requested.

"What?"

"Lower. Please, sir. A little lower if you please."

"What is it that you're asking me? I don't—"

"Lower!" the man snapped, jabbing the muzzle of his AK-47 solidly against Sharif's right side.

"All right! We're going lower." When they skimmed almost within arm's reach of the treetops, he asked the gunman, "Is that better? Are you satisfied?"

"Yes, sir. Thank you."

The answer was incongruous, but there was no more pressure of the weapon digging hard between his ribs. Sharif glanced over as the African unclipped his safety harness, turned and started fumbling with the door on his side of the cabin.

"Wait! You can't do that! We're in the air, for God's sake! Don't—"

Rushing wind drowned out the rest, as his companion forced the door ajar, bent forward and lunged head-first into space. The door slammed shut again behind him, while Sharif fought the controls for mastery.

He felt hysteria encroaching on his mind, another scream building somewhere inside his chest. Wildly, he wondered if the chopper would get better mileage now that he had dumped the extra weight. A quick glance at the fuel gauge showed him that it made no difference.

The radio was crackling, Gaborone's taut voice requiring his attention. "Angel, we have the coordinates. Please listen carefully. They are—"

The needle on Sharif's fuel gauge touched Empty, sank beyond it, settling at rest. As if on cue, he heard the Lama's engine sputter, cough and die. Sharif knew Gaborone was speaking to him, offering encouragement, but it was wasted now.

The great, ungainly aircraft nosed over, angling

toward the treetops as it lost momentum and surrendered precious buoyancy.

Once more, without a hint of rage behind it now, Adnan Ibn Sharif began to scream.

IT HAD BEGUN TO RAIN again, the first drops on his scalp and face distracting Bolan from his thoughts of Val Querente. He'd been wondering if she was worried yet and whether anyone had tipped her to the change in plans.

Johnny might get in touch with Hal Brognola, to find out what was happening, but the big Fed would play the cards close to his vest. Family or not, it was instinctive. Even if Brognola wanted to provide details of what was going on, he couldn't transmit information he didn't possess.

So Val would simply have to wait.

The rain was neither enemy nor friend. It helped to hide their tracks but also slowed them at the same time. It likely wouldn't last long, but while it was falling and for some time afterward they'd have to watch their step more carefully on winding, muddy tracks.

A backward glance showed Quinn still coming on behind him, lurching now and then, using his bare hands for support from trees and dangling vines. Quinn had the AK-47 slung across his back, twin bandoliers crossed on his chest. He wore a dead man's boots and called to mind the image of a demented Robinson Crusoe, armed for the twenty-first century.

"We're getting there," Bolan assured him, speaking softly.

"Right."

And it was true, after a fashion. Five or six more hours on the march, and Bolan thought they should be spitting-close to Gaborone's compound. He wondered, not quite worrying about it, if the place would act on Quinn with some kind of religious tidal pull, drawing him back—if not into the fellowship, at least into the basic tenets of the faith.

Was there enough of Gaborone's indoctrination left in Quinn to make him freeze up on the fight-or-flight threshold? If so, Bolan supposed that there was nothing he could do about it now. He'd given Quinn the opportunity to quit, remain behind, but some part of the young man's dormant conscience had kicked in to make him tag along.

Bolan could only hope it wouldn't be a one-way ride.

He checked the GPS tracker, corrected slightly toward the north, and used a crude ladder of stout, rough vines to scale a muddy slope. Once Quinn had gained the high ground, Bolan tried the radio again, not broadcasting, but simply scanning frequencies for any crosstalk by his enemies. The voice that came out of the radio's small speaker startled him.

"Angel? Angel! Please answer if you hear me. Angel? Over."

Quinn stepped back a pace, as if afraid the radio might strike at him. "That's Gaborone," he said.

"You're sure?"

Quinn nodded. "Positive. There's something odd about his voice, but yes, it's him."

"Who's 'Angel'?"

That elicited a shrug. "I never heard of him. Or it. Whatever."

Bolan considered asking once again if he was sure, but Gaborone was on the air again, pleading. "Angel, I give you the coordinates again." Rapidly, the strained voice dictated four numbers, with degrees and minutes, north and east. "Please answer if you copy, Angel. Over?"

Bolan thought he had it now. *Angel* would be a flyer. Gaborone was offering a homing beacon to his helicopter pilot, but the chopper crew didn't respond.

Bolan tried to make sense of it. The helicopter had been airborne when he'd rattled off coordinates at random, to mislead the pilot. Still, he wondered how a flyboy hired by Gaborone could lose his way between Obike and the village where the firefight had occurred. It seemed impossible, but there it was.

And Bolan would accept whatever gifts the universe was generous enough to give him, at that moment.

Had the chopper passed beyond range of Obike's radio? That was unlikely, if his handheld set could pick up Gaborone's transmission.

What else would prevent the pilot from responding, in the circumstances? He'd been running low on fuel when Bolan had spoken to him some time ago. Had he been on the air, pleading for help, while Bolan had his set switched off? What did it mean when Gaborone broadcast the urgently desired coordinates and got no answer?

Bolan killed the pleading voice to save the walkie-talkie's battery. Quinn spoke as he was busy reattaching it to his web belt.

"Why don't they answer from the helicopter?"

"My best guess," Bolan replied, "they're on the ground."

"Landed?"

"It's possible."

"But you don't think so," Quinn said, pressing him.

"I don't," Bolan confirmed. And in the silence that ensued, he said, "Let's move. We've got a bomb to find."

DESPAIRING, GABORONE at last set down the microphone, removed the sweaty earphones from his head and placed them gently on the plain wood table, by the radio. The bird was lost, and he'd lost contact with the rest of Mbarga's team, as well.

All gone.

Or were they?

Many things could happen in the jungle to a fragile two-way radio. Perhaps someone had dropped it into water accidentally, or fallen so that it was damaged on impact. Mbarga's silence didn't mean that he or any other member of his team was dead.

Except Sharif, of course. The Arab's silence, after begging on the airwaves for direction to the landing site, told Gaborone that he'd run out of fuel and crashed the helicopter at some unknown point northeast of where Samburu Changa's team was slaughtered.

So much death, Gaborone thought. And yet, the people whom he needed to eliminate were still alive.

He would forget about Sharif and hope Camacho still survived, with Mbarga and the rest. Removing competition meant that Gaborone might not receive top dollar for his merchandise, but he could halt the sale if need be, wait until more interested parties joined the bidding for another round.

How long would that take? Days, at least. More likely weeks, for the preliminary bargaining, vetting potential buyers, waiting for them to arrive in Brazzaville. Delay meant heightened risk, with Quinn and his unknown companion still at large, the helicopter smoldering someplace where passersby might find it and investigations sifting clues around Lee Rathbun's disappearance.

How much longer could he hold the yapping dogs at bay?

More to the point, how could he justify further postponing Armageddon and the Final Days when he was called to answer for his actions by Almighty God?

A mounting sense of desperation haunted Gaborone. He wanted to be somewhere, *anywhere,* as far as trains and planes could take him from Obike and the noose that he felt tightening around his neck. But now, the means of swift escape was lost to him. He'd have to radio the outside world and make arrangements for a charter flight, select the faithful who'd accompany him in exile.

And he would have to take the package with him.

Otherwise, all of his work would be for nothing, wasted. He would simply be another madman, shouting at the wind and rain, of no account.

No, Gaborone decided. He had to wait and see what happened next. Determine if Camacho was alive and find out if he still wanted the package that had brought him halfway round the world. If so, then Gaborone would make the deal.

If not, he might devise a way to light the Armageddon fuse himself. Why not? Perhaps, when all was said and done, he was supposed to take the lead and strike that blow, instead of leaving it to other hands.

Outside the commo hut he found his runner waiting, stopped and ordered him to fetch Jomo Tekle. Returning to his nearby quarters, Gaborone sat waiting for the sergeant of his bodyguards to come.

Five minutes later, Tekle stood in front of him, nervously avoiding eye contact. "How may I serve you, Master?" he inquired.

"Select six men," Gaborone said. "Outfit them for a march. Go south, after the others, and discover what's become of Nico's party. When you find him, tell him to return at once."

Tekle absorbed the order, swallowed hard, and said, "Yes, Master. But if I may ask it, please, what should I do if…if…"

"If you can't find him?"

"Sir, if I *do* find him and he…if he's…"

"Dead?"

A child's voice answering. "Yes, sir."

"Then you must find his killers, Jomo. Track them down and bring their heads back here to me."

THE RAIN HAD STOPPED for half an hour, then resumed with new intensity. Drenched to the skin, Quinn wondered why the weather hadn't bothered him as much when he was living in Obike, as it did while he was on the lonely trail with Cooper.

There had been shelter in the village, obviously, but he didn't think that was the answer. It was more a question of attitude, his view of life in general and Quinn's goals in particular.

He'd been part of the hive with Gaborone, one worker out of hundreds, told precisely where to go and what to do each day, his labors calculated for the good of all. Most tasks could be delayed for heavy rain, put off until tomorrow or the next day after that. He rarely felt a sense of urgency surrounding anything he did. It was a lazy kind of life where things got done in their own time and no one seemed to care, as long as Master Gaborone was served without delay.

But everything was different now. He had a deadline, with the emphasis on *dead*. No task master except himself, this time, since Cooper had already shown his willingness to carry on alone. It wasn't teamwork or ambition driving Quinn to keep up with the soldier's tireless pace. Rather, he felt he owed it to himself.

And to the thousands who might die if he and Cooper failed.

There was a new sense of responsibility Quinn

hadn't felt before. With Gaborone, the prophet and his flock were all that mattered. Sinners in the outside world might be converted to the Process, but the vast majority who turned their backs on Gaborone were simply doomed. Their fate had been detailed in scripture long before Quinn's great-great-grandfather was born. He hadn't wept for those who saw the warning signs and chose the road to Hell with eyes wide open.

Now, Quinn thought the narrow, muddy half trail that he followed just might be the road to Hades of a sort. The heat was more or less what he'd expect from Satan's hideaway and half-seen rustling shapes that scuttled through the undergrowth reminded him of imps from Dante's crazed imagination. As for the fires of Hell, he guessed they still might sample those, if Cooper couldn't manage to defuse the Armageddon bomb.

Sometimes Quinn played the futile what-if game, imagining how life might be if he had never stopped to pass the time of day with Process members on his college campus in Wyoming. Who could have predicted that a simple conversation would lead Quinn into the heart of darkest Africa, slogging through rain-drenched jungle with an automatic rifle strapped across his back?

Who would've thought the quest for peace would leave him with blood on his hands?

Quinn didn't mourn the two men he had killed. Both would've done the same to him, given the chance. One had been rushing straight at him, in fact, and firing from the hip. Camacho would've finished Cooper in another moment, if Quinn hadn't cut him down, and where would he be then?

Right where he was. Lost in the rain.

Except he wasn't lost. Or, more correctly, *Cooper* wasn't lost. The soldier knew where they were going, had a fix on what he called their target, formerly Quinn's home. Quinn thought he'd been through happy times there, but he couldn't fix one in his mind right now. There had been work and conversations focused on the master, on some point of doctrine. Parables extolling sacrifice and labor for a common cause. Generic laughter over mishaps on a job, perhaps, but nothing more.

He'd been contented in the sense that livestock was supposed to be, grazing or dragging plows around in service of a species light-years more sophisticated than their own. If there were any memories of tenderness along the way, Quinn guessed they had to have slipped his mind.

He glanced up from the track and saw that Cooper had lengthened the distance between them. He was still in sight, but far enough ahead that Quinn would have to raise his voice for any kind of conversation. Not that Cooper was the chatty type, but still…

He grimaced, picking up the pace, jogging instead of walking as he closed the gap. Quinn never saw the root—vine, snake, whatever—that rolled underneath his right foot as he brought it down, the fresh mud acting like an oil slick. Falling, he had time to squawk before the world tilted and he found himself sliding down a chute of muck he hadn't even seen.

Where had it come from?

And where in hell was he going?

Quinn splashed down in a pool of water layered with moss and scum on top. It felt like oatmeal on his skin and smelled like sewage.

Leeches!

His first thought was of the creeping, slimy bloodsuckers, but they were driven from his mind when he attempted to stand. His feet thrashed uselessly beneath him, and the surface layer of algae rose two inches higher on his neck.

Quicksand.

Before the panic seized him, Quinn had time to call out Cooper's name.

GRIMALDI TOOK the sat phone from his pocket, checked its power level, then replaced it. He could go another six or seven hours with recharging it. If Bolan hadn't called within that time, he'd need to find someplace where he could bum or rent a wall socket and make sure that he didn't lose his one link to the jungle.

Sipping coffee didn't help Grimaldi's nerves, but it was all that he could think of at the moment to help kill the time. He wasn't hungry, didn't want to watch another movie that he couldn't understand. If there was sleeping to be done, he'd do it in his car, parked close enough for him to watch the rented whirlybird and chase off any other would-be flyers if the owner tried to double-deal him.

He had the information Bolan had requested on Pablo Camacho and Adnan Ibn Sharif, hot off the line from Stony Man, but he had no way to communicate it without calling Bolan, which he'd promised not to do. The knowledge he'd acquired made Jack more anxious than he'd been when Bolan simply had a cult to deal with, and until the warrior called him back he couldn't even vent.

Camacho was a ranking member of the Medellín cartel, megamillionaire with ties to narcoterrorism documented by the DEA and FBI. Grimaldi was surprised a dealer of his stature would fly halfway around the world to buy a bomb himself, when he had to have a small army of soldiers at his beck and call, but maybe it was understandable. Some thugs who fought their way up from the gutter to the pinnacles of crime retained a taste for handling the dirty work themselves. Coupled with a mistrust of others, it might be enough to put Camacho on the ground in Africa.

Whatever, he was there, together with his bankroll, and the Executioner would have to deal with him. God only knew what use Camacho might have for a nuclear warhead, but any way Grimaldi tried to study it, the outlook ranged from bleak to pretty freaking grim.

Adnan Ibn Sharif was something else, entirely. Where Camacho was a mercenary hoodlum in designer threads, Sharif was rated as a die-hard zealot. He'd been working to destroy the state of Israel since he quit school in the seventh grade, attached to paramilitary groups including Black September and Hamas. He led his own faction these days, the Lance of God. It was less sophisticated than al Qaeda, but Sharif had tapped a well of Saudi cash that kept his troops in guns and ammo.

Now, it seemed, he was prepared to splurge.

Whether the Congo bomb was earmarked for a date with Bogotá or Tel Aviv, Grimaldi knew Bolan would do his best to stop it cold.

But would his best be good enough this time?

Grimaldi understood that second-guessing Bolan was a waste of time. He wasn't on-site to assess the situation, didn't know how many opposition troops were standing in his old friend's way, or whether he'd get any help at all from Patrick Quinn. There were too many variables, and he had no way inside the game.

Unless the phone rang.

Only then could Grimaldi attempt to assist his best friend. Assuming it was not too late.

In that case, he supposed, Brognola and the crew at Stony Man would find another way to go. Grimaldi guessed that wheels were turning even now, behind the scene, to deal with any possibility of failure. No one had expected Bolan to discover nukes in Africa, but once the threat was recognized, action would follow.

Grimaldi supposed that, if that happened, he'd be frozen out of it, but he might still have a surprise or two in store for those who pulled his strings. If Bolan didn't come back from the jungle this time, the pilot had made a promise to himself.

Payback was never pretty, but it could be satisfying.

If he was too late to help Bolan and Quinn, he might not be too late to settle up the score. A little one-on-one with guru Gaborone, perhaps.

For the first time in hours, he remembered how to smile.

THE CRY BROUGHT Bolan back. He'd missed Quinn's fall, another bit of wet noise in the pelting rain, but heard the young man's voice and doubled back to see what had become of him. The slope down which he'd tumbled was a muddy ramp with gnarled roots jutting out of it at random, thick vines training from the trees that loomed above. Bolan peered through the murk and saw Quinn floundering in water topped with slime.

"Can you get out of there?" he called to Quinn.

A single sputtered word came back. "Quicksand!"

Instead of racing down to feed the pit, Bolan reviewed his options. He had rope coiled in his pack, or he could trust the trees and creepers already in place to hold his weight. Whichever way he went, it was a fact that some trees in the rain forest had shallow roots and toppled easily, crushing whatever stood in front of them when they fell. There'd be no way to change his mind when he was halfway down the slope, so Bolan used a precious moment to be sure at the beginning.

"Hurry!" Quinn burbled.

"Hold still!" Bolan commanded. "Try to float. Don't fight it."

"Easy…you…say."

"Save your breath. I'm coming down."

He used the rope, tied it around a tree and threw his weight against it twice. The roots held fast—so far.

Approaching the quicksand, he saw that Quinn was buried to his neck, with green smears of the upper muck layer plastered to his cheeks. One hand protruded from the quagmire, and his rifle stock was barely visible behind his bobbing head.

"You may need both hands for the rope," Bolan said.

Quinn craned his neck. "You told me not to move."

"Grab with your right hand first, then raise the left."

He tossed the rope's free end to Quinn, missing his face by inches. Muddy fingers clasped it, and the muck seethed briefly as Quinn shifted, then his left hand broke the surface, lunged and gripped the rope.

"All right, hang on."

"I'm trying!"

Bolan started walking backward from the quicksand pit, heels digging in for traction in the mud. He put his back into it, hauling deadweight from the bog's death grip. Quinn tried to help, kicking against the muck and water, but he seemed to make no forward progress.

Finally, by inches, Quinn regained a semblance of dry land. The rain had stopped again, no shower from the sky to wash him clean as he knelt panting on all fours, the AK-47 plastered to his back.

"You'll need to clean that weapon and those magazines," Bolan informed him.

"Can it wait a minute, till I catch my breath."

"Take all the time you need," Bolan replied. "But bear in mind that if another gang of trackers catch you this way, you're defenseless."

"Great. That's perfect."

Wearily, Quinn slipped the rifle's sling and bandoliers over his head. "You want to show me how to do this?" he asked Bolan. "Seems I missed that day in boot camp."

Bolan might've smiled at that, in other circumstances, but he felt the weight of fleeting time upon his shoulders, threatening to crush him if he stood still any longer than was absolutely necessary. Still, Quinn couldn't strip an unfamiliar weapon without guidance, and it didn't serve their common interest to leave the youth unarmed.

"All right," he said, kneeling across from Quinn. "I'll do this once. Next time's on you. We don't have any way to dry it off, but we can get it clean. I have an oiler you can use. It shouldn't rust before we reach Obike, anyway."

"I'm ready," Quinn replied.

"Not yet," Bolan said. "But you're getting there."

CHAPTER FOURTEEN

Jomo Tekle felt the burden of his new responsibility as a physical weight on his shoulders, heavier by far than the backpack and bandoliers he wore. The men spread out behind him on the trail were watching him, he felt it, waiting for their new commander to do something wrong, make some mistake that might unseat him.

It was Tekle's right to lead the search, he being next in rank and in seniority among the master's bodyguards, but he had never seriously thought that it would ever come to this. Nico Mbarga was a man of strength, endurance and intelligence, Samburu Changa much the same. Who could predict that both of them would be eliminated in a single day, leaving Jomo Tekle in charge?

Perhaps the master might've seen it coming, but if so, he hadn't bothered warning Tekle. It was a rude surprise, not altogether welcome, when the mantle had been thrust upon him, with an order to collect a team, find out what had gone wrong with Mbarga's search and fix it.

There was talk around Obike of disaster in the making, and while Tekle didn't pay attention to such gossip as a rule, he knew that parts of what he'd heard were true. The master's helicopter *had* gone off somewhere yesterday with five men in it, all of them his friends, and it had not returned. Mbarga *had* reported finding Changa and his people dead, before his own team broke contact. There *had* been a desperate radio message that morning, the Arab in Master Gaborone's airship, pleading for landing coordinates, then nothing.

It was Tekle's bad luck to get his big break just when all those before him had failed. He would be in the spotlight now, and he had no one to consult on strategy. He couldn't even ask his former commanders what mistakes they'd made, since both of them were dead.

Officially, the master thought Mbarga still might be searching for the white boy and his mystery companion, but Tekle had seen the grim truth in Gaborone's eyes. He'd written off Mbarga and the others as lost, no matter what his lips might say. Tekle was being sent to find their killers and avenge them, not in any hope of finding them alive.

Where to begin?

The trail led south, that much he knew. Tekle had picked a hunter whom he trusted, and the man was on a scent, rushing along the trail cut by Mbarga's party when it left Obike the previous day. Despite sporadic rain, the trail had been no great challenge to find or follow. As to whether it would lead them anywhere, Tekle reserved judgment until he reached the other end.

How many enemies were waiting for him there? Who were they? Why had they decided to attack the Process now?

He couldn't answer any of those questions, but his eight-man team was well-armed, eager to avenge the insults that their adversaries had inflicted. He didn't know where Patrick Quinn stood in the matter, but Tekle had vowed to take no chances with him, where his soldiers and his own life were concerned.

Unfortunately, Tekle's team was starting out a day behind the others, covering old ground. They would presumably pass through the village where Changa's party was slaughtered, but unless the villagers had come back home to roost, what would he gain from that?

Nothing.

Beyond that point, the trail would lead him…somewhere. Mbarga's men had found the helicopter, tried to use it in their search, but something had gone wrong. Tekle assumed the bird had crashed for want of fuel. As for Mbarga and his men, they'd simply broken off contact, no threat described, no explanation offered.

Would he find them in the jungle, dead? And if so, would the killers still be waiting with the corpses? Tekle thought it most unlikely, but he couldn't rule it out. And if the slayers had moved on once more, how would he find them?

Trust the tracker.

Tekle much preferred to trust himself, but he was now in unfamiliar territory, tramping over ground he'd never walked before, searching for enemies he'd never seen. They could be bandits, rebels, even agents of the government in Brazzaville.

But why would they choose this time to attack?

Tekle believed that he could answer that question, at least. The foreigners whom Master Gaborone had welcomed in Obike had to have brought this trouble down upon their heads, first the Americans with cameras, then the Arab and Colombian with money in their pockets. If they hadn't—

Tekle caught himself before the thought went any further. He was dangerously close to criticizing Master Gaborone, if only in his mind, and that was heresy. He needed all the spiritual strength that he could get right now, and challenging the master was no way to reach that goal.

Better to trust him and obey, Tekle decided.

At least until that course of action proved too perilous.

BOLAN RECHECKED the GPS set, pleased to find that they were still on track. Another seven weary miles and change still separated them from Gaborone's compound, but they should make it short of sundown, if they had no more encounters with quicksand or crocodiles along the way.

What, then?

He already had Quinn's description of the building where he'd seen the bomb deposited. Upon arrival, he'd have Quinn confirm which hut he meant, then they would wait for nightfall to begin their probe. Bolan wanted to leave Quinn in the forest, covering his back if that was possible. Above all, keeping him from being underfoot when trouble started.

And it *would* start. That was certain. Bolan had no reason to believe that he could creep into the village, find and penetrate a certain hut, neuter Gaborone's destructive cargo, then slip out again without attracting some attention to himself. It would be nice if he could don some magic cloak and disappear, complete his business as a ghost, but that was not to be.

With more than seven hundred souls residing in Obike, Bolan knew he stood a decent chance of meeting someone, coming or going. Waiting until the middle of the night would help, when most of the inhabitants should be asleep, but Bolan also knew there was a chance that recent incidents would have the camp on red alert, its people wide awake and ready to defend themselves.

In which case it could be a massacre.

Most of the villagers would be untrained and probably unarmed, except for knives or other simple tools they might convert to weapons in a pinch. That made them dangerous, but they weren't his primary opponents.

Not until they interposed themselves between him and his goal.

In that case, if they menaced him and jeopardized his mission, he would do what had to be done. If Gaborone's disciples weren't enemies per se, neither were they entirely innocent. They'd chosen Gaborone and his bizarre ideas as models for their lives—and like

Quinn, they'd raised no objections when their master slaughtered Rathbun's party to preserve the secrets of his hideaway. Some of them doubtless knew about the Armageddon package and were fine with that, as well.

Not innocent. But neither were they Bolan's usual targets, predators who'd stepped so far beyond the pale that their elimination was a favor to humankind. They were deluded, possibly demented in some cases, but they weren't the enemy.

At least until they cast themselves as such.

A movement on the trail ahead of Bolan stopped him dead. The Executioner crouched and froze, staring across the Steyr's sights into a world of lurking shadows where he had no friends. Behind him, Quinn began to ask a question, then bit off the words.

Bolan was ready for the movement when it came again, closer this time, and somewhat farther to his right. He recognized the human form, the weapon clasped against its chest.

Another scout, but whose? Could he and Quinn afford to wait to see if this patrol bypassed them, unaware? He weighed the risk, and in the time it took for him to formulate an answer, Bolan saw the point man turn to meet his gaze.

It wasn't recognition in the other's eyes, because they'd never met or even glimpsed each other heretofore. But he *saw* Bolan, saw the peril to himself and those he led. If he could see the AUG, the point man had to know his time was up, and still he tried to gain the upper hand.

Bolan was ready when his target spun to face him more directly, leveling his AK-47. It was all he needed, an excuse to squeeze the Steyr's trigger and dispatch a 3-round burst to close the distance. Grim-faced, Bolan watched his target fall, while he knelt, waiting for the other gunmen to reveal themselves.

A moment later hell exploded just in front of him and sent him lunging facedown to the earth.

THE FIRST SHOTS triggered Jomo Tekle's instinct for self-preservation. Without waiting to learn their source or direction, he triggered a burst from his rifle and threw himself behind the nearest tree. His only true concerns just then, in order of importance, were to save himself and spare their tracker.

Everyone was firing by the time he got his wits about him. Tekle slid into a prone position, risked a glance around the tree and ducked back as a bullet gouged the bark six inches from his face.

Incoming, that had been, from somewhere up ahead. He hadn't seen a muzzle-flash, there'd been no time for that, but reaching cautiously around the tree to probe the furrow with a fingertip he made out the approximate direction of the bullet's travel.

That accounted for one shooter, if he didn't move, but how many others were waiting to spring out with weapons and threaten his men? Threaten *him?*

Tekle called out the tracker's name and heard no answer. It was possible the point man hadn't heard him, with the racket going on, or that he feared to reveal his position by speaking, but Tekle feared that he was dead. The first shots had been fired near the head of the column. Who else would a sniper engage but the point man?

Tekle cursed through clenched teeth, furious. If he emerged victorious from the ambush but lost his tracker, how could he proceed? He'd grown up in the slums of Brazzaville, and while he'd later spent time in the countryside, he wasn't native to the rain forest by any means. His tracking skills were minimal, and Tekle wasn't sure he had another man among his chosen soldiers who could lead them to find Nico's team.

Amid the hammering of automatic weapons, Tekle had a sudden thought. It seemed improbable that three patrols from Obike, all probing southward, would be ambushed by different enemies within a span of twenty-four hours. Rather, Tekle decided that their foes had to be the same or, at most, different units of one single force.

He fired a burst around the tree, felt better for it even though he had no target, and ducked back again. Something eluded him. Some aspect of the problem that—

He had it!

Changa's force had been annihilated farther south, and Mbarga's team had found their bodies, pressing on from there before contact was lost. To ambush Tekle's team, it meant the enemy was heading north.

They were advancing toward Obike!

Tekle didn't have the radio. He'd detailed Oko Koroli to carry it, and now he'd lost track of him, as with the others. They'd scattered around him, all firing at shadows, but calling to Koroli would only draw fire to himself.

Tekle sat trembling with frustration and the urgency that gripped him. If their enemies were moving toward Obike and the master, they could easily have split their forces to surround the village. Tekle couldn't take for granted that his adversaries of the moment were the *only* hostile soldiers in the area. And that made warning Master Gaborone even more urgent in his mind.

But where had Koroli gone?

Tekle tried whispering his name, but couldn't even hear himself above the gunfire. When he spoke it in a normal tone, the end result was much the same. At last, in desperation, he hunched down and called, "Oko! Oko Koroli! Answer me!"

The voice came back from somewhere to his left. "I'm here!"

Another straining look showed Tekle nothing. "Oko! I can't see you! Signal for me!"

It took courage, Tekle knew that, but at last an arm was raised to fan the air some forty yards due west. He couldn't make out the man's face at that range, but he reckoned no one else would risk drawing more fire just to deceive him.

He considered calling Koroli to join him, but the shouted order would pin a special target on the radio man. Likewise, he couldn't call across the battlefield for him to alert the master, since that order would be overheard and might bring forward some other punitive reaction, possibly accelerating the attack upon their village.

Tekle's only choice was one he dreaded, but he could find no way to avoid it. He had to go to the radio man, do his best to make it there alive and thus warn Master Gaborone of danger moving toward him through the jungle.

Taking a deep breath, Tekle burst from cover, running for his life and everything he valued in the world.

QUINN SAW THE RUNNER moving, raised his AK-47 smoothly and remembered what Cooper had told him about leading moving targets. How far should he aim ahead?

He chose a point and fired, sweeping his rifle left-to-right while his target ran right-to-left. He couldn't swear that it had worked, but something happened with the runner, tripping him it seemed, so that the moving figure staggered, stumbled, fell.

Quinn felt like cheering for an instant, till it hit him that he might've killed another human being, and the shout died in his throat. It would've been a bad idea, regardless, since the other riflemen were firing at him now, driving him back and under cover of a rotting log. Bullets sprayed bark and pulp around him, but they couldn't reach him in his hidey-hole.

Of course, he couldn't reach them, either. If he meant to be of any further help to Cooper, he would have to move, get out and mix it up with their opponents. Dropping one man hardly counted, even if he *was* responsible for knocking down the runner. From the sound of it, there were at least another six or seven guns against them, keeping them from where they had to be.

The bomb was waiting.

But he had to sweep these men aside to reach it.

Quinn started crawling to his left, westward, behind the massive log. He didn't know where Cooper was, exactly, but the sharp sound of his weapon came from somewhere to the east, behind Quinn. Separating was a good idea, he reckoned, since it would prevent the enemy from dropping both of them at once.

How odd it was to think of other Process members as "the enemy," but was Quinn even counted as a member of the sect today? Had Gaborone already stricken his name from the rolls in one of the periodic shaming ceremonies he used to flay defectors in absentia?

And if he had, what difference did it make?

The gunmen ranged before Quinn clearly meant to kill him without knowing who he was. They wouldn't stop to question him and might not recognize or understand him even if he started shouting out his name. If he was going to survive and help Cooper defuse the Armageddon bomb, Quinn knew he'd have to kill them first.

Again, the thought dismayed him.

But it didn't slow him.

He circled farther to his left, trying to work his way around and flank the Process shooters. If he could surprise one of them, maybe two, it would reduce the odds that Cooper had to deal with and increase their chances of survival. Cooper wouldn't count on him to do much more than hold his ground, so any extra contribution would surprise the grim-faced soldier, even as it served their cause.

Quinn wasn't much at woodcraft, creeping silently through clinging undergrowth, but gunfire covered any sounds he made while sneaking awkwardly around the far end of the battleground. He stayed low, moving in a crouch that cramped his thighs and lower back, hoping none of his enemies would turn in his direction, glimpse him and alert the others. Homing on erratic muzzle-flashes, Quinn advanced with all the caution he could manage, hoping Cooper had a better plan.

The rifleman surprised him, springing upright from a clump of ferns and weeds directly in his path. Quinn gasped and squeezed his AK-47's trigger in reflexive action, hammering a burst into the wide-eyed stranger's chest. It was enough to put him down, but not before the falling gunman fired a short burst of his own.

He nearly missed.

Quinn heard and felt two of the bullets ripple past his face, before a third clipped his left shoulder, gouging deep, half spinning him. He gasped a wordless cry of pain, aware that he was falling, but he couldn't catch himself. Quinn landed on his wounded shoulder, squealed once more and twitched over onto his back.

It took a moment for him to assess the damage, realizing that his arm and shoulder weren't disabled, though the bloody furrow etched into his flesh bled freely and produced dull waves of nauseating pain. Quinn clenched his teeth and moved the arm, groaning, until he satisfied himself that it would function on command.

He waited, then, to find out if his adversary had survived, but nothing stirred in front of him in the undergrowth. After another moment, he could see two feet protruding from the ferns. His eyes picked out a small hole in the sole of one athletic shoe.

Rising, Quinn clenched his wounded shoulder, drew his hand back bloody from the touch and wiped it on his pants.

He'd have to stop the bleeding soon, but first he had to see what he could do in Cooper's aid. Too many of their enemies were still alive and well, still firing in the night at shadows they mistook for human beings.

Let's just keep it that way, Quinn silently implored as he crept forward, seeking prey. Just give me one more chance to do it right.

Another chance to trim the odds was all he craved.

It didn't sound like much to ask.

THREE SHOOTERS REMAINED, by Bolan's count, but they were scattered on a front spanning some thirty yards. It didn't sound like much, but in the jungle thirty feet could mark the outer range of visibility, and covering three times that distance in a rush would leave him vulnerable to triangulated fire.

He'd have to take his adversaries one by one, and try not to alert the others while he did it. One way or another, Bolan knew he couldn't leave the field while they were still alive.

He thought briefly of Quinn, wondered where he had gone, but there was nothing he could do about that now, no profit from allowing the distraction to divert his full attention from the task at hand. Alive or dead, Quinn was beyond his reach, beyond his help, until Bolan had dealt with his remaining enemies.

He closed in on the nearest of them, stealthy movements calculated to produce a minimum of sound. Ferns whispered as he passed, but no one with the sounds of battle ringing in his ears would notice. With any luck at all, the soldiers sweating over guns and praying to survive the next few minutes wouldn't hear him coming for them.

Not until it was too late.

He didn't draw his knife this time, uncertain whether he'd get close enough to use it, but he set the Steyr for semiauto fire, to keep the noise down and preserve his ammunition. One shot was as good as three or four, if placed correctly, and he didn't plan to miss.

When he had closed the gap between himself and his first target to some twenty feet, Bolan eased down against the gnarled roots of an ancient tree and found his mark. The gunman had no clue that he was framed in Bolan's sights, rising to fire short bursts away to southward, ducking back again, and then repeating the procedure every ten or fifteen seconds.

Bolan waited for the mark to rise again, the AK-47 spitting fire, before he stroked the trigger of his AUG and drilled the nameless gunner's skull. It was a clean shot, in and out, dropping the lifeless body like a sack of laundry in the weeds.

One down.

He moved on, creeping like a primal thing, which in a sense he was. The jungle welcomed predators. They helped maintain its balance, culling out the weak and ill.

Sometimes they culled the evil, too.

His second mark was crouched behind a log, firing less frequently now that his own gun and one other were the only weapons still in active play. Where were the others? Bolan had disposed of three, but that left two still unaccounted for. He wondered whether Quinn had dealt with them, or if the others had devised a strategy to wait him out and spring from cover when he next revealed himself.

He circled left around his latest target's flank and found a spot to watch and kill from. A moment later his eyes picked out the human outline from its leafy background, making sure his all-important first shot didn't miss.

He might not get another, and it wouldn't matter where Quinn was, alive or dead, if Bolan was eliminated. That would be the endgame, with no instant replays, no time-outs or second chances.

It was do-or-die time, and he didn't plan to be the one who died.

The mark was moving, rising to his knees. Bolan had all he needed in the way of target, lining up and squeezing off his shot from fifteen feet. The hit was clean and solid, square between the stranger's shoulder blades. It pitched him forward, draped him across the log he'd used for shelter.

The third man had to have been advancing just as Bolan was, but in the opposite direction, for he burst from cover and rushed the Executioner, his AK-47 lighting up the night. Bolan recoiled, triggered two rapid shots that missed their mark, and rolled out to his left in search of cover.

As he found it, the soldier heard a second AK join the action, both guns hammering away in tandem for a second, maybe two, before silence descended on the forest once again. He waited, counting off four heartbeats, then leaned out to risk a look across the killing ground.

Quinn stood over the man he'd killed, sweeping the field with haunted eyes. By moonlight, Bolan saw the blood jet-black against his khaki sleeve.

"You're hit," he said, rising.

Quinn blinked at him and shrugged as he replied, "You ought to see the other guy."

CHAPTER FIFTEEN

Perhaps the radio was cursed.

Ahmadou Gaborone didn't believe it, though his ancestors might have. Still, it was a convenient explanation for the way his people seemed to disappear almost as soon as they left camp. One or two radio contacts, and then they were gone.

Jomo Tekle was the latest, vanished from the air, *into* thin air, without a trace or hint of what had happened to him. First Nico Mbarga, then Samburu Changa and the helicopter, and now this.

Flustered and frightened, Gaborone had to count up the losses on his fingers. Seventeen of his own trusted men, plus his two foreign buyers, Camacho and Sharif. The loss not only weakened his security, cutting his private army by one-third, it also spoiled his larger plans.

At least for now.

Gaborone hadn't reached his present position—humble in appearance, but wealthy in dollars and influence—by giving up the first time he met with adversity. If that were the case, he'd never have left Africa for the brave new world of America. He wouldn't have some 750 loyal disciples in Obike, with at least two thousand more scattered around the globe. He wouldn't be a close friend of important men in Brazzaville.

And he would not be on the verge of making Armageddon real.

A key mistake his adversaries often made was taking Gaborone for just another huckster, one more in the endless line of preachers with their hands out, peddling salvation at so much per head and skimming whatever they could for themselves. When they saw Gaborone in that light, they made a critical mistake.

He enjoyed living well, absolutely, though no one visiting his quarters in Obike would suspect he was a multimillionaire. Much of his income had been carefully invested—in precious metals, gems, selected real estate that likely wouldn't suffer greatly in the Final Days.

He would emerge from the Apocalypse a leader among men, entitled to their adoration, living like the kind he was. And all because he understood the word.

All because he *believed*.

A major weakness of the so-called "moral" leaders, whether Christian or Muslim, was that they paid lip service to holy writ while stealing with both hands. They spoke in glowing terms of Allah or Jehovah, Christ or Yahweh, but they never really counted on a reckoning, in this life or the next.

For them, religion was a means of gaining or maintaining power. But for Gaborone it was the truth. He knew that Armageddon and the Final Days lay waiting for humankind. He knew it and was ready to accelerate the process in accordance with God's plan.

But now a snare was laid before him. He was being tested, and the form of his response might change the course of human history. If he failed now, who else would lift the torch and carry on his holy work?

Gaborone had already decided that he would waste no more men searching the jungle. He had thirty-five bodyguards left, plus weapons for more of his people if they were attacked. He wouldn't distribute them yet, he decided, since most were untrained and the mere act of passing out guns would disturb them, pushing the community closer to panic.

Thus far, Gaborone thought that most of his sheep were still unaware of the losses he'd suffered. They knew of the fires yesterday, and the patrols that he'd dispatched, and while some might be speaking of soldiers who left camp and never returned, the words hadn't yet reached his ears. Gaborone trusted his guards and his selected spies to keep him instantly informed of discontent within Obike. If the mood turned mutinous he'd know about it, and he would respond with platitudes or force, whichever seemed appropriate.

He hadn't worked this long and hard to let a handful

of sob sisters ruin everything. Before that happened, he would see them all in hell.

But preferably not this day.

His plan, for now, was simply this: to guard the village and to wait. If Jomo Tekle's hunters broke their silence or returned to camp, he would find out what they had seen. If they didn't return, as Gaborone now felt might be the case, he would be ready with his soldiers for whatever move their enemies should make against the village.

And while they waited, he would think about the disposition of his special merchandise.

It did him no good in Obike, did the Lord no good at all until it was employed as God intended. Why were men allowed to build weapons of mass destruction, if those weapons weren't a part of God's eternal plan? This weapon in particular would play a grand historic role—if he could find the proper ally soon, to take it off his hands.

He didn't care who used the bomb or what cause they espoused. All that mattered was the timing and location, the inevitable chain reaction one explosion could ignite. From that point onward, no one could subvert God's master plan. It only took a willing hand to set the primer charge.

And if he couldn't find one, Gaborone had already decided, he might have to do the job himself.

Not that he planned to watch the mushroom from ground zero. God forbid. But it would be his finger on the trigger, and the Lord would know it when He came into His glory. Gaborone would be rewarded for his part in helping bring the prophecy to life.

And on that day, he would be king of all the Earth.

THE SHRILL SOUND of the sat phone jarred Grimaldi from uneasy sleep. He'd barely closed his eyes, not even meaning to, but now the sound revived him like a jolt of pure adrenaline. He answered on the second ring, breathless.

"I'm here."

"We're not," Bolan replied. "We've got a ways to go yet."

"What's the holdup?" Grimaldi asked.

"Opposition on the trail. We handled it, but my associate's been winged."

"I need to get you out of there right now," Grimaldi said.

"Can't do it. If we leave the merchandise behind, no telling where it might show up tomorrow or next week. Nobody wins that game."

"Stand down and blow the whistle, then, why don't you? Brazzaville won't take it lying down. And if they do, we'll go to the UN."

"No time," Bolan said. "Any full-scale move would only push the plunger. I need to get in and fix it first, before the clock runs down."

Grimaldi didn't like to play the devil's advocate, but he asked anyway. "Are you equipped for that?"

"Let's hope so."

"Okay, then," Grimaldi said. "I got that background on the buyers you were looking for."

"Camacho's out," Bolan informed him brusquely. "What about Sharif?"

Grimaldi blanked out all he learned about Camacho's role in the Colombian cartel and shifted gears. "Adnan Ibn Sharif is Palestinian. He came up through the PLO and Black September, as you might expect. Today he heads the Lance of God. Supposedly, they're based in Syria, but Saudis pay most of their bills. He's not Osama yet, but with a package like the one you're looking for, he could be, and then some."

"I'll keep an eye open," Bolan said.

"What's your ETA?" Grimaldi asked.

"Four hours, give or take. There's no way to predict how long we'll be tied up in town."

Or whether you'll get out alive, Grimaldi thought, immediately wishing that he hadn't. It was always there, lurking in some dark corner of his mind, but there was nothing to be gained by voicing it out loud.

Instead he told the Executioner, "So I'll just wait then, till I hear from you again."

"Sorry," Bolan said. "If I had a way to pin it down—"

"I know. Forget about it? Just call me when you're ready for a lift. We never close."

He got a laugh for that, and it surprised him. He imagined Bolan standing in the jungle, Quinn somewhere around him nursing bloody wounds, and then the big guy smiled. He *laughed.*

Grimaldi would've given everything he owned to be there with his friend, but that wasn't the role he'd been assigned to play.

"I'll be in touch," Bolan assured him.

"Right. I'll see you then."

"I'll see you," came the echo, and the line went dead.

Four hours to the village, if they didn't meet more opposition on the way, and then the party would begin in earnest. If they'd had coordinates worked out, Grimaldi could've lifted off before he got the call. Two hours and a half, say, maybe three, to put him on the scene as soon as possible.

But Bolan wouldn't hear of it. He didn't want Grimaldi out there on his own, exposed, if anything went wrong. That was the way he looked ahead, thinking of others first. It was the reason that he risked his life on missions others wouldn't touch. For Val. For old times' sake. Or for the whole damned human race.

Grimaldi couldn't jump the gun, because he didn't know where Bolan would be waiting for him when the smoke cleared, and he'd do more harm than good if he picked out the wrong LZ.

All he could do was sit and wait, be ready to fly when the call came. Ready to fight and die beside his friend when he was summoned.

"SO, HOW'S THE SHOULDER?" Bolan asked.

"It's fine," Quinn answered. When he raised his arm to prove it, though, a jolt of pain lanced through his shoulder and across his chest. He couldn't hide the grimace, even as he muttered, "Like I said, it's fine."

"Be careful with it," Bolan said. "Those stitches aren't the best."

They felt all right to Quinn, considering that Cooper had sewn up his shoulder without anesthetic, giving him four lousy aspirin for the pain while he was working. Quinn had clenched his teeth around the canvas strap of his ammo bandolier, tasting his own sweat and maybe someone else's while he moaned and muttered through the operation, fat tears streaming down his dirty face.

And he'd been proud when it was over, that he'd managed not to scream.

There'd likely be a scar, Cooper had told him, but he didn't mind. It would be something he could show his wife, assuming that he ever found one. Something for their kids to ask about, if they had any. And grandkids, maybe, too. Quinn could sit back and tell them all about the time when he was young and stupid, when he bought into a pipe dream and it nearly got himself killed.

All that, of course, presumed that in the end it wouldn't get him killed, and at the moment that was far from certain. Six more inches and the bullet that had scarred his shoulder could've drilled his heart, maybe ripped into his lung and left Quinn drowning in his own blood.

The hasty bid to kill him hadn't worked, this time, but Quinn knew there'd be others waiting for him, either on the trail or in Obike. They were still outnumbered and outgunned, though after watching Cooper work, Quinn wouldn't say they were outclassed.

But class was one thing. Breathing was another.

Everybody died, and every fast gun met a faster one

someday. He'd learned that from the Westerns he had watched while growing up. One man could take out half a dozen on a lucky day, but it was different when he faced down thirty-five or forty, much less seven hundred plus.

Quinn might've led a sheltered life before he joined the Process, but he could still spot killer odds. And Obike, he knew, was likely to be the end of their trail in more ways than one.

"I'm ready," he told Cooper. "We should go."

"Agreed." The soldier had his pack on and his rifle slung, all ready for the next phase of their march.

"Was that good news?" Quinn asked him. "On the phone?"

"It was…informative," Bolan replied. "I wouldn't say it helped our situation."

"So, it's still just the two of us."

"That's right."

"Maybe we should avoid the hunting parties for a while and save our strength. You know, be ready for the main event and all that."

"I'm with you." Cooper surprised him with the bare suggestion of a smile. "Let's see if we can pull it off."

The march resumed. Quinn knew it had to be midday, but he couldn't use the sun to help him guess the time more closely, since the great trees hid it from his view. Two hundred feet below the canopy, there was a kind of twilight broken only in those clearings where light poured down in a golden flood, reminding Quinn of illustrations from an old-time Bible.

They'd been rain-free for the past two hours, and Quinn hoped that it would stay that way, to let his clothes dry. He was tired of feeling clammy all the time, between his perspiration and the intermittent drizzle from above. Sweating made him feel dirty, and the rain somehow had failed to wash him clean.

He wondered now, trudging along the narrow jungle track, when he'd feel clean again, if ever. Did the blood wash off, or would he always see its dark stain on his hands? And if this trip was any indication of his life, how did his escort live with all the men he'd killed?

Too many questions.

Quinn concentrated on his footsteps, welcoming the dull pain in his shoulder as a distraction from conscious thought. They'd reach Obike soon enough, and he'd be tested once again.

Quinn prayed he wouldn't fail this time.

KUMI KWABENA WAS nervous, and not without reason. He'd been summoned to the master's presence, told to drop whatever he was doing and to come at once. As one of Master Gaborone's handpicked bodyguards, he knew that could only mean trouble.

So, what else was new?

They'd had nothing but trouble the whole past two days. First fires in the village, then one of the white boys went missing, and three teams of searchers had gone out to find him.

But none had come back.

Kwabena hadn't given up on Jomo Tekle's hunting

party yet, but he knew Samburu Changa's men were dead, and he believed Nico Mbarga's team had met the same fate, somewhere in the jungle to the south. A summons now most likely meant that *he* had been selected as the next team leader, the next human sacrifice, and suddenly Kwabena wasn't quite as zealous in the master's service as he had been moments earlier.

The thought shamed him, or should have, but Kwabena didn't want to throw his life away for nothing. He had pledged himself to Master Gaborone and to the Process, vowing that he would defend both to the death, but there was something sinister and terrifying in the way his friends had lately vanished into nothingness.

The day before he'd stood and watched Mbarga's team depart, and did the same for Tekle's squad that very morning. There were dangers in the forest, certainly, and human enemies, as well, but never in Obike's history had armed men simply disappeared without a trace.

They knew that Changa's team was dead, of course, because Mbarga had found them and reported back. That was before he'd lost contact and strange panicky messages had come in from the Arab visitor, replacing Danso Beira at the helm of Master Gaborone's helicopter.

The bird was gone, too. Perhaps crashed, lost forever.

Now it was Kwabena's turn, and while he feared the orders Master Gaborone might give him, he still couldn't bring himself to cut and run.

A guard outside the master's quarters recognized him, snapping to attention. That was strange enough, in itself, since he was only a corporal, and newly promoted at that. It shocked him to think that he might be the highest-ranking bodyguard remaining in the village.

For the first time since he'd joined the Process, recognition struck Kwabena as a curse.

He knocked and waited to be summoned inside. Lights powered by one of their generators burned inside the bungalow, a privilege of leadership, since most Obike residents made do with lamps and candles. It was daylight still, but barely in the master's quarters, since he had the blinds drawn. Kwabena saw him sitting in the corner farthest from the door, and faced that direction as he bowed.

"Master, you called for me?

"I did." The voice was weary, like the master's sagging face. "You are aware of our most recent difficulties, I assume?"

"Yes, sir."

"It seems that Jomo Tekle and his men are lost to us, as well. I am not certain of it, but the signs are bad. The team has broken contact and we cannot raise them on the radio. They do not answer calls on any frequency."

The words were out almost before Kwabena knew he meant to speak. "What can I do, Master?"

"My faithful servant." Gaborone's lips twitched, as if in feeble imitation of a smile. "You have been recently promoted, I believe?"

"Yes, sir. To corporal."

"I name you captain now," Gaborone said, "and place you in command of my remaining bodyguards."

"But, sir—"

"You feel unequal to the task? Perhaps you wish to nominate another for the post?"

"No, Master!"

"Good. I know how anxious you must be to find out what has happened to your comrades."

"Yes, sir." A bitter lie, between clenched teeth.

"But I'm afraid we cannot spare you for another fruitless search just now," Gaborone said. "We must secure our own defenses first, make sure Obike is not vulnerable to intrusion from outside."

Kwabena coasted on a wave of sweet relief. "Yes, sir! I have some thoughts on how to make the village more secure. We can—"

The master raised a hand to silence him. "Better to show than to explain, Captain. Command your men and do your best. We may face danger soon."

"I will send three more men at once to guard your quarters, Master."

"Yes, a capital idea. By all means do so, and be quick about it. We may soon face danger in our very streets."

"Yes, sir!"

With a salute, he fled the master's presence, thrilled where he had been afraid short moments earlier. Promoted once again, and to the leadership of Master Gaborone's elite army!

Granted, the thirty-odd men who remained weren't much of an army, but Kwabena reckoned he could pad the ranks with able-bodied villagers and get the force back up to fighting strength. If there was trouble on the way, it wouldn't take him by surprise.

The master trusted him.

Kumi Kwabena wouldn't let the great man down.

ADNAN IBN SHARIF WAS fairly sure that he had not reached Paradise. Despite his years of service to God, the blood of enemies that he had shed in his jihad against Israel and all its allies, he had somehow missed the great reward that should've automatically been his at death.

Where was the milk and honey? Where, oh where, were the succulent virgins he'd dreamed of on so many nights in his cold, lonely tent?

Sharif was hanging upside down, his head throbbing from its impact with some solid object, warm blood dripping from his lacerated scalp. In front of him, the world was blurry and shot through with jagged cracks, as if his eyes were shattered. An oppressive heat enveloped him, and odors that he couldn't place at first.

If this was hell, why did it smell of motor oil?

He remembered the crash, then, shifting cautiously in his inverted seat before new flares of pain forced him to stop. Also, there was a creaking sound he didn't like and for a moment it had felt as if the whole world tilted, maybe slipped a little toward the brink of some unseen abyss.

Unseen.

His vision cleared by slow degrees, until Sharif knew he was staring through the helicopter's bubble windscreen. It had cracked and buckled when they nosed into the jungle canopy, but seemingly had stopped short of imploding when the helicopter had flipped over on its back. They had to have settled sometime after he was knocked unconscious, for Sharif could see no sky ahead of him or to either side. He was immersed in leafy green on every side, suspended in a web of vines and groaning branches.

Cautiously, he turned to look for his companion, then remembered how the African had leaped to meet his death as they went down. He had to laugh at that, a quick snort of contempt. The fool had killed himself for nothing, while Sharif survived.

But for how long?

The chopper slipped again, bringing the Arab's heart into his throat. He knew that he had to get out soon, and somehow make his way down to the forest floor. Sharif wasn't a botanist. He knew nothing of how the forest giants grew, or whether it was even possible, but one thing struck him as a certainty: if he remained where he was dangling now, he'd surely die.

Cautiously, clinging to his seat with one hand, Sharif used the other to unlatch his safety harness. Gravity reached out to claim him, and he barely had the strength to keep himself from plunging through the broken windscreen into darkness far below. Moving with literally painful care, his muscles bruised and screaming from their new ordeal, he eased down to a point where both feet touched the cabin's ceiling, turning toward the nearest cockpit door.

It had been torn off in the crash, praise God, so he wouldn't have to kick and hammer on it to escape. He *would* have to crawl out, one slow step at a time, and pray with every move that his own shifting weight wasn't enough to send the chopper plummeting.

Sharif took baby steps at first, then realized that they didn't reduce his weight, but simply wasted precious time. A long stride brought him to the open doorway, poised upon its lip, still clinging with one hand to his inverted pilot's chair. He craned out through the doorway, groping for a branch or vine that would support his weight, and clutched a green liana that seemed thick enough.

He tested it, first tugging with his right hand, then releasing his grip on the seat to lock both hands around the rough vine. Sharif closed his eyes at the moment of truth, swinging out of the cockpit and into the moist embrace of crackling leaves. They brushed his face, some as smooth as velvet, others knife-edged with serrated teeth, but all he felt or cared about was the supporting vine.

It held.

Without a conscious plan, he started lowering himself hand over hand. He also clamped his legs around the vine, gripped with his feet as he'd been taught to do when climbing ropes, long years ago in his guerrilla training. Up or down were all the same, sharing the weight with arms and legs, gripping with hands, knees, feet.

Five minutes later, as he cleared the lower canopy, Sharif experienced a sudden rush of dizziness. A void yawned underneath his feet, the forest floor a murky patch of shadow far beneath him. In a panicked moment, he almost lost his grip, then clung more tightly to the vine in grim despair.

How long was the drop? At a guess, he would've estimated sixty feet, but it just as easily could've been eighty. Either one would break his legs and pelvis, snap his spine and leave him helpless, dying, if he fell.

But then he glimpsed the miracle.

The stout vine that supported him dangled as far below Sharif as he could see. For all he knew, it might reach to the ground. As long as it supported him, as long as he could keep his death grip on that rough lifeline, he could descend with no more injury than muscle cramps and some abrasions on his palms.

Praying nonstop for the strength he needed, inching down the length of nature's rope, Sharif made progress at a snail's pace toward his goal of safety. When he'd covered half the distance to the forest floor, he paused to blink the cruel sweat from his eyes and saw that his supporting vine would leave him ten or twelve feet short.

Ten feet was nothing. He was nearly six feet tall, himself. He'd simply climb down to the bottom of the liana, then dangle by his outstretched arms and drop— how far? Perhaps four feet, at most.

Simple.

It was a combination of the sweat and muscle strain that beat him. Twenty feet above the forest floor, Sharif began to feel the liana slipping through his fingers. Though he clutched it desperately, he couldn't stop the muscles in his arms from cramping when he needed them the most.

He fell, first clutching with his ankles so he dangled

upside down, then losing that grip, too, and somersaulting to the ground. He landed on one shoulder, twisted at the waist, and heard a dull snap somewhere deep inside himself.

A bright pain flared between his hip and armpit. He hoped it was a dislocated shoulder or a cracked rib, something he could live with. Nothing that would keep him prostrate on the forest floor. A broken arm was bearable. He could survive that. But a broken hip…

Sharif began to test his body, piece by piece. The all-important legs were first, slowly extending, flexing, feet rotating on their ankles. They responded well enough, which meant he should be able to stand up and walk.

Unless it was his spine.

But if the legs moved, if he felt the pain between his hip and shoulder, then Sharif knew that he wasn't paralyzed. His spine hadn't been severed. Certainly his neck hadn't been broken.

Tears of sweet relief coursed down his cheeks. Sharif was muttering a prayer of thanks when he heard a low-pitched grumbling sound nearby.

He turned his head, craning his neck to find its source. That movement cost him pain, but it was nothing next to the surprise and fear that flooded through his veins a heartbeat later.

Crouching less than ten feet distant from him was a leopard, lips drawn back from two-inch fangs to loose another rumbling snarl. It sounded angry. Was that rage or hunger in its yellow eyes?

Sharif groped for his pistol, never mind the pain, but searching fingers told him that the holster on his hip was empty. He had lost his only weapon somewhere in the crash or while he scrambled from the airship.

"Damn you," he told the cat in Arabic. "Damn you to hell."

The leopard blinked at him, then sprang and clamped its jaws around his face, as if to swallow Sharif's dying scream.

CHAPTER SIXTEEN

Another GPS check showed the warrior they were still on course, if not exactly up to speed. Bolan had to admit he was impressed by Quinn, marching despite his wound. It wasn't major, but experience told Bolan that it would be hurting now. More to the point, it was a shocking lesson in mortality for one who'd never fired a shot in anger prior to that hellacious day.

So, sure, the kid was holding up all right.

But would he go the distance?

Bolan didn't have a crystal ball and didn't trust them anyway. He was his own best "psychic friend," and any ESP he had was limited to judging new acquaintances and sniffing danger down the road.

He didn't smell any right now, at least not close enough to count, but they were following the scent toward big-time trouble in the village where he'd first seen Quinn.

Unless...

His mind kept coming back to that *unless*. It nagged him, drew his thoughts in much the same way that the socket of a missing tooth drew a probing tongue.

There were at least three circumstances that could foil his bid to locate and defang the Armageddon bomb. The first, denied by Quinn but still a possibility in Bolan's mind, was that there'd never been a nuke at all. Rumors and scuttlebutt aside, the crates that Quinn had seen could've contained anything from guns or generator parts to new robes for the choir. Without a look inside, no one could say for sure.

A second possibility was that the bomb existed, but was no longer in Obike. Gaborone's men could've moved it anytime between the day of its arrival and the present hour. Bolan's raid to kidnap Quinn might've provided the incentive for a move. If not, the sudden deaths of Gaborone's two buyers and three squads of shooters could've done the trick. And if the bomb was gone, that meant interrogations would be necessary to discover its new hiding place.

Would there be time and opportunity to locate someone who possessed the crucial knowledge, wring the information from him and move on to find the bomb before it moved again? He couldn't absolutely rule it out, but Bolan didn't want to bet the farm—much less his life or several thousand others yet unknown—on that eventuality.

The third bad-news scenario didn't involve a missing bomb. Rather, it hinged upon a bomb already armed and activated, one that Bolan lacked the knowledge and equipment to defuse. He understood the basics from a training session taught at Stony Man, but he was also painfully aware that any high-tech backup systems, secret triggers and the like could easily defeat him.

Which would leave a giant smoking crater in the Congo, possibly irradiated to the point where even the aggressive jungle couldn't plant new roots. Deforestation with a vengeance, right.

But it could still be worse.

If Gaborone's surprise package exploded in Obike, there would be investigations, inquiries, foreign commissions and UN inspections, but there was little chance that global conflict would erupt. The Congo had been plagued by strife for generations, but it wasn't Israel, wasn't London, wasn't New York City or the U.S. capital. Part of the Congo's homegrown tragedy was cultural and economic isolation from the outside world. A nuclear explosion there would cause more ripples than starvation in Sudan or ethnic slaughter in Rwanda, but it wouldn't light the Doomsday fuse.

Not even close.

And with that grim realization, Bolan found Plan B.

If he couldn't deactivate the Armageddon bomb, particularly if he found it marking time in countdown mode, he was prepared to let it blow on-site, rather than slip away and wind up in Miami, Paris, Tel Aviv or Moscow. If tragedy was unavoidable, at least he had the wherewithal to minimize the body count and the political fallout.

Maybe.

In fact, as Bolan knew too well, it was sometimes as difficult to blow a nuke as to disarm one. That was by design, of course, to ward off catastrophic "accidents." A certain detonator was required, including a specific primer charge. He couldn't simply thump it with a hammer, shake it like a jug of nitro or haul off and dump it in the nearest campfire.

None of that would do the trick. None of the foolish hype from Hollywood, where bullets fired into a stick of dynamite produced fireworks without the benefit of fuse or blasting caps. It simply didn't work that way. Never had, never would.

Nukes were sensitive, sure, but the only risk of detonation came when they were armed and activated. Otherwise, the main risk was a radiation leak if clumsy handling cracked the shields installed around the bomb's hot core. It wouldn't blow in that case, but might spend the next millennium or two bleeding a steady flow of silent death into the jungle atmosphere.

"How much longer?" Quinn asked from behind him.

Bolan didn't have to check his watch. "We're getting there," he said.

And heard the small voice in his head, But you're taking too damned long.

KUMI KWABENA PLUNGED into his new assignment with unbridled energy. When others asked if he was going out to look for Jomo Tekle, he frowned and shook his head, informing them that Master Gaborone had overridden his desire to scour the jungle with commands of much greater importance. He had been appointed to defend them all from deadly enemies, and he required their help.

None dared refuse whatever he demanded of them. In most cases, he required only a sharp eye, extra vigilance to strangers lurking near the village. For two dozen of the prophet's able-bodied followers, men without wives or children, there were guns and orders to augment the camp's perimeter patrols. Four guards were posted at the master's residence, one at each corner of the bungalow to cover all approaches. Others stood outside the generator shacks, the commo hut, the arsenal, food stores and motor pool.

Kwabena left nothing to chance.

He couldn't absolutely guarantee no strangers would invade the village after nightfall, but the extra guards would make an infiltrator's work more difficult. The watchtowers were double-manned, with extra ammunition laid in for the gunners, just in case. Kwabena's strategic sentries scattered through the village guarded everything of critical importance to their life as a community.

And still, self-doubt returned to haunt Kwabena as the afternoon wore on toward dusk.

He had reported his achievements to the master and received congratulations in return. That should've put his mind at ease, but he couldn't help thinking of the countless things that might go wrong.

His men were only human. Some of them might fall asleep or simply turn away by chance as hostile forces

made their crucial move. Kwabena knew he'd get no
sleep that night, compelled to make the rounds incessantly, changing his pattern on the hour, to keep his
troops alert and fighting fit.

That part of it was drudgery, a process of attrition
wearing down his strength and nerves over the long haul,
but it wasn't Kwabena's greatest fear. His *real* anxiety
sprang from the fact that he knew nothing of their enemy.

How many were there in the hostile force? Where did
they come from? Were they native African or white? If
white, were they American or European, mercenaries
or the agents of some outside government? Did they
enjoy support from Brazzaville, or were they renegade
intruders? How did Patrick Quinn relate to the attacks,
or was his disappearance mere coincidence?

Logistics mattered more, just now, than motives in
Kwabena's mind. What weapons did his adversaries
bear? Were they commanded by an officer who knew
the territory? Were they numerous enough to ring the
village and annihilate its people in a storm of automatic
fire?

Did they have air support?

Kwabena doubted that, although the master's helicopter had gone missing under most suspicious circumstances. Nothing he had planned would save them if
their enemies could drop out of the sky or launch a rain
of bombs and bullets from above.

Kwabena yanked the leash on his imagination, hard,
before it got away from him.

If there were hostile aircraft in the area, he reckoned

they'd have buzzed the camp by now. As for the master's precious bird, the last communication from its pilot led Kwabena to believe that it was lying somewhere in the jungle now, a twisted mass of smoking wreckage.

That left only infantry to threaten him, and while the enemy had killed more than a dozen of his friends so far, they'd done it piecemeal, picking off five here, six there, likely in ambush situations where the targets never saw it coming. One or two men could accomplish that, if they were trained, well armed and ruthless.

Before he lost contact, Nico Mbarga had reported following two sets of footprints through the forest, heading southward. One, he'd been convinced, was Quinn's. The other had been unidentified, perhaps a friend of Quinn's who'd helped him flee Obike after setting three convenient fires as a diversion.

Kwabena didn't know what friends the missing acolyte might have outside Obike. Quinn was an American and white, thus doubly suspect in Kwabena's eyes, but if he'd shown signs of disloyalty prior to vanishing, Kwabena had no knowledge of it.

Moving restlessly about the village, searching for weak points, Kwabena realized that a small force—say, one or two men—stood a better chance of evading his guards than a blundering army of dozens. Two men—or one, if Quinn had been discarded—couldn't overwhelm Kwabena's security force, but they might infiltrate, conceal themselves, perhaps get close enough to Master Gaborone that they could—

He paused again to rein in his imagination. It was like a rude, unruly child, intent on disobeying him and causing problems where none should exist.

He would not lose the master to assassins, would not let a turncoat or a stranger slip into the village and destroy the harmony that Master Gaborone inspired.

New orders were required, and he would issue them at once. It gave Kwabena a new sense of purpose as he set off briskly to resume his rounds.

"I RECOGNIZE THIS place," Quinn said.

Bolan stopped in his tracks and turned to face him, raising a quizzical eyebrow. "You're sure?"

Quinn nodded. "Yes, I am." He moved left, toward the base of a huge tree were two hash marks were etched into the trunk, pointing. "I was on a nut-and-berry run. I marked the way, going out, so I wouldn't get lost. Obike's ... that way, maybe half a mile."

Bolan removed the GPS tracking device from its belt pouch, consulted it, then tucked it out of sight again. "You're right. Good work."

"Dumb luck," Quinn said, but he still felt inordinately pleased by Cooper's praise.

"Okay," he said, before Cooper could respond to his self-deprecation. "What's the plan, now that we're almost there?"

"The usual, to start," Bolan replied. "Watch out for guards. Make no unnecessary noise. When we get close enough you can direct me to the building where you saw the crates."

Quinn noticed that he didn't say *the bomb*. Cooper believed him, he was sure of that. They wouldn't have come back here, otherwise. But there was still a measure of reserve, a hint of doubt.

And why not, anyway?

It wasn't as though the two of them were lifelong friends who'd forged an ironclad bond of trust over the years. They'd known each other for a day and change, with Quinn resisting and reviling Cooper roughly half that time. His late conversion *should* feel strange to Cooper. And assuming that the soldier trusted him completely, there was still a chance that he'd been wrong about the bomb.

I wasn't, though, Quinn thought. God help us all, I'm not wrong.

Wishing that he were, Quinn followed Cooper through the shadows that were stretching into dusk. Another hour, give or take, and night would fall around them like a shroud. Trail markers wouldn't matter then, but he supposed they'd be within sight of the village by that time.

Within sight, maybe, of the place where they were destined to be killed.

Quinn was surprised to find the prospect didn't terrify him as it might've done. He'd lived through close encounters with the Reaper, wore a bullet's brand to prove it, and while he had no desire to die right now, Quinn wasn't quaking in his stolen boots.

Maybe I'm just too tired to give a damn, he thought.

Or maybe he was thinking past himself for once, the

first time that he could remember since he'd hooked up with the Process, trying to prevent a needless holocaust.

He still believed in scripture—some of it, at least— but Quinn no longer bought the argument that God required a helping hand from mortal men to make His prophecies come true. And if He *did* need human help launching a global war, initiating the Last Days, Quinn was convinced that the Almighty wouldn't call on "Master" Gaborone.

Distracted, he almost collided with his escort, lurching to a jerky halt as Cooper stopped in front of him. This time, instead of checking on the GPS to plot their route, the soldier held his sat phone.

"I just need to make a quick call," Bolan said. "Then we'll be on our way."

"Take all the time you need," Quinn answered as he settled in to wait.

GRIMALDI WASN'T SLEEPING this time, when the sat phone's shrilling voice demanded his attention. He'd been leafing through a glossy magazine, appreciating the models though he couldn't translate any of the French captions or text. Who needed words when they were draped in next to nothing, anyway?

He grabbed the phone before it rang a second time. "Grimaldi."

Bolan's voice asked him, "How long for you to reach the compound?"

Jolted with adrenaline, Grimaldi made the calculation. Ninety miles per hour if the Hiller UH-12 gave him the best performance of its life, and Bolan's target was two hundred miles from where Grimaldi sat.

"Two and a quarter hours, give or take," he said.

"You know the airstrip?" Bolan asked.

"Affirmative. It's on the aerials. I think it's five miles east or something."

"Meet us there, ASAP," Bolan said. "But if we're not visible when you show up, don't hang around."

"I'm on my way. Confirm no loitering unless I see you on arrival."

"Right. We're going in as soon as it gets dark. I'll see you."

"See you. Right."

The line was dead again. They didn't traffic in goodbyes because it sounded too damned final, like the slamming of a casket's lid.

Grimaldi took his gym bag with the 12-gauge pump and extra ammunition, locked his rent-a-wreck and wondered if he'd ever see the car again.

Who cared?

The chopper's owner wandered out to watch his takeoff, standing well back from the rotor wash with arms folded across his chest. Grimaldi wondered whether he was rooting for the bird to crash, letting him keep the fat deposit that would likely buy a newer one, or if he had some fondness for the chopper in his heart.

Again, it made no difference as he lifted off and aimed the aircraft north. He would feel better when he cleared the city and was truly on his way. Grimaldi almost felt like this was another test run, practice for the main event, instead of jumping off into the wild blue on a mission that might claim his life.

Bolan was going in at nightfall, still roughly an hour away. That meant he'd only be exposed to peril for an hour and a quarter, more or less, before Grimaldi reached the airstrip Gaborone used for his charters, in and out.

Only an hour and a quarter, sure.

That was like saying he would *only* spend a year or two in hell before the lifeline dangled fleetingly in front of his face. Most killing confrontations could be timed in seconds, minutes at the far outside. Bolan, meanwhile, would be exposed to hostile guns for seventy-five minutes or more.

Unless he killed them all.

Grimaldi didn't know if he could bring himself to do that, even in the interest of survival. Quinn might be some help, but who could say? They'd need time for the bomb, deactivating it, whatever Bolan had in mind, and more time for the five-mile hike to reach the airstrip.

That could be a bitch, Grimaldi thought, with hunters on their trail the whole damned way, but he supposed escaping was the least of it. After the penetration and whatever fighting went along with it, finding the bomb, defusing it if that was possible, withdrawal from the camp should be a piece of cake. Like falling off a log, Grimaldi thought.

Into an open grave.

And if they didn't make it to the LZ, he was just supposed to leave. He'd promised not to hang around and wait for stragglers from the fight. No loitering. He'd pledged his word.

Too bad.

If there was any chance at all of getting Bolan out alive, with or without the young man he'd originally gone to find, Grimaldi was prepared to take the risk. It wasn't that he loved a fight, just couldn't get enough of it, or even that he simply didn't mind the risk.

The rub was that he knew he couldn't face himself tomorrow or the next day, any time at all, if he let Bolan down tonight. He couldn't live with that unless he knew for damned sure that he'd come too late. Not seeing Bolan wouldn't mean his friend was dead and gone.

Grimaldi had to know.

And God help anyone who tried to stop him finding out.

AHMADOU GABORONE listened patiently, nodding now and then, while Kumi Kwabena reported his progress. He had increased perimeter patrols, placed guards at every vital point in camp, and he would personally tour the posts all night, insuring that none of the sentries fell asleep or shirked his duty.

There was nothing more to do.

So why, then, didn't Gaborone feel safe?

He kept the dark, uneasy feeling to himself as he told Kwabena, "You've done well, Captain. Your efforts are appreciated and shall be rewarded, I assure you."

"Master, please, it is an honor but to serve."

"Of course. Then I won't keep you from it."

Turning from his new security commander, Gaborone went back inside his bungalow and closed the door behind him. He would spend the night alone, with guards outside, and pray to see the morning light break fair over the village. But if enemies or demons came upon him in the night…

He longed to flee the village altogether, but he couldn't get away. Without the helicopter, he was limited to travel overland on winding trails, most of which led ultimately to dead ends. He'd always flown into Obike, had supplies delivered the same way, and welcomed only airborne visitors. The isolation that had pleased him once upon a time now made him feel as if he were in prison, under lock and key.

For months on end he'd lectured his disciples on security, preparing them for an assault by enemies, which, in his heart, he'd never really thought would happen. Now the day had come, and Gaborone discovered that, of all Obike's residents, he was the least prepared.

What should he do about the package?

He could hide it somewhere in the jungle, but that meant dispatching soldiers—half of them, at least—just when he needed them the most. Another problem, too: what if he moved the package, only to encounter his advancing enemies, and thus deliver it into their hands? What would become of it, of him, in that case?

Gaborone tried praying, but it didn't help. The lines weren't open as of old. His ears rang with a kind of psychic busy signal and he heard no voices from on high. Perhaps the Lord was currently preoccupied with other business, but His humble servant thought He might've made time for a grave emergency affecting Armageddon and the Final Days.

Thus spurned, Gaborone rose from his knees and paced the little parlor of his bungalow. He lived in luxury, compared to those who slept in dormitories, segregated by their gender, but today his home felt like a cage. Even with windows open, he was stifling, suffocating. He was tempted to dispatch a runner for the camp physician, but he feared what might ensue if word got out that he was ill.

Panic. Despair. The physical unraveling of all he'd worked so long and hard to build with others' labor, sweat and cash. The hopeless dissolution of a dream.

He paced and fretted, focusing on Patrick Quinn. The face eluded him, although he had to have seen it at some point. Was Quinn a victim or a Judas? Would this man whom Gaborone couldn't remember bring him down?

Would God allow that, after all that Gaborone had done on His behalf?

Perhaps.

Pacing, he thought of Job, once the most righteous man on Earth. Scripture told Gaborone that no man was more faithful to the Lord, or better loved by Him. And yet, one morning, God had made a spiteful, childish bet with Satan, tossing Job into the pot. Satan was given leave to kill Job's wife and children, strip him of his worldly goods and plague him with all manner of diseases. All to see if Job would still be faithful to his Lord.

The sheer injustice of it rankled Gaborone. He raged on Job's behalf, and on his own. When faithful servants were betrayed and cast aside, what could they do except rebel against the masters who abused them?

But the Bible said that Job hadn't rebelled. With each new trial, his faith in God grew stronger than before, his love for the Almighty more intense.

Which raised a question. What in hell was wrong with Job?

Was he insane? A masochist, perhaps?

"Not me," the prophet muttered as he paced. "Not me. Not me."

He wouldn't be a hapless pawn in anybody else's game.

And he wouldn't be cast aside. Not even by the Lord.

THEY'D CIRCLED TWICE around the village, pausing frequently to stare at it from different vantage points, before Quinn pointed to a structure in the northeast quadrant and told Bolan, "It's in there. At least, it was, last time I saw it."

"Fair enough."

It was a place to start, and if he didn't find the bomb inside that building, then what? He assumed it wouldn't be inside one of the barracks dorms, wouldn't be hidden in the mess tent, wouldn't be planted beneath the prophet's bungalow. The generator huts were out, based on Quinn's estimate of size, and Bolan didn't think he'd find it in the commo shack, either.

That narrowed down his search to seven buildings Quinn identified as storehouses or shops. Bolan would have to check each one in turn, if he found nothing in the first, which was supposed to be the village armory.

What better place to stash a megaweapon, then? Unless, of course, it was supposed to be a secret from the prophet's guards, as well.

If the bomb existed, someone in the village had to know where it was. The drones who carried it from one point to the next might not have been informed about a crate's contents, but Gaborone surely would know.

And that would be Plan B.

If Bolan couldn't find the Russian packages where Quinn had seen them last, he'd try to reach the self-styled prophet for a little one-on-one. They could negotiate, one life for thousands, and if that deal wasn't satisfactory for Gaborone, if the guru decided that he couldn't life with it, then he could die with it.

And Bolan would go on without him, searching for the bomb until he dropped.

"You know the airstrip?" he asked Quinn. "Have you been there?"

"I have, yeah."

"What I need for you to do right now is go there. It's a hike, I realize, but if you start now and avoid the sentries, you can make it by the time our pickup's ready."

"Wait a minute, now."

"I don't have time for arguments," Bolan said. "If you're not some kind of nuclear technician, then from this point on you'd just be in my way. I don't need any obstacles beyond what we've already seen, and I can't cover you inside the village. Are we clear?"

Quinn answered stiffly, "Crystal. But—"

"No buts. Just find the airstrip. Do it now."

"I can—"

"You *can't*. If you try helping me, you'll get us both killed. Now get over it and move."

"All right," Quinn said, "if that's the way you feel."

"That's how it is."

"I'll see you at the strip, then."

"Right."

Bolan left Quinn without another word, tired of debating what could only go one way if either one of them was to survive the night. His way, whatever happened in the village, Quinn would still be going home to Val and to his family. If Bolan made it to the strip on time, so much the better, but if he was unavoidably delayed, he stood a chance of getting out alone.

The jungle wasn't Mars or Jupiter. He knew it well enough to make his way out, find a crib in Brazzaville and reach out for another contact with the Farm. If it came down to fleeing overland, Quinn would be nothing but a ball and chain around his ankle, slowing Bolan and making him a fatter target.

Satisfied that he had made the only choice available, he moved toward the perimeter and the guards who waited there.

CHAPTER SEVENTEEN

Obike's troubled residents tried hard to keep the night at bay. They had a bonfire burning in the middle of the village, and lamps had been hung outside some of the barracks, resembling porch lights in a stateside residential neighborhood. That effect was compromised, however, by the jungle that surrounded Gaborone's community on every side, and by the troupe of armed guards on patrol.

The sentries had to cope with darkness on the village outskirts, since Obike wasn't wired for floodlights all the way around. Its two guard towers both had lights mounted on high, but neither one was lit as Bolan made his second entry to the isolated village. He guessed that the big lights sucked power from the generators at alarming rates, and that gasoline was hard to get. The prophet would preserve them if he could, for bona fide emergencies.

And with a bit of luck, he'd have no use for them this night.

Bolan had come in from the west on his first visit to Obike, and had left the village heading south. Trusting that someone in the compound had to have marked both points by now, he changed his angle of attack to enter near his target, via the northeast perimeter. Crouching inside the tree line, masked by shadow, Bolan estimated that the compound's armory was fifty-odd feet distant over open ground. A rifleman was posted on the door, and others passed around the village outskirts in rotation, one team moving clockwise while the other circled counterclockwise.

Bolan was confident he could evade the roving sentries, but the guard outside the armory was something else. Unless he wandered off to visit the latrine sometime within the next few minutes, Bolan would be forced to take him down, as quietly as possible.

But even silent attack left a risk of being seen. There were no lights on in the armory, nor was it near the central bonfire, but a dormitory just beyond it had a lamp suspended from its doorpost. Anyone inside could glance through a window and observe him grappling with the sentry, as could the inhabitants of two more barracks in the same vicinity.

It would be tight, but there was no alternative. Inaction, in this case, could spell disaster on a scale Bolan didn't care to contemplate.

He checked his pistol, knowing before he made the move that it was ready, nestled in its holster. He waited for the next two sentries to pass by in opposite directions, then broke cover, jogging through the semidarkness toward his goal. The angle of approach he'd chosen put him on the solitary watchman's blind side now, unless the guard turned more than halfway to his left rear for some reason, peered around the corner and caught Bolan on the move.

The soldier ran swiftly, eyes darting to left and right, watching for any threat along the way. A shouted warning could undo him, bring the guards rushing to take him down with volleys of converging fire. He'd fight them, take some with him, but it would be difficult—perhaps impossible—to take them all at once.

When he was halfway to his target, Bolan drew the pistol and slowed a little, not wanting his pounding footsteps to announce him, but he couldn't risk any significant delay. Behind him more guards were on the move, pacing the night away, and others might be coming to relieve them soon, from who knew where. He had one chance to do it right, and if he failed there would be hell to pay.

It was a blitz attack with no finesse to speak of. Bolan charged around the northeast corner of the armory and slammed into its watchman on the run, pounding the weapon's butt into the guard's temple. They fell together, Bolan dealing another rapid blow to the young man's head.

Bolan rose to a crouch, used duct tape to silence the guy and bound his wrists with plastic riot cuffs. He scanned the darkened windows overlooking him, searching for startled faces and finding none. No cry was raised to bring the soldiers down upon him.

Quinn had predicted that the door would be padlocked, and he was right. Bolan was ready for it, crouching with the bound man just behind him as he palmed and plied a set of supple picks. It was a large padlock, but old and inexpensive. Gaborone had counted more on loyalty and guards than on a single block of metal, and the oversight betrayed him now.

In thirty seconds, Bolan had the padlock open. Forty saw the guard tucked up inside the armory, door closed behind him. There was nothing he could do about the hasp or missing lock outside, except to hope that no one noticed soon enough to foil his plan.

Leaving the guard to one side of the threshold, Bolan turned and had a hasty look around the armory. There wasn't much to see. Extra Kalashnikovs in upright racks, with three shotguns. Cases of ammunition stacked against the far wall from the door.

And in the center of the hut, two wooden crates with black Cyrillic writing on their sides.

KUMI KWABENA WAS as nervous as an antelope in a hyena's den. Most nights, on duty, he would drink a pot of coffee to prevent himself from dozing off, but he was light-years past caffeine this night. His very skin felt tighter than it should, as if his own body was trying to imprison him, restrict his movements, and the only way to free himself was by incessantly patrolling the compound, checking his troops to verify that they were on alert.

Tonight will be the worst, he told himself.

If there was no attack this night, when they had lost so many men within twenty-four hours, Kwabena was prepared to rethink the danger. If they were spared, it might mean that their enemies had chosen to withdraw, bloodied perhaps, or simply running low on ammunition and supplies. Perhaps he'd been mistaken in believing Jomo Tekle's team was ambushed by an enemy advancing toward Obike. After all, he didn't know where Tekle's men had fallen, wouldn't know for sure until their bodies were recovered, gnawed by scavengers.

He had jumped to a conclusion under stress and might be wrong.

Or maybe not.

Kwabena checked his wristwatch and scowled at what it told him. They were still hours away from sunrise, and the camp was only quiet now because he had decreed a curfew with the master's blessing, trying to eliminate needless confusion for his men on guard. As jumpy as some of them were, especially the new draftees, he had imagined accidental shootings that would spread panic like wildfire through the village.

Not a problem, now.

The master's children had been ordered to remain indoors unless they had some vital duty to perform, cleared with Kwabena in advance, or if a call of nature absolutely couldn't be contained. Guarding against that likelihood, he'd detailed men to supervise a long procession through the camp's latrines before bedtime, like it or not, with no excuses tolerated.

He believed he'd thought of everything, but logic told him there was always something else.

Leaving the men on the perimeter alone for now, he walked a zigzag pattern through the village proper, checking in on stationary guards he'd posted outside various facilities. All quiet at the motor pool and the infirmary. A young cobra had come into the mess tent, but he found its severed body twitching on the ground in thirds, around his smiling sentry's boots, blood fresh on the machete in the young man's fist.

Congratulations there, and he moved on. The four guards posted on the master's bungalow snapped to attention when they saw Kwabena coming, making too much noise to suit him. Whispering, he told them to forget about that part of military discipline tonight and let the master sleep, reminding them once more as he passed on that they had to stay awake.

No unforeseen disturbance at the commo hut or the first generator shed, where young men bobbed their heads and promised to remain alert. Kwabena reached the eastern watchtower and started to ascend its wooden ladder, twenty feet straight up and never mind his vertigo. A leader overcame such foibles, or he was replaced.

When he was halfway up the ladder, concentrating on the trapdoor overhead, something distracted him and drew his eyes off to the right. It was a dizzy feeling, peering down into the compound, but he'd turned before he had a chance to think about it.

What had drawn him? There was something...

No, that wasn't it. His eyes weren't drawn off target by an object. Rather, they had been attracted by its absence. There was something—someone—missing from the scene laid out below him.

The armory! There was no sentry on its door.

Clenching his teeth, fighting his fear of heights, Kwabena started down the ladder once again. Inspection of the watchtower could wait. First thing, he had to find the guard he'd left outside the armory, and when he'd finished with him, the absconder would feel grateful if Kwabena let him live.

Once more on solid ground, he jogged across the compound to the doorstep of the armory. He circled once around the building, finding no trace of the man he'd left on guard, and only then discovered something infinitely worse.

The padlock from the door was missing, too.

Kumi Kwabena drew his pistol with a trembling hand and reached out for the doorknob. He twisted it and lunged across the threshold.

He required a moment to assess what he was seeing, but he didn't have that time. A strong arm locked around his windpipe from behind, trapping his breath and any warning cry inside. Kwabena felt the blade lance deep between his ribs, and in the flash of consciousness remaining squeezed the trigger of his pistol once, and then again.

QUINN WAS A HALF MILE from the village, following the narrow track between Obike and the airstrip, when he had a change of heart.

He had balked at leaving Cooper in the first place, finally relented rather than provoke a confrontation with the soldier he was sure to lose, but Quinn turned back now, running toward the village. Praying that he wouldn't be too late.

For what?

To help.

Quinn couldn't leave him to it. There must still be something he could do, even if Cooper wasn't there to help or see him try.

Defusing bombs was totally beyond his field of expertise, an exercise he'd only seen in movies out of Hollywood. Quinn knew he would be worse than useless in attempting that, might even activate the bomb or set it off while trying for the opposite effect.

But Cooper had taught him something on the trail. They'd talked about the A-bomb long enough for Quinn to know that certain elements or steps were necessary to produce a detonation. Something called a primer charge, connected to a trigger that he wouldn't recognize if it was lying on the trail in front of him. It took one charge to detonate another, like a blasting cap with dynamite, and if that primer charge was damaged or removed, the big bomb wouldn't work.

Again, Quinn wasn't sure if he could pull that off, but there was something else Cooper had said that stuck with him. If the lead shield around the bomb's nuclear core was broken, it became a different kind of weapon, leaking radiation strong enough to kill whoever handled it, unless they wore protective gear, which, to his knowledge, wasn't found in Gaborone's jungle community.

If he ran out of options, if there was no other way to go, Quinn thought an AK-47 burst would do a fairly decent job of rupturing the Armageddon bomb and letting its destructive rays escape.

Of course, the man who fired that burst would likely be the first to suffer radiation poisoning, but at the moment Quinn could only think of picking up the job where Cooper had left off. If he could manage that, at least—

There was firing from the village. Automatic weapons. He heard AKs and a lighter weapon that might just be Cooper's.

Quinn picked up his pace, sprinting headlong through darkness toward the camp. If Cooper was alive and fighting, they still had a chance. However slim, he couldn't turn his back on that.

Not even if it brought him to a slow and screaming death.

AHMADOU GABORONE WAS nearly certain that he'd lost his mind. Inside his head, chaotic thoughts spun aimlessly, like bits of litter in a cyclone. Panic sizzled through his veins and made him skittish, flinching every time another shot rang out, ducking as if the slug was meant for him.

The first two shots had caught him on the verge of

sleep, worn out by worry and attempting to anticipate the moves of nameless, faceless enemies. He had reached out to Brazzaville by radio, near dusk, and sought help from a man of some authority who had accepted Gaborone's largess on various occasions. The reply was sympathetic, but it still came down to a rejection. Troops couldn't be sent unless a state of insurrection was declared, which was a presidential call. And if the chief executive should issue that decree, there might be pressure from the nation's clique of rich conservatives to wipe Obike off the map.

So Gaborone was on his own this night, with thirty-odd armed men to guard his body and his dreams. The prospect frightened him as nothing had before, at least since childhood.

He was so close to success, and now there was a real threat that the victory would be denied him, snatched out of his very hands by strangers.

"Oh my God," he muttered as he paced the bungalow, "why have you forsaken me?"

No answer.

Gaborone cursed bitterly, then clapped a hand over his mouth. Too late to take the words back, so he babbled an apology to the Almighty. Normally, he drew upon God's power in a crisis situation, to increase his own, but that no longer seemed to work.

What would he do if God truly deserted him?

More gunfire from outside, staccato bursts fired at erratic intervals. He couldn't guess how many guns were firing at a given time, much less whose finger pulled a given trigger, but it sounded like a dozen weapons, maybe more.

Firing at what, or whom?

He risked a quick glance through the nearest window, looking past the bonfire in the middle of the village toward a point where muzzle-flashes winked and fluttered. An alarm bell sounded in his mind before he realized that they were clumped around the armory.

Forgetting any thought of danger, Gaborone burst from his quarters, rushing past the startled guards who flanked his door. One of them tried to stop him, then thought better of it and ran after Gaborone, the other trailing both of them.

"Stop that!" he shouted as he ran. "You fools! You don't know what's in there!"

And that was his fault, an executive decision based on need-to-know security demands. Of all his followers, only Nico Mbarga knew exactly what was in the wooden crates with the Cyrillic legends printed on their slats. It hadn't seemed important to him that the rest should know; in fact he thought it was a terrible idea. But now his caution had come back to bite him on the—

"Stop! Stop firing, for God's sake!"

A handful of the guards had heard him, turned to face him and spread the word to others. Awkwardly, the firing sputtered out, then stopped.

"Master!" Kumi Kwabena was beside him suddenly, gripping his elbow. "You should not be here. It isn't safe."

Gaborone shook him off, drove Kumi back a pace

with his wild-eyed expression. "You must not fire into that building," he commanded. "If you do, it spells death for us all!"

QUINN STOPPED a hundred yards short of the village outskirts, caught his breath, then moved ahead more cautiously. The gunfire had increased while he was running back along the unpaved jungle road, then petered out again just as he reached the tree line.

Once again he felt despair. The emotion had weight, like one of those lead vests the dentist used to make him wear for X-ray sessions. It was more than just fatigue, his wild sprint through the darkness or the rifle in his hands and bandoliers around his neck.

Quinn knew that he was feeling Cooper's loss, then caught himself again before it totally defeated him. He wasn't absolutely sure the prophet's guards had finished Cooper. There was still a chance, however small, that the soldier could be alive.

Quinn found no one guarding the perimeter as he entered the village, ducking from one building to another as he made his slow way toward the focal point of the excitement. Floodlights from the towers guided him, and he could see more than a dozen riflemen surrounding what he knew must be the armory.

Cooper had made it that far, anyway.

But was he still alive inside?

As Quinn crept past a dormitory, someone pulled the door open and gaped at him with frightened eyes. Before the watcher had a chance to speak, Quinn raised a warning finger to his lips and hissed for silence, saw the nod and watched the door swing shut once more.

Sometimes the blind obedience was helpful, after all.

Quinn moved in closer to the action, though he couldn't really call it action now. The guards were standing poised around the armory, some taking advantage of the lull to reload their weapons, others covering the bullet-riddled structure as if it still posed a threat to them.

Seeing the walls pockmarked with bullet scars, the door half off its hinges, Quinn nearly gave up hope that Cooper was alive. Nearly. A small spark of that hope rekindled when he saw that Gaborone was with his bodyguards, speaking to them in urgent, low-pitched tones. Quinn moved in closer, so that he could catch the words.

"You must remove him from the armory without more shooting," Gaborone told his elite. "I know it's dangerous, but if a bullet strikes the detonator, we may all be killed."

He didn't mention leaking radiation, probably because he wanted those around him to go in and check the armory, to find out if Cooper was alive or dead and drag him out into the firelight. Quinn supposed even the royal elite might balk at radiation poisoning, sterility and a protracted death.

"But, Master—" one of them began.

"No arguments!" Gaborone snapped. "It must be done as I have said."

Some of the soldiers huddled, muttering among

themselves, then one of them called out in French, "Are you alive in there?"

No answer, so he tried the question in Kikongo, with the same result.

"English!" Gaborone commanded.

Another stepped up in response. "Inside the bungalow! Are you alive?"

And the familiar voice came back at them, "Why don't you come inside and see?"

Grinning despite the circumstances, Quinn shouldered his AK-47, sighting down the barrel from a range of fifteen yards.

He couldn't reach Cooper to fight and die beside him, but he still might have a way of helping. A diversion could be useful, Quinn supposed.

He found a target, let his finger curl around the AK's trigger and began to squeeze.

"INSIDE THE BUNGALOW! Are you alive?"

He was, but it was touch and go. Bolan lay prone between a stack of ammo crates and a coffin-size box with the nuke packed inside. Part of it, anyway, since he'd identified the detonator in a separate crate and moved it well away from the Armageddon bomb. He'd gotten that far and had removed the larger box's lid before his first surprise visitor dropped in to chat.

Now he was in the soup, clearly surrounded, and only dumb luck had kept the storm of incoming fire from striking him or the crate he lay behind. Several rounds had drilled the ammo cases on his other side, but since there'd been no tracers, the spare rounds weren't cooking off around him.

So, when the call came, there was nothing left for him to do but play it out. "Why don't you come inside and see?" he answered, goading them.

They hadn't fired again, although he half expected it. Instead, there was a shuffling of boots outside the shed and whispered conversation Bolan either couldn't hear or couldn't translate. Either way, it sounded like his enemies were working up their nerve to rush him.

Had they been warned not to fire blindly around the nuke? If so, it might give Bolan a small edge against the team that tried to root him out. He could fire at will against any attackers, while troops restrained from using deadly force would have to overwhelm him physically, with numbers. He assumed they'd snap, forget their orders after he had killed a few of them, but in the meantime…

Bolan almost risked it, rising to attack the Doomsday package while he had a little breathing room, but as he reached all fours another burst of gunfire echoed through the night outside. Someone was shouting, questions by the sound of it, and then a dozen AK-47s started firing all at once.

He dropped again, facedown, but after half a second realized the slugs weren't coming his way. There was chaos in the camp, but it was moving rapidly away from him, as some of those who had surrounded him pursued another enemy

Bolan made no attempt to puzzle through it. He had

minutes—maybe seconds to complete his vital work, and he couldn't afford to waste a single one.

Keeping his weapon close at hand, Bolan rose to a crouch and reached into the oblong crate.

CHAPTER EIGHTEEN

Quinn had no conscious plan other than to distract the assembled guards from Cooper and the armory. Beyond that, he was simply playing it by ear and hoping that they didn't kill him instantly, before his sacrifice could do some good.

His first shots were directed at a soldier he had recognized by firelight, something of a bully who enjoyed authority too much for his own good. Three bullets put the tough guy down and started his companions scrambling, turning every which way as they sought the source of danger.

Quinn had Master Gaborone framed in his sights, frozen in shock and gaping at the corpse laid out in front of him, and he nearly took the shot. His finger had begun to tighten on the trigger when he hesitated, found he couldn't fire.

Quinn had discarded his illusions that the man was

chosen by some higher power, much less a divinity on Earth, but still he couldn't pull the trigger, send death screaming through the air between them.

Something stayed his hand, and then it didn't matter anymore, as one of Gaborone's defenders spied him, shouted out a warning to the rest and fired a burst in Quinn's direction from his own Kalashnikov.

The bullets came too close for comfort, but they didn't panic Quinn the way they might've the previous day. He ducked, turned toward his snarling enemy and answered with a rattling spray of fire that made the shooter dance, twitching, before he fell.

Then it was time to run, before the rest of them cut loose in unison and shredded him. Quinn used his knowledge of the camp to duck and weave while gunfire blazed behind him, bullets striking dormitory walls on either side of him and screaming into darkness overhead. The shadows welcomed him, while flood-lights from the towers crisscrossed in a frantic bid to find him, pin him down.

One of the blinding lights swept over him, moved on, then veered back to the point where Quinn had stood a heartbeat earlier. He wasn't there, but something flick-ered in the shadows farther on, prompting the tower sentries to unleash a hail of automatic fire. Some of their bullets drilled tin roofs and spent their force inside the dorms, while frightened occupants dodged here and there in search of cover. Other rounds gouged divots in the dirt, but none of them found Quinn.

He'd gone to ground again by that time, hoping that

a game of cat and mouse would buy more time, lead his pursuers farther from the armory. They wouldn't all leave Cooper, he supposed, but any he could draw away would be a help.

Having accomplished all he meant to, Quinn now focused on survival. It was probably a futile effort, but they hadn't killed him yet, and while he still had ammunition left, while he could run and fight, he didn't plan to make things easy for his would-be executioners.

The mess tent loomed in front of him, flaps raised for ventilation and to let the roving guards see through it without offering an infiltrator anywhere to hide. The broad view cut both ways, however, and Quinn saw the lone guard moving in to box him while the man was still some twenty yards away.

Quinn knelt, aimed, fired in record time, half expecting to miss, but his slugs cut the sentry's legs from under him and left him thrashing in the dirt. Not dead, but down, his AK-47 out of reach.

Quinn could've finished him but let it go, dashing away before the others could obtain a fix on his position and react. He was a laboratory rat, running the maze, but in his case no tasty treats awaited him. He wasn't running *to* something, and there was no reward beyond a brief extension of his life.

He thought of Cooper, hoped the soldier wasn't wasting this brief opportunity to neutralize the Armageddon bomb. Quinn reckoned neither one of them had much time left, but with determination and a little luck, they both might make it count.

I'm sorry, Val.

He wasn't certain where the thought had come from, in the midst of running for his life, but maybe she could hear it somehow, somewhere. He *was* sorry, for failing here, his family and for whatever happened to her other friend, because he—Quinn—had been a thoughtless fool.

He'd chased a pipe dream all the way from home to Africa, and by the time he woke to recognize the nightmare, it was too damned late to take it back.

But not, perhaps, too late to make it right.

Quinn stopped dead in his tracks, leaning against a barracks wall to catch his breath. The hunters, some of them, were closing on him now. He couldn't get a head count from their clomping footsteps, but he had a decent fix on their position. They were drawing closer by the second, and if he was bold enough, he had a chance to stop them now.

Quinn filled his lungs with air and held it, braced himself, then doubled back the way he'd come. In front of him, five runners faltered, gaping at their prey, uncertain why the man who'd once been one of them was running toward them with a rifle in his hands.

Quinn bellowed in the night, an incoherent howl of rage, and met them with a spray of death from his Kalashnikov.

DREAMS DIED HARD, but they could die, and Gaborone's great vision for the Final Days was slipping though his palsied fingers as he cowered in the shadows, waiting for a bullet from the darkness to obliterate all conscious thought.

It would be merciful, he felt, to let that pain sear through him, followed by oblivion. Or would he somehow find his way to Paradise despite his failure on the earthly plane? Would God somehow forgive him for the bungled effort to fulfill His prophecy?

No hope remained, as far as Gaborone could see. His men were chasing enemies around the village, while a steady stream of his disciples fled into the jungle. Faith and prayer had failed them, just as he had. They would rather take their chances in the dark, with hungry beasts, than to remain with Gaborone and fight to save their homes.

Of course, he couldn't blame them. Gaborone wanted to run, but he was paralyzed by fear and had no refuge. There was nowhere safe to hide within the village now, he understood that much, and with the helicopter gone he couldn't make it back to Brazzaville.

Do something! shrieked a voice inside his head.

And so he ran. Not toward the mess tent and the sounds of battle rising there, but toward his bungalow. The guards who ringed the armory ignored him, focused on the man inside who'd challenged them to go inside and bring him out.

Their master left them to it, if they had the nerve. As for himself, he'd seen and heard enough.

His quarters stood apart from other nearby structures, giving Gaborone an extra bit of privacy befitting one who sometimes spoke with God on urgent matters of the heart and soul. No guards remained to see him as he rushed inside and went directly to his bedroom, where he thrust a hand beneath his pillows and withdrew a Skorpion machine pistol. He checked the stubby weapon's 20-round box magazine and took another from the drawer of his small nightstand, thrusting it into a pocket.

Gaborone was now as ready as he'd ever be to face the hostile world outside the bungalow. His plan was rudimentary—cross to the motor pool, select a vehicle and race five miles through darkness to the airstrip. Maybe he could hide there, even if he had no pilot and no wings. Sometime tomorrow or the next day he could creep back to Obike, find out what remained of his jungle community and try to radio for help.

But first he had to make it through the night alive.

Gaborone moved to the threshold of his bungalow. He hesitated there, clutching the Skorpion so tightly that his fingers ached, then found his nerve and plunged into the night.

BOLAN HAD STUDIED diagrams, committed them to memory. He had schematic diagrams for nukes of half a dozen nations locked inside his head, but it had been a while since he'd accessed that information and the clock was running, putting him on edge.

And simple nukes aside, the detonators were a bitch.

The good news first: they hadn't tried to arm the bomb. Its detonator occupied a separate, smaller crate, as Bolan found after he'd opened both. That was as far as he'd proceeded when the armed intruder interrupted him, and only now was he returning to his crucial task inside the shed that had become a sieve.

He set the smaller crate between the ammunition pyramid that sheltered him on one side and the coffin with the nuke inside it on the other. Working with a penlight held between his teeth, he scanned the detonator's face for any clues as to what made it tick—and hoped it wouldn't start ticking while he was huddled over it.

There'd be no nuclear explosion if it blew, but Bolan knew there had to be enough plastique inside the detonator to remove his head and hands at contact range. He had to do this carefully, and never mind the fact that half a dozen goons with AK-47s might burst in upon him any moment, spraying lead around the room.

He thought about it, and the tools he had at hand, deciding any operation he attempted would be crude at best, and might well trigger any covert backup system built into the detonator. He could likely crack the casing, poke around inside to try to find the batteries, the ground wire, something to deactivate the primer charge. But if he failed, the countdown would begin, and Bolan wasn't sure that he could stop it.

He had a sudden inspiration, turning from the detonator to the fat nuke in its casket. Taking an all-purpose tool from his belt, he bent over the north end of the Doomsday egg, where anyone who planned to set it off had to first attach the detonator. There, he started stripping screws and shoving them into his pocket, lifted off a faceplate and began to slash the multicolored wires within.

There as no system to it and no risk. Without its primer charge, the nuke was perfectly inert. And in a few more seconds, thanks to Bolan, it would need a major overhaul by qualified experts before a detonator could be used to spark its cataclysmic chain reaction. Bolan left the detonator's socket gaping open, torn wires dangling where they hadn't been completely severed, half a dozen crucial bolts and screws no longer in the package.

That should slow them, but Bolan wasn't finished yet. He didn't plan to leave the detonator behind for Gaborone to use or sell. Instead, he took it from its crate, gripping the recessed handle on one side, and pressed a button that he judged to be the timer's activator.

It was green. Why not?

The digital display blinked at him, showing zeroes straight across. Bolan bent closer, found the time selectors that were really little different from those on the average alarm clock, and prepared to press one with his index finger.

How much time?

Twelve seconds sounded right.

He keyed it in, then pressed another button—red, this time—to start the countdown. As the readout blinked eleven, Bolan rose and took the detonator with him, hoisting it left-handed, spinning once around like an Olympic shot-putter before he pitched it toward the door.

It struck the door on nine and impact pushed the door open. The detonator, round and heavy like the door of a small office safe, sailed through and landed on the ground outside.

Bolan dropped back behind the casket-crate as two Kalashnikovs cut loose outside, both riddling the doorway where his enemies expected him to be. The bullets fanned thin air and punched new patterns in the walls, while Bolan stayed below their line of fire.

He'd lost a second in his head, somehow. There was no blast when he mouthed zero, but it came a heartbeat later, more or less equivalent to a grenade's explosion in the open air. He didn't know what kind of shrapnel it would generate, nor was it relevant. Bolan was up and running as the echo rattled windows through the village, firing from the hip as he burst from the shed.

The nearer of his guards was down on one knee, wiping fresh blood from his eyes. The other stood to Bolan's right, still reeling from the blast but aiming his Kalashnikov with shaky hands. The first short burst from Bolan's AUG stitched him across the waist and put him down, before a second sent the kneeling shooter sprawling on his back.

The other guards had gone, apparently pursuing whoever had fired into their ranks short moments earlier. Before Bolan could analyze that problem, he heard footsteps rushing up behind him, trailing a familiar voice.

"They're right behind me," Patrick Quinn gasped. "So, what's Plan B?"

Bolan suppressed a smile and said, "Let's take a ride."

GRIMALDI SAW the red-orange flash of an explosion far below and to his left, perhaps a quarter mile away. There was a fire down there, as well, and he supposed it was the village where the final act of Bolan's mission had to be playing out.

Or maybe not the final act.

If Bolan managed to disarm the nuke, he still had plans to meet Grimaldi at the airstrip. That was five miles from the village, coming closer by the second as Grimaldi skimmed the treetops, homing on the prearranged LZ.

Five miles.

Grimaldi covered that in three and one-third minutes in the Hiller UH-12, but running it was something else entirely. The standing record for a one-mile run was just a hair under four minutes. The record for a twenty-six-mile marathon was something like two hours and five minutes, for an average speed of five minutes per mile from a world-class performer.

Bolan was good, a natural athlete, but Grimaldi knew that he wasn't world-class. On top of that, he'd been humping around the damned jungle for two days, fighting for his life and lugging forty-odd pounds of gear around on his back. He wasn't rested, and he wouldn't have the luxury of a straight run through daylight, over cleared and level ground. Add Patrick Quinn, if he was still alive, and that would slow the soldier even more.

How long, then?

The pilot decided forty minutes would be optimistic, but he wouldn't mind the wait. It gave him time to deal with any opposition at the landing strip and make sure he was ready when Bolan appeared, with or without the kid he'd come to fetch.

He saw the airstrip now, a shack to one side with a faint light showing through its single window. As Grimaldi circled once around the field, a door opened, spilling more light, and two men stepped out of the shack.

Grimaldi reached across for his gym bag, resting in the copilot's seat, and unzipped it. He reached inside and found the Winchester 12-gauge, lifting it clear and placing the gun in his lap.

No more circling.

He hovered briefly, then descended, far enough from the shack that the men would be forced to approach him. He watched them conferring, pretended to run through a checklist while he switched off the engine and listened to the rotors slowing overhead.

The watchmen huddled for a moment, arguing, then took the bait. Grimaldi tracked them with his eyes, not seeming to, the shotgun lying ready in his lap. When they were fifteen feet away, he popped the door on his side, beamed a smile, and asked them, "How's it going, men?"

"What you are doing here?" the taller of them angrily demanded. "We are not expecting you."

"Emergency," Grimaldi said. "I've got the paperwork right here."

The pair came closer, moving in lockstep. One carried a Kalashnikov; the other had a pistol tucked into the waistband of his khaki trousers.

"What is paperwork?" the tall one asked.

"It's like a death certificate," Grimaldi said, and shot him in the chest. The buckshot charge lifted his target off the ground and punched him through a clumsy backward somersault.

The other watchman tried to draw his handgun, but he didn't have the time. Grimaldi pumped and fired again, misjudging height and taking off most of the shooter's head. The dead men lay together on the grass, soaking its roots with lifeblood from their veins.

Grimaldi sat and wondered how much longer he would have to keep them company.

IT WASN'T EASY GETTING to the motor pool, when Gaborone sought cover after every six or seven steps. His terror nearly paralyzed him, sheer will keeping him in motion at a jerky, halting pace. He lurched from one deep shadow to another, dodging his own supplicants as if they were a mob of hostile strangers.

Which, for all he knew right now, they were.

The exodus was still ongoing, those who'd pledged their love and lives to Gaborone evacuating Obike as fast as their legs could propel them. Here and there, he saw one of his bodyguards attempting to restrain them, sometimes firing on the frightened sheep, but nothing slowed them. Those who survived to reach the darkness of the jungle would be lost.

It wasn't only fear that slowed him, however. Twice, so far, his own men had fired shots at Gaborone. They didn't recognize him, he supposed, but rather took him for another traitor on the run. The first time, he had ducked machine-gun fire from one of the guard towers, nearly freezing in the spotlight's beam before raw panic goaded him to run. His shooters had moved on to other targets, while he hid behind a dormitory, but the threat of death was everywhere around him now.

His second near miss came mere seconds after an explosion rocked the village. Gaborone thought it had come from the direction of the armory, but he couldn't be sure. Had someone fired into the shed against his orders, hit the detonator with a careless round and caused it to explode?

If so, the enemy concealed in there was either dead or dying, no more threat to Gaborone in this life. But the blast might well have cracked the Armageddon bomb's protective shields, in which case radiation could be leaking from the long crate even now.

Ahmadou Gaborone wasn't a physicist, had never even finished the equivalent of high school in his homeland. He had no idea how radiation traveled, or how swiftly, other than the fact that it could not be seen, smelled, heard or tasted. But it could be felt, oh yes, after it penetrated flesh to cause a slow and agonizing death.

New panic spurred him on to greater speed. He ran through shadows, hiding from the lamps that hung outside some of the dorms. He'd covered half the distance to the motor pool by now, at least.

A soldier suddenly appeared in front of him, one of his own, shouting for Gaborone to stop. He obviously couldn't see the prophet's face, might not have recognized him in the circumstances, anyway. The gunman's manic shouting and the weapon leveled from his shoulder drove a spike of mortal fear through Gaborone.

The Skorpion erupted in his fist, before Gaborone was conscious of squeezing the trigger. It blazed off half a magazine, shredding the soldier's face and chest before he got control and raised the smoking weapon from its target.

Incredible.

He had done that, and if he had the strength to kill an armed man in a stand-up confrontation, who could stop him?

Emboldened, Gaborone skirted the twitching body of his victim and proceeded toward the motor pool. Just another few yards more and he would see the jeeps, the old bus, waiting for him to select his chariot. Five minutes, maybe less, and he'd be on his way to safety, leaving death and fear behind.

He saw the vehicles a moment later, checked both ways before he sprinted toward them, breathless. Halfway there, he realized that someone else had got there first. Two men were seated in the last jeep on the left, as if preparing to depart. An instant later, and the engine revved, snarling like any other jungle beast.

Taking the men for two of his own soldiers—maybe cowards, but at least not fools—Gaborone ran toward them, waving his gun overhead and shouting at them to wait. In God's name he beseeched them to help him escape, find a safe place where all three could hide.

The headlights flared, immediately blinding Gaborone. He stumbled to a halt, holding the Skorpion in front of his face, to shield his eyes. He heard the jeep approaching, felt the makings of a smile tug at the corners of his mouth before he realized it wasn't slowing for him.

It was speeding up.

The jeep's square nose struck Gaborone dead center, crushing his rib cage, snapping both legs above the knees. He fell, sucked underneath it, twisting briefly in a haze of dust, before his head collapsed beneath the left-rear tire.

The prophet's final vision was a bright light swallowing the world he knew and fading swiftly into black.

"DO YOU KNOW who that was?" Quinn asked.

"I didn't get his name," Bolan replied.

"Him! It was *him!*"

"You mean—"

"The master! Gaborone!"

"Damn it! Hang on!"

He swung the jeep around, a roaring U-turn in a space that seemed to narrow but that somehow tolerated the maneuver. Roaring back toward where he'd struck the running gunman, Bolan saw the crumpled body in his headlights. Gaborone could answer certain crucial questions, if he would, about the source of his black market warhead and the possibility that others had been offered in the same job lot.

Braking beside the body, Bolan saw he was too late. Whatever secrets Gaborone had carried in his head were leaking now into the soil.

"What are we doing?" Quinn demanded.

"Getting out of here," Bolan replied.

But saying it and doing it were worlds apart.

He gunned the jeep through yet another U-turn,

circling tight around the prophet's battered corpse, and headed back in his original direction. That way lay the road between Obike and its private airstrip, where Grimaldi should be waiting for them even now.

In normal circumstances, he supposed vehicles passed around the village outskirts, but that route would leave them more exposed to gunfire than a straight run through the compound, barracks looming close on either side to shield them from the tower guns.

Not that the gunners on their pedestals weren't trying for a shot. Excited by the action down below, uncertain as to who was friend or enemy in the confusion, they were firing here and there around the village, strafing dorms and chasing runners through the narrow streets. From the cries that fire elicited, they had to be scoring somewhere, but the jeep rolled out without a hit from either of the tower guns.

It was a different story on the ground. There. remnants of the palace guard were scattered randomly throughout the compound, trying to make sense from chaos and determine where they ought to be, what they should do to help the cause. And in the absence of a leader to direct them, violence seemed to be a popular response.

One guard leaped in front of Bolan's jeep and fired a burst across the hood, then ducked back out of range when Bolan swerved to hit him. Quinn was waiting, swiveled in his seat, when the shooter popped out again behind them, rattling off a burst across the backseat with his AK-47.

"Did you get him?" Bolan asked.

"Beats me. He fell, at least."

"Close one," Bolan said, peering through the shattered windshield.

"Close is right. I'm hit again," Quinn said.

Bolan glanced over for a heartbeat, seeing Quinn wipe bloody streamers from his face, then wipe the red hand on his pants.

"Looks like a glass cut," Bolan said, "but I can't stop to check it here."

"I hope not," Quinn replied, firing another automatic burst toward someone rushing at them from the right. A cry rewarded him, and they passed on, leaving the dead and wounded in their wake.

It couldn't be much farther to the road, Bolan thought. They were nearly through the village, running out of street before the tree line loomed in front of them, and if the damned road wasn't there, he didn't have a backup plan on tap.

He'd hoped they wouldn't need one.

From his left, a stream of bullets tracked the jeep, clanging on impact with the left-rear fender. Bolan swerved to spoil the shooter's aim, while Quinn returned fire in an aimless spray. It finished off his magazine, and Bolan heard him busily reloading from his captured bandolier.

"We need to get away from here." He echoed Bolan's thoughts.

"I'm working on it."

And like that, they cleared the village street and

Bolan saw the dark mouth of the unpaved forest road that would convey them to the airstrip. Veering to his right, he powered toward it, milking every ounce of power from the jeep that he could get.

"We've got it," he told Quinn, who had turned back to face their rear again.

"I hope we're not too late," Quinn answered. "Someone's coming after us."

THE HEADLIGHTS BLAZED in Bolan's rearview mirror like the bright eyes of a jungle predator pursuing them into the night. The size was wrong for it to be another jeep, but what did that leave?

At the motor pool he'd counted jeeps, one dirt bike and an ancient bus. It had to be the bus behind them now, and Bolan wondered how many of Gaborone's armed guards had climbed aboard before it started chasing them. He hadn't noticed it until Quinn sounded the alert, but that could mean the bus was running parallel, along another village street, until they cleared Obike's outskirts and prepared to take the forest road.

"It may not be the guards," Quinn said. He sounded skeptical and hopeful, all at once. "I mean, maybe it's just some of the others bailing out."

Could be, Bolan thought. If a group of villagers had stuck together, looking for an out, they might've seen him take the jeep. And then what? In their panic, maybe they supposed it was their "prophet" fleeing toward the airstrip and they chose to follow him. Maybe they'd follow anyone who seemed to know where he was going, since they didn't have a clue themselves.

But Bolan couldn't trust to luck this time, with Jack Grimaldi waiting at the airstrip and a busload of potential enemies straining to close the gap between them. One way or another, he was bound to find out who they were and what they wanted.

"Get a grip!" he cautioned Quinn, then hit the brakes a second later, skidding to a crooked halt across the narrow track.

The bus, some sixty yards behind them, slowed on the approach but didn't stop. He couldn't see the bus driver, with the headlights blazing in his eyes, but Bolan knew the driver could see *him*. Standing behind the jeep, he raised the Steyr to his shoulder, peering through its scope directly at the bus's windshield, where the driver's seat should be.

"What are you doing?" Quinn demanded. "Are we shooting them?"

"Hang on."

Quinn followed his example, raised the AK-47, but his young voice had a tremor in it when he said, "Okay, I'm with you."

Bolan knew it cost Quinn something, every time he fired his weapon, and he didn't want to fire on innocents himself, but if the other driver held to his collision course—

A muzzle-flash erupted from the right side of the bus, to Bolan's left. He couldn't tell if it was someone firing from a door or window, but it hardly mattered. The shots told Bolan all he had to know, and he returned fire instantly, ripping two short bursts through the bus's broad windshield.

Beside him, Quinn was firing longer bursts, but still exhibiting control. Head-on, the bus was windshield, grille and headlights, nothing more. They peppered it with bullets while it closed the gap to thirty yards, then twenty, steadily advancing like a juggernaut immune to injury.

At fifteen yards, Bolan was braced to run, his rifle's magazine almost on empty. Quinn was fumbling with another hasty reload, muttering, "Come on, come on, come on" like it was all one word, a hopeless mantra, flicking glances up and down between his weapon and the bus.

And suddenly, the bus veered to their right, tires digging new ruts in the turf as it accelerated, one last burst of strength before it crashed into the trees. The diesel engine didn't die, but kept on wheezing fumes into the night.

From that perspective, Bolan saw the open door directly opposite the driver's seat. He crouched behind the jeep, reloading swiftly, while he waited for their adversaries to emerge.

There'd been at least two people on the bus, one driving while the other tried to shoot them, but he saw no movement now beyond the starboard row of windows.

"Do we check it out?" Quinn asked.

"I'd rather not."

"So, what? We just stand here?"

"We leave," Bolan informed him.

"Just, like, *leave?*"

"Unless you'd rather miss our ride."

"No way!"

"Then get aboard."

Quinn scrambled for the shotgun seat, keeping a sharp eye on the bus, his AK aimed in that direction all the while. Bolan did likewise as he slid into the driver's seat, but he had to set his weapon down to take the wheel.

"Go on," Quinn said. "I've got them covered."

Bolan trusted him enough to put the jeep in gear and pull away. Quinn held his rifle steady on the bus until they couldn't see it anymore, then turned and slumped into his seat.

"I hope that's it," he said. "I mean, we're done, right?"

"Not exactly."

"What, you mean there's more?"

"We've got the flight to Brazzaville ahead of us," Bolan said. "You'll need some fresh clothes there, before you pay a visit to the embassy."

"The U.S. Embassy? What for?"

"You'll need a passport, if you plan on going home. That *is* the plan right?"

"Right," Quinn said, and smiled through layers of blood and grime. "That definitely is the plan. Except—"

"What will you tell them?" Bolan finished for him.

"Jeez, you're reading minds now?"

"Give the truth a shot," Bolan advised. "You never know. It just might work."

The airstrip wasn't much to look at by moonlight, but Bolan could've cheered when he saw Jack Grimaldi standing by a vintage helicopter, one hand raised to shield his eyes from the jeep's headlights. He was carrying a shotgun, with a pistol tucked into his belt. Two dead men armed with weapons of their own lay off to one side of the chopper, leaking quietly into the grass.

Grimaldi clasped his hand and said, "Man, I was hoping that was you and not another bunch from the unwelcoming committee."

"There may be some more behind us," Bolan said. "We left a partial roadblock, but it won't be hard to shift."

"In that case," Jack replied, "what are we waiting for?"

"We'll ditch the hardware once we're airborne, closer to the city," Bolan said.

Grimaldi smiled. "Suits me. It never hurts to be prepared."

A moment later they were airborne, Quinn seated in the rear, Bolan in the copilot's seat. The moon was bright above them, and the jungle dark below. Like always, Bolan thought. There was a razor-thin dividing line between the darkness and the light.

He leaned back in the seat and closed his eyes, trusting Grimaldi for the first leg of their journey home. Tomorrow, he decided, would be soon enough to think about the rest.

EPILOGUE

"And, so, you had no trouble after that?" Johnny asked.

They were seated in a corner booth of Alvarado's Steak House in Cheyenne, platters of beef and mugs of beer in front of them. Valentina sat between them, with a Caesar salad and an iced tea on the side.

"Well," Bolan said, "the guy who rented Jack the chopper thought he'd pull a fast one and hang on to part of the deposit. Something tells me that his average clientele is on the shady side and doesn't like to argue with police."

"What did you do?" Val asked.

"Jack talked him out of it."

"Oh, my."

"No hassles at the embassy?" Johnny asked.

"Not a one. Apparently someone had called ahead and smoothed the way."

"I'm thinking Hal," Johnny replied.

"Or someone from the Farm. In any case, it did the trick. They had to walk Quinn through the passport questionnaire and do a physical, something the CDC requires for expats who've 'gone native.' He passed the monster virus test, and that was it."

"I hardly recognized him," Val remarked. "He's just so…different."

More than you know, Bolan thought, but he didn't push it. Quinn would tell Val what he chose about his time in Africa, especially the last two days. If he had qualms about describing their last bloody trek together, Bolan didn't feel it was his place to spill the details.

"Was it terrible?" she asked, intruding on his silent thoughts.

"It wasn't good," he told Val honestly, "but I've seen worse. We both have."

There was a catch in Val's voice as she told him, "I should say I'm sorry that I brought you into it, but I'd be lying. Patrick was—is—someone special. If you'd known him earlier, before all this, you would've seen it."

Bolan sipped beer and said, "He showed me something on the trail, Val. If there's more, I'll leave it up to you and to his family."

"Speaking of which, they want to thank you personally." Val could read the look on Bolan's face, quickly adding, "But I explained that wasn't possible. Security and all."

"Okay."

"They want to make some kind of a donation now, but—"

"Have them take a long vacation with their son," Bolan replied.

"That was my first suggestion, too."

"What was the get-together like?" Johnny asked.

"Mostly tears, as you'd expect," Val said. "Pat kept apologizing, then his father started, and they just went round and round like that until I left."

"Crying and stuff," Johnny suggested.

"Big-time," Val agreed.

"Oh, well."

Val mock-glared at him. "Hey, don't tell me you two haven't got soft hearts."

"Soft?" Johnny teased.

"Hearts?" Bolan echoed.

"All right, be that way. But he's going back to school this fall, I think. He has a chance to put this all behind him."

"Fair enough," Bolan said.

"What about the others?" Johnny asked. "From the Process, I mean."

"You likely know as much as I do, if you watch the news," Bolan replied. "Some never made it out. I'd guess two-thirds or more broke for the jungle when the shooting started. Some of them have started surfacing. The rest, who knows? Maybe they just kept going."

"They've found more than a hundred still alive," Johnny remarked. "At least, that's CNN's version. It doesn't sound so bad."

"I wonder where they'll go," Val asked of no one in particular. And got no answer from her men.

"What happened with the bomb?" Johnny asked.

"The Farm says Brazzaville sent people in to 'handle it,' but they got nervous and the UN had to fly a special team in to collect it. For a while, the locals wanted to hang on to it, but someone tipped them that the media would have a field day with them hijacking black market nukes. They let it go."

"Go where?" Val asked.

A shrug from Bolan. "Someplace where they can dispose of warheads, I suppose."

"Is anyone tracking the source?" Johnny asked.

"That's affirmative. It's Russian, but that doesn't really pin it down. We knew before the nuke popped up that Gaborone was having Russian visitors, and others from Sudan, the Middle East. He didn't keep a bill of sale. My guess, unless somebody comes out of the dark to drop a dime, we'll never know."

"That's horrible," Val said. "Doesn't it frighten you?"

"They're out there," Bolan said. "Not only nukes, but viruses, bacteria, a world of WMDs. We can't all live in fear, or else the bad guys win."

"Speaking of bad guys," Johnny said, "what happened to Sharif?"

"Unknown," Bolan replied. "The locals found some helicopter wreckage traceable to Gaborone, but there was no one at the site. Maybe he made it out. If he shows up again, we'll know."

"And if he doesn't?"

. Bolan shrugged again. "What can I say? The jungle's like a roach motel. Some who check in never check out."

"It has to be a setback for the Lance of God, if they've lost him."

"He's expendable," Bolan replied. "They all are, in the terror game. When they're recruiting teenage kids to volunteer as walking bombs, there won't be much protracted mourning for Sharif. Odds are, if he's not home by now, he's been replaced already."

"And Camacho?" Johnny asked.

"He's gone, for sure," Bolan said. "As to what impact that has on the cartel, I guess we'll have to wait and see. My guess, it won't slow down production in Colombia."

"But maybe it will help their people crack the gang," Val said.

"You always were an optimist." Bolan couldn't resist a smile.

"What's wrong with that?"

"Today, nothing."

"I'll drink to that," Johnny said, picking up his mug. Their glasses clinked as Bolan answered, "So will I."

AleX Archer
THE CHOSEN

Archaeologist Annja Creed believes there's more to the apparitions of Santo Niño—the Holy Child—luring thousands of pilgrims to Santa Fe. But she is not alone in her quest to separate reliquaries from unholy minds who dare to harness sinister power. A dangerous yet enigmatic Jesuit, a brilliant young artist and a famed monster hunter are the keys to the secrets that lie in the heart of Los Alamos—and unlocking the door to the very fabric of time itself....

Available January 2007 wherever books are sold.

GRA4